TEXAS PROUD

As Rana watched the seeds of genuine friendship being sown between the two men, she suddenly realized the complexity of her own situation. Both men were now her lovers. She could very easily be the wedge that could destroy this partnership, or she could be the glue to keep it together. She had to keep them together no matter what it took...

Rana took a drink of her coffee, then was silent for a long moment.

"Rana?" Sue Ellen asked again.

Rana sighed. "The father could be either Gamblin or Jason," she said.

"My God," Sue Ellen said. "Well, do you know which one?"

"Yes," Rana said. "I know which one. But I can't let them know."

TEXAS PROUD

ROBERT VAUGHAN

PaperJacks LTD.

TORONTO   NEW YORK

AN ORIGINAL

PaperJacks

TEXAS PROUD

PaperJacks LTD.

330 STEELCASE RD. E., MARKHAM, ONT. L3R 2M1
210 FIFTH AVE., NEW YORK, N.Y. 10010

PaperJacks edition published June 1987

This original PaperJacks edition is printed from brand-new plates made from newly set, clear, easy-to-read type. No part of this book may be reproduced or transmitted in any form or by any means, electronic or mechanical, including photography, recording, or any information storage or retrieval system, without permission in writing from the publisher.

ISBN 0-7701-0599-8
Copyright © 1987 by Robert Vaughan
All rights reserved
Printed in the U.S.A.

TEXAS PROUD

Chapter One

"The inside lane is closed by construction, and a minor accident has brought traffic to a standstill on the Eastex Freeway. If you're coming into town from Houston Intercontinental, you might want to try another route. I-45 is good if you are far enough out; closer in, I would suggest you use Hirsh Street, Jensen Drive, or Hardy Road. Traffic seems to be moving reasonably well on those three routes. This is Carl Sinclair reporting from *Jet-Copter One*."

"Thanks a lot for telling me now, Carl," Rebel Hewlitt said as she snapped the car radio off. She drummed the steering wheel impatiently as she sat motionless in her lane. The lane just to her left was blocked off by bright orange cones; its surface was torn up for new construction.

After a few minutes of waiting, Rebel narrowed her green eyes, looked around to make certain there were no policemen nearby, then shifted her Jeep into four-wheel-drive and pulled out of the stalled traffic between two of the orange cones, onto the lane under construction. While the other cars sat locked in the traffic grid, Rebel bounced along over potholes, concrete rubble, and perforated-steel planking. When she reached the place where the road-construction gang was using jackhammers to break up the old pavement, she edged around them onto the shoulder and passed the startled workers with a triumphant laugh and a jaunty wave, her red hair flowing in the wind. Three minutes later she passed the spot of the traffic accident, then pulled back onto the empty highway and accelerated to seventy miles an hour.

For her last birthday Rebel had been given a red sports convertible, a Mercedes 450 SL. She used it occasionally — when she played tennis at the River Oaks Country Club or planned to meet friends at some elegant place like the free-form pool at San Luis. She drove it to the Western Heritage Sale last April where, along with a personal invitation, formal wear, and a bluebook rating of more than ten million dollars, Rolls-Royces and Mercedes were practically a requirement for admission. But so far, the car, like formal wear, was something she used only for special occasions.

Rebel smiled, recalling a comment she had overheard one evening as she was getting out of her Mercedes. "I'll tell you what, pardner. If God ever made anythin' better to look at than a beautiful girl in a red convertible, He kept it for Himself."

She did like her Mercedes, but most of the time she preferred to drive her six-year-old Jeep, leaving the red car sitting in the driveway at home on River Oaks Boulevard. She certainly couldn't have taken the Mercedes onto a lane under construction.

Fifteen minutes later Rebel turned into the parking lot at the Adams' Mark Hotel. She saw an empty slot next to Deke McClarity's Seville, slipped her Jeep in alongside, then, after restoring her wind-blown hair with a few quick brushstrokes, walked across the parking lot to the hotel entrance.

The doorman smiled at the beautiful young woman as he held the door for her. He turned to watch her walk toward the two glass elevators at the back of the lobby. The woman, as usual, didn't even stop by the desk. She knew exactly where she was going, even though she wasn't registered as a hotel guest. She was there to meet someone.

The doorman put his hand in his pants pocket and fingered the one-hundred-dollar bill he had been given. He didn't particularly like what he was going to do, but he needed the money. Besides, if the woman was cheating on her husband, she should be caught. He had a wife like that once and he could still remember the bitterness he had felt when he found out about her.

The doorman looked over toward one of the sofas in the sunken lobby. There, a rather plump man sat reading a newspaper. When the reader looked up the doorman nodded, then glanced toward the woman who had just come in. The man folded the newspaper, saw the girl get into one of the bubble elevators, then watched it rise until he could see where it stopped.

Ben Anderson got up from the sofa and walked over to a telephone. He made a credit-card call to

Washington, D.C., and listened to the beeps and clicks as the long-distance circuits fell in place. His call was answered by Evan Hewlitt himself.

Evan Hewlitt of Texon Oil was one of the wealthiest and most influential men in the world. He conversed regularly with presidents, prime ministers and kings. He was a man who could stand nose to nose with Armand Hammer, T. Boone Pickens, the Hunts, the Rockefellers, or anyone else. It gave Anderson a tremendous sense of power to have access to Hewlitt through the unlisted number in his private office.

"Mr. Hewlitt, this is Ben Anderson."

"Who?"

"Ben Anderson, of Anderson Confidential Investigations? You hired me to..."

"Yes, Mr. Anderson, I remember," Evan said. "What do you have for me?"

"It's just like you said, Mr. Hewlitt. I followed Deke McClarity and she showed up."

For a moment there was silence from the other end, then a slow, resigned sigh. "Where are you now?"

"I'm in the Adams' Mark Hotel in Houston."

"Are they both there?"

"Yes, sir. They're together."

"In the lounge?"

"No, sir. In a room."

Evan was silent for a moment. Then he spoke, asking in a quiet, painful voice, "What room?"

"I don't know."

"You don't know? What the hell good is your information if you don't even know what room?" Evan sputtered.

"I'll know within half an hour," Anderson promised.

"I have people working on it."

"You call me back as soon as you know."

"Yes, sir," Anderson said.

Rebel already had the hotel room key. She opened the door and stepped inside. Deke was on the other side of the room standing in front of the smoked-glass window, looking out over the Houston skyline. When the door opened he turned toward her and smiled.

"You made it. I heard there was a big traffic tieup on Eastex Freeway. I was afraid you wouldn't be able to get here."

Rebel crossed the room and put her arms around his neck, then leaned into him.

"Neither rain nor snow nor gloom of night can stay this woman from her appointed rounds," she quipped.

"Appointed rounds, is it? You mean I'm just one of your appointed rounds?" Deke's blue eyes flashed with humor.

"I'll never tell," Rebel replied. She slid her hands up his chest, then to the sides of his head as her fingers slipped into his dark, expensively groomed hair. She could feel the charge of passion leap between them and, as his mouth closed on hers, she parted her lips, drinking deeply of his kiss.

Deke's hand slipped down from Rebel's neck to her back. He pulled and pressed her against himself, molding her pliant body against his. Rebel's heart hammered as she breathed the musky scent of him and tasted his lips and tongue, stimulating a desire for more.

Deke's hands slid underneath Rebel's cotton shirt, squeezing the bare flesh of her back, and Rebel shuddered as the waves of intense wanting swept over her.

"Don't...don't you think we ought to close the drapes before we get too carried away?" Rebel asked.

"If anyone climbs this high just to watch us, they deserve a thrill," Deke said thickly. As he spoke, his tongue probed into her ear, sending such intense desire quivering through her that she heard herself cry out his name, not protesting, but pleading with him to go on. And because at this moment she could think of no words so sweet as his name, she said it again.

Deke slipped his hands from beneath her shirt and slowly, but very deliberately, began undoing her buttons until the blue oxford shirt she was wearing hung open, exposing skin and a lacy half-bra. The white mounds of her breasts spilled over the top of it, and Rebel could feel the air delicately touching her pulsing, incredibly hot skin.

He slipped the shirt down over silky shoulders that were lightly dusted with freckles. With the shirt out of the way, he unsnapped the bra and let it drop. One hand reached up to cup one of her breasts gently, the milky whiteness of it contrasting sharply with the rest of her skin. She felt an extraordinary heat in it as her nipple hardened into a knot of pleasure. Deke's other hand moved down, unsnapping the top of her jeans and then, slowly, slipping under the waistband. His hand slid across her navel, then moved farther down, and farther still, until all of Rebel's being cried out for more.

Her jeans were a barrier, but it was of little consequence as they were removed as easily as her shirt had been. After that came her lace bikini panties, freeing her full, aching flesh of all hindrance. Now she stood before him in all her naked glory, a spade of fire glistening at the junction of her thighs.

"Okay, so you want to leave the blinds open. But do

we have to do it standing up?" Rebel teased. "Or may we use the bed?"

"Standing up might be fun," Deke answered with a ribald chuckle. He began shedding his own clothes. "But it would be easier in bed."

Rebel stretched out on the big, king-sized bed and looked at Deke's naked body as he came to her. She loved everything about his body: the smooth skin, the muscle definition of his chest, arms, and abdomen, even the puffy scar tissue on his thigh, where he had taken a Viet Cong bullet seventeen years ago.

Deke joined her on the bed and his hands returned to her skin, trembling with eagerness and hunger, burning her with their touch. He pulled her almost roughly against his lean, athletic body and she felt herself joined to his flesh so closely that it was hard to sense any separateness anymore. Once again Deke's lips and tongue probed Rebel's mouth, plumbed the depths of her soul. It was much more than a kiss of passion; it was also a kiss of exploration and wonder, a lover's kiss, tasting of something deep and mysterious.

Rebel opened her mouth to take in his lips and tongue. Then, when the ultimate connection was made, she gave herself up to receive him deeply inside her and rushed headlong with him down some silken tunnel toward the rapture that waited for them in all its deep potential.

When it first started it was a tiny sensation that began somewhere deep inside the innermost chamber of her soul. She could feel it moving out in ripples, spreading forth in a series of concentric circles like waves from a pebble cast in a pool. The waves began gathering power with more and more urgency, moving with unbounded energy until finally they crashed upon the shore of her soul, causing a burst of ecstacy to sweep through her as her body attained the pure release and satisfaction it was seeking.

A million pins pricked her skin and involuntary cries of pleasure sprang from deep in her throat. She felt as if time stood still while brightly colored lights flickered before her eyes and her body jerked in orgasmic, convulsive shudders.

There were two more exquisite charges of ecstasy after that: one nearly as strong, then another not quite as powerful but still intensely satisfying. Then, when she felt Deke's shuddering body reach its own goal, a new, totally unexpected orgasm burst over her, sweeping away all that had come before and bringing her to a peak of fulfillment so supreme that every part of her being, from the tips of her toes to her very scalp, tingled with its sweet rapture.

Rebel balanced precariously upon the precipice for several seconds, and during those moments of pleasure her body became so sensitized that she experienced not only her orgasm, but she could feel, through Deke's body, the ecstatic release that was his own completion. The waves of pleasure that swept over him delved into her body, too, so that his climax and hers became one massive explosion, seemingly without end.

As Rebel coasted down from the peak, floating like a leaf, she met new eddies of pleasure, rising back up a bit before gently slipping farther down. Finally, after all the peaks and valleys had been explored, there still remained the warm, well-banked coals of a blazing fire and Rebel lay exhausted in Deke's arms, wishing this moment could last forever.

Ben Anderson had seen her get off the elevator on the

third floor, so he began his search there. He had already given a description of the girl to the maids, along with ten dollars apiece to keep their eyes open. He promised another twenty dollars to the one who could tell him what room Rebel entered.

No one on the third floor saw her, and he was beginning to get frustrated when he noticed that in addition to the glass elevators there was a more conventional one. He smiled as he realized that Rebel had exited on the third floor just to throw someone off, then continued on in the enclosed elevator.

"Not a bad move, honey," Ben said under his breath. "But I've followed the scum of the world...no little rich-bitch Maid of Cotton is gonna lose me."

Two years ago Ben Anderson, along with millions of other Americans, had sat in front of a TV with a six-pack of beer to watch Texas win the Cotton Bowl. As part of the halftime festivities, the National Maid of Cotton was introduced...

"...and now, ladies and gentlemen, while the University of Texas marching band plays 'The Eyes of Texas,' we proudly introduce Miss Rebel Hewlitt, the National Maid of Cotton!" Rebel Hewlitt had sat on the back of a convertible as she was driven around the field, waving and smiling at eighty thousand screaming fans in the Cotton Bowl.

Now, here he was, Ben Anderson, chasing that same girl through the corridors of the Adams' Mark Hotel. It was things like this that made his job interesting.

Two hundred fifty dollars a day plus expenses wasn't bad either. Ben had been prepared to come down to two hundred, but Evan Hewlitt never blinked when he heard the price. He just told him to get the job done.

Ben finally found a maid on the sixth floor who remembered seeing the girl. He gave her twenty dollars to point out the room, then another twenty to disappear for five minutes.

"What are you going to do?" the maid asked.

"Nothing that's gonna cause trouble, honey," Ben said. He showed her his P.I. license. "I'm just trying to gather some evidence, that's all. If you're around, you might get caught up in it and wind up having to go to court as a witness. That's gonna cost you a lotta time and money, and I don't think you wanna do that."

"No," the maid answered quickly. "No, I can't afford nothin' like that."

"Then be a good girl and go take care of some rooms at the other end of the hall."

The maid pushed her linen cart to the far end, leaving Ben alone. Ben went down to the room and stood just outside the door, listening. The average person walking down the hall would have heard nothing from the room, but Ben did, and he knew exactly what he was hearing.

Ben looked up and down the hall and when he was certain the coast was clear, he took a small device from his pocket and pried out the peephole in the door, then slipped it in backward. He put his eye to the hole and looked inside. The room was distorted and the figures looked far away, but he could see a man and woman on the bed. The woman was on the bottom, with long, shapely legs raised to either side of the man's naked hips. Her red hair was fanned out on the pillow, and her hands moved up and down the man's naked back. The bed was jiggling under their thrusts.

"The eyes of Texas are upon you," Ben sang softly. He watched for a few moments longer, just long enough to make sure that he was seeing what he thought he was seeing, but not long enough to give in to voyeurism. He couldn't afford to give in to that vice; the opportunities for such diversions were too great in this job. If he didn't discipline himself, he could wind up spending all his time watching such shows.

Ben pulled his eye away from the door, turned the peephole back around, then took the elevator down to the lobby. He was going to call Evan again. This time he would have all the information his employer required.

Rebel was still coasting with the aftereffects of making love, so the shrill ring of the telephone startled her. She raised up on one elbow and the nipple of her breast brushed against Deke's shoulder. It tightened at the contact.

"Who could that be?" Rebel asked. "Deke, does anyone know you're here?"

"No," Deke said easily. "Whoever it is, they have the wrong room."

The phone rang again and Deke reached for it.

"Hello?"

"Deke, this is Evan Hewlitt. I want to talk to Rebel."

Evan's voice was so strong that Rebel could hear it. She felt a jolt of fear course through her body and, involuntarily, she covered her nakedness with a sheet.

Deke looked at Rebel as if asking her what she wanted to do. With trembling hands she reached for the phone.

"Yes, Daddy?" she said in a small voice.

Chapter Two

Business Weekly:

For a time this winter, it appeared that eighty-two-year-old Rana McClarity would lose her iron grip on Texon Petroleum Corporation to archrival Evan Hewlitt. But the "Baroness of Black Gold" began fighting back. When all was said and done, there was no doubt that Rana McClarity would still be running the energy conglomerate in the same way she has administered it for the last sixty years... more like a reigning queen than a chairman of the board.

"There were some who thought Mrs. McClarity's age would cause her to let power slip through her fingers," a Texon source said. "But when J. W. Remmington, backed by Evan Hewlitt, attempted an unfriendly takeover, Mrs. McClarity fought him off."

In March, Mrs. McClarity used $212,000,000 of Texon's precious cash to buy back Remmington's 6% stake in Texon's common shares, at 40% premium over market.

Mrs. McClarity is currently negotiating an oil-lease arrangement with the government of Mexico. Inside sources say this complicated contract, if successful, could chart the direction of Texon for decades to come, but if unsuccessful, could bring about her downfall. As expected, President and C.E.O. Evan Hewlitt is opposed to this, and should Rana McClarity fail, Hewlitt stands ready to pick up the Texon reins of power. Success is by no means guaranteed for Mrs. McClarity. Resistance from within could be the lesser problem, however, as opposition continues to mount from Washington. There are some high-ranking government officials who feel Texon's proposal may threaten the overall balance of trade for the U.S. Ironically, her strongest ally in the government at this point is New Jersey Senator Morgan Carmack. Carmack, normally a thorn in the side of Texon Petroleum, has threatened to summon Hewlitt before his Multinational Business Committee to question him about alleged kickbacks to certain foreign officials. These allegations, whether proven or unproven, can only be embarrassing for Evan Hewlitt, so embarrassing that he may lose valuable support from within the company.

Maggie St. John looked through the smoked-glass window of the limousine as it glided down I-45. On the plush leather seat across from her sat her employer of the last twenty years, Rana McClarity. Rana was on the telephone, while Maggie, her pencil and secretarial pad momentarily stilled, waited patiently for the conversation to end.

"You're the governor of this state, Tom," Rana was saying. "If you can't see that those concessions are granted, then who can? Well, can't you convince the subcommittee that it's good for Texon, and what's good for Texon is good for Texas? Tell them it means more than twenty-five hundred additional jobs, and that means Texas wages and Texas taxes. That should be worth something.... Yes, I understand the problems you are facing, but I'm depending on you to get everything taken care of. I'm counting on you.... Yes, I'll give your regards to the president. Good-bye."

Rana handed the receiver to Maggie, who put it back on the mobile-phone base.

"Thank you, Maggie," Rana said. "Now, where were we?"

"We were discussing your itinerary for Washington," Maggie went on. "From one until seven you'll be meeting with the senators and congressmen who are your supporters. At seven, you have a meeting with Stewart Jackson. He's the president's advisor on petroleum, and he is very much Evan Hewlitt's man."

Rana smiled. "Yes, I know. As Gamblin used to say, Evan has Mr. Jackson's pecker in his pocket."

Maggie laughed. "My God, how awful! But quite accurate, I'm afraid."

"Go on," Rana said. "What's next?"

"At nine you'll have dinner with the president and the first lady in the White House."

"The dinner is confirmed?"

"Yes," Maggie said. "They had to reschedule some

ambassador, but it's arranged. I chose a Trevor Wade dinner dress for you in a striking shade of blue. Your star-sapphire necklace will be the perfect accent."

"That sounds good," Rana said. "And my hair?"

"Michael will be flying with us. He'll be on the plane to get you ready for your first meeting, and then again before your dinner with the president."

Rana smiled, then reached over to pat Maggie on the hand. "Maggie, I couldn't live up to my image without you."

At Hobby Airport a DC-8-61, better known as the "Stretch 8," sat at a gate at the extreme end of the boarding concourse. Instead of a gate number, there was an announcement board inside the airport reading PRIVATE — AUTHORIZED TEXON PASSENGERS AND PERSONNEL ONLY. There were gate attendants, just as there were at the other gates, but these attendants were employees of Texon.

In the designated seating area more than twenty people, all members of Rana McClarity's traveling entourage, awaited permission to board the plane. Petroleum engineers, financial advisors, multinational business consultants, a landman, and the senior member of the King Norton law firm were among those making the trip to Washington. In addition, the hairdresser, two bodyguards, and a personal maid were included.

The captain and his copilot came through the gate, waved to their passengers, then walked along the boarding chute to the airplane. Captain Bivens had completed his ground check at the airplane and had already received his weather briefing. They were greeted at the door of the plane by a pretty Hispanic woman named Maria, the senior cabin attendant.

Once Rana's car reached Hobby, her chauffeur drove out onto the parking apron, where he snaked his way between the hoses and fuel trucks, the baggage carts and food-service vans, and under the wings and behind the tails of the jets, finally coming to a stop beside the Texon DC-8.

Two ground crewmen were pumping fuel into the airplane while a third stood in the uplifted bucket of a cherry picker changing a light in the high, sweeping tail. A dark-blue, three-pointed star, the symbol of Texon, presented a sharp contrast against the pristine white of the tail. All work halted as the huge limousine stopped near the nose of the airplane.

"Your elevator is here, Mrs. McClarity. Do you want to board now?" the chauffeur asked.

"Yes, I'm ready, Marty," Rana answered.

Marty got out of the car, opened the back door, and held it as first Maggie, then Rana, stepped out. Rana, who was a little taller than Maggie, took long, purposeful strides toward the mobile elevator, which was in position. No stranger would have suggested that this powerful-looking woman was eighty-two years old.

"Was that her?" one of the two fuel handlers asked. "Was that Mrs. McClarity?"

"Sure. Haven't you ever seen her before?"

"No. Why did she come out here to board?"

"She's worth about five hundred million dollars. You think she's gonna come through the airport with the common people?"

"Sumbitch! Five hundred million bucks, huh? Sumbitch! Wouldn't that be somethin'? What would you do if you had that much money, Leroy?"

"Get a hot piece of ass and a cold piece of pie," Leroy answered sarcastically. "Now, get on up there on the wing and make certain the nozzle's grounded. I don't want you to blow us all to hell while you're spendin' Mrs. McClarity's money."

Maria greeted Rana and Maggie as the door opened to the boarding chute. She smiled and escorted them onto the plane.

Rana spent a lot of time on board this plane, so she took a particular interest in how it looked, and the way it looked pleased her. The inside had been decorated by G. Thomas Swain, one of the most exclusive interior decorators in Houston. Swain had been the chief decorator for several of the million-dollar private boxes at the Astrodome in Houston and Texas Stadium in Irving, but Rana believed he had done some of his best work on this plane.

With the exception of the flight crew, Rana and Maggie were alone on the plane.

"Maria, you may board the others now," Maggie said as they walked through the galley.

"Yes, ma'am," Maria replied.

When they reached the lounge, Rana settled into her seat. There was a command console beside her that would allow her to speak directly to the pilot, or through the flight engineer, with any ground telephone. Beside the seat was the latest issue of *Texas Monthly*, and Rana picked it up. One of the cover stories dealt with the Alamo, and Rana chuckled.

"What is it?" Maggie asked.

"I was just thinking of my great-aunt Tyna Mae," Rana said. "I wonder what she would think if she knew I was involved in a twenty-billion-dollar deal with Mexico. She never trusted Mexicans, you know. Her father — my great-grandfather — was killed at the

Alamo. The Alamo seems like such ancient history, yet my life was touched by the life of someone whose father actually died there. When you think of it as the span of a couple of human lifetimes, it doesn't really seem so long ago, does it?"

"No, if you put it that way, I suppose not," Maggie said.

Up in the cockpit, Joe and Eddie were going through the checklist. Joe picked up a telephone receiver and clicked the flight attendant's call button.

"Yes, sir?" Maria answered.

"Is everyone on board?"

"Yes, sir," Maria answered.

"Then close the door and we'll light the fire."

A few minutes later all four engines were running and he called the tower.

"Hobby ground control, *Texon One*. Request taxi and clearance."

"*Texon One*, you're cleared to thirty-one left. Ceiling is twenty-five hundred overcast, visibility three miles, altimeter two-niner-niner-seven."

"Thank you, Hobby." Joe moved the thrust levers forward slightly and, under its own power, the huge airplane began taxiing toward the active runway.

Deke McClarity paced the floor, telephone in hand, as he looked out over the Houston skyline from the thirty-eighth floor of the Texon Tower Building, where they'd rushed after leaving the hotel. Deke's physique paid homage to the many hours of jogging and tennis he put in. The reward was that his forty-year-old body still remained in much the same shape as it had been in 1966, when he played quarterback for Texas. His jet-black hair, his deeply tanned skin, and his six-foot frame completed the picture of a man both healthy and successful.

Rebel came over to stand beside Deke, and he put his arm around her. He found the base of her neck beneath the long copper hair and began to drum his fingers lightly as she laid her head on his shoulder. As he waited for his phone conversation to resume, his thoughts were of Rebel. She was a one-hundred-ten-pound bundle of energy and joy to him. He had watched her grow up, and now that she was twenty-three, he knew she was what he wanted.

Then came the telephone call from Rebel's father... the telephone call that threatened to take her away from him. Over and over in his mind he repeated, *Please, God, don't let it be true. Let it just be another of Evan Hewlitt's tricks.*

Mercifully, in the midst of these thoughts, the phone became alive on the other end.

"Yes, this is Deke McClarity. Has my grandmother's plane left yet?" Deke said into the phone. "It's pulling away from the gate now? What position is it in for takeoff? Okay, look, I want you to take a truck-mounted boarding ladder out to the end of runway thirty-one left.... That's what I said, a truck-mounted boarding ladder to thirty-one left.... Okay, thanks."

Deke hung up the phone. "Come on," he said as he grabbed Rebel's hand. "We have to hurry."

"Where are we going?"

"We're going to catch a plane," Deke answered. "It has already left the gate."

"Deke, you're crazy! We don't have a chance of catching that plane!"

"Sure we do, if you'll get a move on," Deke said.

Half leading and half pulling, Deke took Rebel up the

flight of stairs that led to Texon Tower's rooftop heliport. A Bell Jet Ranger was sitting in readiness on the pad, and a pilot was in the small operations office, reading a paperback novel.

"Is this thing ready to go?" Deke shouted.

"Yes, sir, Mr. McClarity," the pilot answered. He stood up quickly and put the book down, spine up, on the table. "Where to?"

"Thirty-one left, at Hobby Airport," Deke said. He opened the door and practically pushed Rebel into the helicopter.

"Thirty-one left? You mean at the end of the runway?"

"That's it," Deke said. "Come on, hurry. I want to catch my grandmother before she takes off."

"My God! Are they already out at the active?"

"I just spoke with Hobby ground control. *Texon One* is taxiing now and there are six airplanes ahead of them."

The pilot jumped in, then pulled the starter trigger. The turbine whined and the igniters snapped as the blades started spinning. In half a minute the spinning rotor blade was a blur overhead and the pilot lifted up from the pad, then, nose down, headed southeast. Hobby Airport was four and a half minutes away.

At that very moment halfway across the country, in Washington, D.C., Evan Hewlitt turned his swivel chair around so he could look out over the city. Through his window he had a sweeping panorama of the mall from the Washington Monument to the Capitol. Off to the left he could see the Ellipse and the White House.

Stewart Jackson had told him that Rana McClarity had wrangled a dinner with the president. *Okay,* he thought, *let her eat at the White House*. He still had a few cards to play. In fact, he'd just played one of the cards with Deke and his daughter. In a way, he hated to do what he had done... but he had done it for Rebel's sake. It would be easy for people to think he was trying to break up his daughter's romance for his own purposes. In fact, he would admit to anyone who asked that he didn't want Rebel with Deke. But basically the telephone call he made a short while ago had been for her own good.

Evan's telephone buzzed and he picked it up.

"Mr. Hewlitt, Mr. Jackson is here."

"Send him in," Evan said.

Evan's back was still to the door when Stewart Jackson came into the office. He heard Jackson cross over to the desk, but he still didn't turn around. He waited until Jackson cleared his throat softly, discreetly.

"You don't have to clear your throat, Stew. I know you're here," Evan said. He turned around, slid his glasses up his nose, then put his hands behind his head. Evan was lean and trim, a tribute to his daily regimen of racquetball.

"You asked me to come to see you?" Jackson inquired.

"And you came. Thank you."

"Mr. Hewlitt, you must know that as one of the president's advisors on energy, it's not good for me to be seen coming to your office. I have to keep my position as neutral as I possibly can."

"Nonsense," Evan said. "Everybody knows the administration is against the deal Rana is trying to put through."

"Perhaps so, but my position is most tenuous now.

You must know that Senator Carmack is investigating you thoroughly."

Evan chuckled. "What's the matter? You afraid he might find out about that fifteen-thousand-dollar bribe I slipped you during the takeover bid?"

"That was a consultation fee," Stewart said quickly.

"Consultation fee, bribe...what the hell difference does it make? You're in for a penny, you may as well get in for a pound."

"Perhaps things will work out by themselves," Stewart suggested.

"Horseshit!" Evan replied. "Nothing works out by itself, and you damned well know it. If we're going to beat Rana, it's going to take an all-out effort. Don't ever make the mistake of underestimating that woman. A lot of people have made that mistake in the past and they've been crushed."

"It's not that I'm underestimating her," Jackson said. "It's just that I feel...that is, the president feels we would be better off staying out of this one."

Evan sighed, then leaned forward and dropped his arms to his desk. He'd pussyfooted around enough; it was time for some action.

"Jackson, I want you to get to the minister of petroleum in Mexico City. I want you to convince him that they don't want to sign those leases with Texon."

"I've already explained to you, the president feels that might be construed as improper influence on our part."

"And that's your only reason? Because it might be construed as improper influence?"

"Yes."

"Maybe we can come up with a reason that would be

compelling enough for you to take some action on your own."

"Oh, no, I don't think so," Jackson stammered. "It would be much too dangerous."

"Think, Stew. I'm sure you can come up with a reason. In fact, you might come up with a million reasons."

"A million reasons?"

"Two million, actually," Evan said. "A million for the minister of petroleum, and a million for you."

Beads of perspiration broke out above Jackson's upper lip, and he put a hand on Evan's desk to steady himself. He took a shallow breath before he spoke again.

"Mr. Hewlitt, that is precisely the type of thing that Senator Carmack is looking for. Am I hearing what I think I'm hearing?"

Evan picked up a gold pen and began tapping it lightly against the palm of his left hand.

"I don't know," Evan answered. "That depends on how it sounds to you."

"It sounds..." Jackson stopped, took a breath, and started again. "It sounds damned good," he said.

"I thought it would," Evan said as he nodded his head. "Then I can count on your support?"

Jackson smiled. "We'll have her caught in the middle," he said. "There's no way she can win."

Evan held up his finger and wagged it slowly back and forth. "Uh-uh. I told you — don't count the old broad out."

Chapter Three

"Texon One, this is Hobby tower. Change now, to your company freq."

Joe tuned the radio to the private frequency used only by Texon Oil Company.

"This is *Texon One,* on company push," he said.

"Texon One, this is helicopter three, one mile from you and approaching from the north. Prepare to take on two passengers."

"What? Helicopter three, are you out of your mind? We've already left the gate...we're damned near to the runway."

"I understand that, but I have priority passengers and they wish to come aboard."

"What priority?"

"Joe, this is Deke McClarity. I'm coming aboard."

"Yes, sir, Mr. McClarity. I'll return to the gate."

"No need," Deke said. "Look out your left window."

Joe twisted around to look through the window, then saw a yellow ramp truck, with a collapsible boarding ramp attached to it, coming alongside. "Okay, Eddie, you'd better go get the door open," Joe said. "I'll tell Mrs. McClarity."

As the helicopter swung around to land alongside *Texon One*, Deke saw the front door open and the portable ramp move into place. He looked over at the helicopter pilot, smiled, and gave him a big thumbs-up as the skids touched down.

"Good job, Bill!"

"Thanks, Mr. McClarity," the chopper pilot answered.

Deke and Rebel hopped out, ran over toward the boarding ladder, up the steps, and into the plane. Once they were on board, Eddie closed the door and dogged it shut. He picked up the phone. "They're on board, Captain!" he said.

"Get everyone in their seats," Joe replied. "The tower's on my ass to expedite the takeoff."

The plane turned onto the runway and began rolling, even as Eddie returned to his station and everyone found a seat. Deke and Rebel settled into the first two seats in the front row. Rebel laughed in pure joy and excitement and reached over to take Deke's hand in hers.

"I really didn't think we would make it!" she cried.

Deke kissed her as the four turbine engines opened up to takeoff power and began sucking in air. The plane rotated about three-quarters of the way down the 7,600-foot-long runway, and by the time they were crossing over the 610 loop, they were already at 2,000 feet. They turned right, providing a striking view of the Houston skyline. One of the most prominent buildings on the skyline was the Texon Tower Building. To the right of their flight path were the refineries that were spilling smoke and fumes into the air. Chief among them was the gigantic Texon facility. And then they were into the overcast and the ground simply disappeared.

When Deke felt the plane settle into a steady climb, he looked over at Rebel, who had her head back, her eyes closed, and a small smile playing across her mouth.

As he had while he was on the phone, Deke began thinking once more of Rebel. This was no infatuation; he was in love with her. It was not something he had intended to let happen...after all, she was so much younger than he was. Hell, he could even remember the day she was born. She had been only four years old when he left for Vietnam, a little red-haired girl running around getting into trouble at his graduation party. By the time she was seventeen, she was already a looker who flirted openly with him in the experimental way young girls will when trying out their new curves. That was during the time of his divorce from Carol.

Deke looked out the window into the gray clouds for a moment and thought of the divorce. It had made gossip columns in the tabloids all across the country, and for a year he kept seeing "Carol's Own Story." Then, last year, she and one of her lesbian lovers had posed nude for a picture spread in *Playhouse* magazine. Stories associating Deke with Carol had just begun to die down, but now the gossip would pick up again; of this he was certain.

He could guess the juicy tidbits that would come out concerning his relationship with Rebel. The age difference would be one, but the biggie, the real grist for the mill, would be that Rebel was a Hewlitt and he was a McClarity. That raised all sorts of possibilities: the Romeo-and-Juliet aspect of battling families; the mongers wouldn't call it a marriage, but a merger. He could just see the tabloid headline now: "A Marriage Made in the Boardroom."

But Rebel said she loved him and she had been proclaiming that fact for over four years now. Because of the problems he could envision, Deke had been denying his own feelings for her, but he couldn't deny them any longer. And if they were really in love, what did anything else matter? Let the gossip columnists and the rumormongers go to hell. Together they could survive anything!

Or could they? Rebel's father was definitely against the marriage, which he perceived as a threat to his own position within the company... as if it were just a way for Rana McClarity to get Rebel's voting proxies. Evan Hewlitt had been against the relationship from the very beginning, but Rebel had defied him.

Then, this afternoon, Evan had dropped the bombshell, announcing that there was a certain impediment to their marriage. That was why they had to get on this plane today. Deke had to see his grandmother... had to find out the truth, once and for all.

Rebel reached over and squeezed his hand. "Deke? Deke, are you frightened?"

"Frightened? No, I'm not frightened."

"But what if it's true? What will we do if it's true?"

Rebel's hair showed the effects of the rotor wash from running under the blades of the helicopter. Deke reached up and pushed an errant strand away from her face.

"Let's not buy trouble," he said. "Let's not worry about things until they happen." He leaned over and planted a very light kiss on her nose. "Come on, let's go."

They got up and walked through the passenger compartment, smiling and nodding at the familiar staff and crew. When they reached the boardroom it was completely empty.

"Wait," Deke said, and he pulled Rebel to him and kissed her. She opened her mouth on his and leaned into him and he thought of this afternoon...the incredible smoothness of her skin, the damp heat of her thighs, the hot rush of orgasm as they had made love. He wished they could make love one more time before they spoke to his grandmother.

The door to the lounge opened and Maria came into the boardroom. She saw Deke and Rebel standing in the middle of the room, locked in a lovers' kiss.

"Oh, I'm sorry," she said, somewhat embarrassed at having disturbed them. "Please, excuse me."

"It's all right," Deke said. "Is my grandmother in the lounge or in her compartment?"

"She's in the lounge with Mrs. St. John," Maria said.

"Thank you," Deke said. He put his arm around Rebel. "Come on, into the breach."

Deke opened the door to the lounge. Maggie stood to greet them while his grandmother remained seated in her chair waiting for them, curious as to why they had come aboard in such a dramatic fashion.

Deke's father had died before Deke was born. His mother moved into the background, completely dominated by her in-laws. She was never more than a shadow to Deke, a quiet woman whose life was lived in a whisper in order to preserve her son's heritage. Deke had been raised by his grandparents, loved by them, disciplined by them, and trained by them. Rana was his grandmother, but she was much more than that. She was the only authority figure he had ever known.

"Hello, Grandmother."

"Hello, Deke," Rana said, offering her cheek to him for a kiss. "Hello, Rebel."

Rebel, too, kissed Rana on her cheek. Then the two of them sat on the sofa near Rana's chair.

"Well," Rana said, "it is pleasant to see the two of you, but I must confess that you've piqued my curiosity. What brings you here?"

"We want to be married," Rebel said.

"I see," Rana replied. She looked at Deke. "Is that right?"

"Yes. Grandmother, I'm obviously not asking for your consent, but..." He sighed and grew silent.

"But?" Rana asked quietly.

"Daddy just called from Washington," Rebel said. "He's been having us watched. He had a detective spying on us. A detective — can you imagine such a thing? Anyway, he knows now that Deke and I have, well, more than a casual relationship. He got very angry. He called me names and said awful things to me. I told him that I couldn't understand why he was so upset. I told him that Deke and I are in love and want to get married, but he... he just laughed. He said that under the present circumstances you would like nothing better than for us to get married, that it would give you everything you need, but he said that we couldn't get married now or ever. Then he laughed and said, 'Rana McClarity has finally been *hoist by her own petard*.'"

"I see," Rana said. "And did you ask him what he meant by that?"

"He said that we couldn't get married and you would tell us why. He said that even you wouldn't let it go through."

"Grandmother, if you know of any real reason why Rebel and I can't get married, I want to know about it," Deke said.

"I see," Rana said. She sighed and leaned her head back on her chair. "So...after all these years it comes back to haunt me."

"Grandmother, you mean it's true? We can't get married? You know what Evan was talking about?"

"I never thought about the consequences," Rana said. "I never considered that it might hurt someone someday. You have to remember, I was very, very young...and that was long, long ago."

Chapter Four

Somewhere in Illinois, early summer — 1923

The clanging of the crossing bells rose in pitch, then dropped off sharply as the train rushed by. It swept around a long curve and Gamblin McClarity had to hold on to the lavatory basin to steady himself. He checked his shave in the mirror, and the image that looked back at him was one of a handsome young man with black hair, deep blue eyes, and a strong chin.

When Gamblin had left the oil fields of Texas eighteen months before, he was under something of a cloud. He left not only to escape an unpleasant situation, but also to seek adventure and travel. He found very little adventure and a lot more travel than he wanted, spending eighteen months at sea working as an able-bodied seaman aboard a freighter. And now, even though he was on board a train a thousand miles inland, he was still wearing the clothes of a sailor: sturdy denim trousers and a black turtleneck shirt.

Gamblin's sailing days were all behind him now. When his ship docked in New York the week before, he chose not to sign on for the next cruise. He had decided that there had to be more to life than sailing on rusting ships through storm-tossed seas to steaming ports halfway around the world, so he took his pay-out and surrendered his seaman's papers. Now he had eleven hundred dollars in cash and he was going home to Texas.

He had sworn never to return to Texas unless he could return as his own man. With eleven hundred dollars in his pocket, he felt he could do just that.

The porter came into the men's room and began cleaning off the shelves.

"Porter, do you have any idea how long it'll be until we reach St. Louis?" Gamblin asked in his easy Texas drawl.

The porter took out his pocket watch and studied it importantly for a moment, then put it back in his pocket.

"I 'spec's we'll be 'rivin' at Union Station in 'bout half an hour," he said. The porter smiled. "Will you be gettin' off in St. Louis?"

"Yes, but just overnight," Gamblin said. "I promised a friend I'd stop by and see someone while I was there."

"Yessuh. Well, good day to you, suh."

An hour later Gamblin was riding in a taxi looking through the windows at the city of St. Louis. They were on Olive Street, and as they passed by Sportsman's Park

Gamblin could see large crowds of people moving through the gates. Vendors were on the streets and sidewalks around the great stadium, hawking Cardinals pennants, hats, and programs.

"The Cubs are in town," the driver said. "You sure you don't wanna get out here? It'll be a great game."

"No, thanks," Gamblin said.

They drove past the stadium and a few minutes later a loud bell clanged, almost in Gamblin's ear.

"Goddamned trolleys, think they own the goddamned street," the driver swore as he reluctantly gave way to a streetcar that rumbled past. After ten more minutes the taxi pulled up to the curb in front of a block-long row of lookalike brick houses that were all connected.

"Here it is," the driver said. "You want me to wait?"

"Could you?"

"Sure, but I'll have to keep the meter runnin'."

"Oh," Gamblin said. "Well... uh... never mind. I'll get another taxi."

"Won't be that easy," the driver said. "This ain't too nice a neighborhood. Not many cabs cruise down here lookin' for fares."

"I'll get by," Gamblin said.

"Have it your way, mister. That'll be fifteen cents."

Gamblin paid the fare, then pulled his sea bag out of the car and set it beside him. After the cab drove away Gamblin turned to look toward the houses to find 2117. There was no number 2117, but there was a 2115 and a 2119, so he knew where the house had to be.

The woman he was coming to see was Mary Cruckshank, whose husband, Phil, had been Gamblin's shipmate. He and Phil weren't really that close, so he was surprised when Phil asked him if he would stop in

St. Louis and say hello to his wife. Gamblin tried to get out of it.

"Go on," Phil insisted. "Believe me, it'll be worth it. Mary'll feed you supper 'n give you a place to stay for the night. The next day you can get back on the train all relaxed and ready to go. Mary likes entertaining my friends. Do it for me, will you?"

Gamblin finally ran out of reasons why he didn't want to do it, so here he was, standing on the front porch of 2117 Fourth Street, knocking on the door.

Gamblin heard the door bolt click, but the door came open only as far as the inside chain would allow it. He saw an eye appear in the crack of the door.

"Who it is?" a woman's voice asked.

"Uh, Mrs. Cruckshank?"

"Yes. Who are you?"

"I'm Gamblin McClarity."

"Who?"

"Gamblin McClarity, Mrs. Cruckshank. I'm a shipmate of your husband's. That is, I was a shipmate, but I quit the ship and Phil said I should come by to see you on my way home."

"Just a minute."

The door closed for a second, then opened again.

"Come on in."

Mary was a small, olive-complexioned woman, with blue-black hair and eyes so deep a brown that it was difficult to tell where the iris stopped and the pupil began. She was wearing a faded housecoat and she clutched it together at her neck while she examined Gamblin.

"What'd you say your name was?"

"Gamblin. Gamblin McClarity."

The woman smiled and the smile did something to

her. He saw then that she was actually a very pretty woman. "Gambling?" she asked. "Do you gamble a lot?"

"Not gambling, Gamblin. It's an old family name."

"So you're a friend of Phil's, huh?"

"Yes. We sailed together on the *Samuel T. Morrison*."

"Is Phil comin' soon?"

"No, I'm afraid not," Gamblin said. "The fact is, he just shipped out on another cruise."

"He did? He didn't tell me that in his last letter," Mary said. "He said he'd be comin' home this month."

"I'm...I'm sorry," Gamblin said. "I didn't know that."

"Did he tell you why he was shipping out again?"

"No," Gamblin said. Gamblin sighed. "Mrs. Cruckshank, to tell the truth, Phil and I weren't really that close. Matter of fact, we worked on different watches. I knew him and he seemed like a decent sort...but we never really hung around together. Actually, I was a little surprised when he asked me to look you up. Now that I've seen you, though, I must confess that I don't know why he keeps shipping out cruise after cruise when he has someone as pretty as you waiting at home."

Mary smiled again, then reached up and touched her hair, as if just then aware of how she looked. "I must look a mess. Why don't you have a seat? I'll go get dressed."

"All right," Gamblin said. Gamblin sat on a small, rather uncomfortable sofa while he waited. He picked up one of the half dozen movie magazines that lay on the table in front of him and thumbed through it for a few minutes.

The wait was much longer than he had anticipated,

but when Mary reappeared, Gamblin knew why it had taken so long. She had gone to great lengths to prepare herself. Her hair was bobbed and combed in a pageboy style similar to that worn by many of the movie stars he had just seen in the magazine. She had put on lipstick to give her lips a bee-sting effect, and her eyes were accented by the heavy application of mascara. She changed from her housecoat into what he knew must be her best outfit, a short-skirted dress of red satin. Gamblin knew and appreciated that she had dressed for him, but in truth he had thought she was prettier before she had applied the somewhat overdone makeup and the rather garish-looking dress. Before, there had been a girlish innocence to her appearance; now that innocence was gone.

"Well," she said, "we will just enjoy a nice visit, won't we?"

Gamblin spent the afternoon telling her stories about the *Samuel T. Morrison*, exaggerating some parts to make her laugh. She prepared dinner for him, just as Phil had promised, and when darkness fell she gave him a place to spend the night...in her own bed.

Afterward, Gamblin lay in the bed with his hands folded behind his head, staring at the ceiling. During the day the little brick house had caught the summer sun and heated up like an oven. The outside air was a little cooler after sunset, so the window was open to take advantage of what breeze there was. Outside, somewhere, there was a streetlamp on the other side of a tree that cast shadow patterns onto the ceiling, and Gamblin was contemplating those shadows. Beside him in the bed, Mary lay naked and flushed with the afterglow of their sex.

Gamblin felt guilty. It was bad enough to sleep with

another man's wife...it was a double sin if that man had been his shipmate. He thought of the *Samuel T. Morrison* and where it would be right now. It was after midnight at sea and the midwatch would be on. Gamblin thought of the times he had pulled midwatch.

He thought of the smell of the engine room, the wink of the moon on the black sea, and the creaks, groans, and rattles of a ship under way. He wondered if Phil had drawn the midwatch. If so, he would be awake right now, totally unaware that the friend he had sent to visit his wife was at this moment in bed with her. He hadn't intended to take her to bed...it had just happened.

No, that was a lie. He had known when she opened the door and stepped back to let him inside, clutching the neck of her faded housecoat in a futile gesture to mask her vulnerability...he had known from that moment where this stopover in St. Louis would end. He was guilty and he was acutely aware of that guilt.

Mary was lying quietly, showing no signs of struggling with the feelings that assailed him. After a long period of silence, she put her hand between his legs and he felt her soft, cool fingers wrap around his penis. He felt himself becoming aroused a second time, but because the guilt was too strong, he pushed her hand away.

"Don't you want to do it again?" Mary asked.

"No," Gamblin said.

Mary chuckled. "Your mouth says no, but this says yes."

"We... we ought not to do it again," Gamblin said.

"Why not? When a man pays to spend the night with me, he has me for as many times as he can find his pleasure."

Her words hit him with impact of a slap in the face with a cold, wet sponge.

"What?" he asked quietly. "Did you say when a man *pays* to spend the night with you?"

Mary raised up on her elbow and looked down at him. The action pulled her breast into an elongated pear and the nipple of it brushed lightly against Gamblin's chest.

"Gamblin, you're a sweet man," Mary said, "but if I let every man I ever found appealin' do it for free, I'd soon be out of business. You wouldn't want me to go out of business, would you?"

"No," Gamblin said. "No, I guess not." He laughed, then reached over for her. "I'll say this for paying you. It does get rid of the guilt."

"What guilt?" Mary asked as she pulled him to her.

Gamblin enjoyed it more the second time. He knew where things stood and this time there were no nagging images of defiled innocence; there were only tactile awarenesses. She was wet and incredibly hot and he felt as if he were submering in a vat of boiling cream. And she was all his...bought and paid for.

At three in the morning Gamblin awakened. The breeze had settled and the oppressive heat was gathering in the room. Gamblin knew there was a six o'clock train heading for Texas. He reasoned that Union Station had to be cooler than this little room, so he decided to leave earlier than he had planned. He knew that the chances of getting a taxi were remote, but the station wasn't more than three miles' distance, and even if he had to walk all the way, it was better than lying here suffocating. Gamblin dressed, left an extra two dollars on the dresser to soothe his conscience, then left.

He had gone no more than a mile when it happened.

He heard a sound, or at least sensed a movement, just before someone hit him, but it hadn't been enough warning. He felt an explosion in the back of his head; then he tasted salt and dirt in his mouth. The salt was from the blood of his lip, cut when his face hit the sidewalk, and the dirt was from the trash in the gutter. He was vaguely aware of someone going through his pockets.

"Son-of-a-bitch!" he heard. "Look at this! This son-of-a-bitch is rich!"

"You mean he was rich," another voice said, laughing.

Gamblin tried to raise up, but as soon as he moved his head he was overcome with dizziness and nausea. He lay back down, just to rest for a second. Only a second, then he would get up.

"Hey! Hey! You drunk or something? Get up!"

Gamblin opened his eyes and was surprised to see that it was daylight. He sat up, once more feeling dizzy and nauseous, but he was able to overcome it.

"Mister, if you got hold of any booze in this neighborhood, you're lucky to still be alive."

Gamblin looked at the speaker and saw a policeman staring down at him. Suddenly, he remembered his wallet and he reached for it quickly.

"It's gone," the policeman said. "The first thing I looked for was your wallet. I wanted to see who you were."

"I'm Gamblin McClarity," Gamblin said. "I am...I was a seaman."

"A seaman, you say? You're a long way from any ocean, Gamblin McClarity. What are you doing in St. Louis?"

"I'm going back to Texas," Gamblin said. "I got off the train here to visit a friend. I was going back to the station when someone — no, there were two of them — hit me." Gamblin put his hand behind his head and felt a bump and dried blood. The police officer looked, too.

"I guess you were hit at that," he said. "Took a pretty good lick from what I can see. Did you get a look at them?"

"No."

"Then how do you know there were two of them?"

"I heard them talking," Gamblin said. He tried to stand and nearly fell. He would have, had the policeman not reached out for him. He looked over at his sea bag. It was still beside him, still unopened.

"Looks like they didn't even bother with your bag," the policeman said.

"I guess when they found my wallet they figured they didn't have to," Gamblin said.

"Oh? What was in your wallet?"

"A little over a thousand dollars," Gamblin said. "Everything I'd saved for the last eighteen months."

The policeman whistled. "I'm sorry," he said. "Do you still have your train ticket?"

Gamblin felt in his front pants pocket and pulled out the ticket.

"Yeah," he said. "Yeah, I do."

"Well, at least you can make it home. I'll go up to the next call box and get you a ride to the station."

"No," Gamblin said.

"No?"

"I'm not going to Texas. I won't go to Texas broke. I left that way. I'm not going back like that."

"Mister, if you've got friends in Texas, it'd be a lot

easier for you to be broke there than to be broke here."

"I don't have any more friends there than I do here," Gamblin said, "so I may as well stay."

The policeman rubbed his chin and looked at Gamblin for a long moment. "I guess you'll be looking for work?"

"Yes," Gamblin said.

"Well, my brother-in-law works down on the river with the Mississippi Barge Company. They move oil on barges. It's hard work, but the pay's pretty good. Maybe I can put in a word for you."

Gamblin smiled. "Yeah," he said. "Yeah, thanks a lot."

"Do you feel up to going down there now?"

"What else do I have to do?" Gamblin answered. "Sure, I'm ready."

"I'll call him. Maybe he'll come get you. I know he was tellin' me yesterday how bad he needs men. Fact is, he needs them so bad I suspect he'd give you an advance on your wages, under the circumstances."

"Thanks."

"I've got to get back on my rounds. I'll go call. You just stay here. Someone'll be by for you after a while."

"Thanks again," Gamblin said.

Half an hour later an open-sided truck pulled up to the curb. It was a very old truck that looked as if it dated back to the war. The gears and brake lever were outside the cab and it clanked and made a grinding sound as the driver came to a stop. The pistons were slapping about noisily and steam leaked from the radiator. Several belching explosions, like pistol shots, came from the exhaust pipe. The driver, who was wearing an oil-stained pair of coveralls, was as dirty as the truck. He leaned out of the open side of the cab.

"Your name McClarity?"

"Yes," Gamblin said.

"Get in, McClarity. We got four barges to work today."

Chapter Five

"Books are the most noble of all man's creations," Tyna Mae Ellison often told her great-niece. "Just think, we can know exactly what people were thinking hundreds of years ago just by what they wrote. It's like having a conversation with the ages. We can never be lonely, not really lonely, if we have our books. Always remember that, Rana."

"Yes, Aunt Tyna Mae," Rana would answer.

Over the last year Aunt Tyna Mae's reading had been drastically curtailed as her eyes had begun to fail. That was perhaps to be expected of a woman who was ninety-eight years old. Her loss of eyesight could have made her a very lonely woman had it not been for her nineteen-year-old great-niece, as books had become her only friends.

The idea of her aunt lying in that darkened room day after day, with only the changing shadows to mark the passage of time, so depressed Rana Marlow that she started a daily routine of visiting and reading aloud.

When Rana first began the visits, she did so out of a sense of obligation to her late father. Tyna Mae had been his only living relative, and now she was Rana's only link to her father. But after a while she began to look forward to the visits almost as much as Tyna Mae did as she discovered her aged aunt to be a fascinating and amazingly lucid woman. "Remember the Alamo" was a phrase Rana had heard all of her life, but her aunt, who was twelve years old when the battle was fought, actually *could* remember it.

Tyna Mae's family had lived in the village of San Antonio de Bexar until Santa Anna's troops were reported advancing. When her father realized the battle was imminent, he sent his family to safety in Washington on the Brazos. He then joined Travis in the Alamo, where he and one hundred eighty-two other brave Texans fought to the death.

Tyna Mae was a living history book, having known personally William Travis, James Bowie, Sam Houston, and Stephen Austin, names Rana had read about. She had married Josiah Hunter Ellison, one of the earliest Texas railroad pioneers, who'd been a millionaire before the Civil War, but had spent all his money outfitting a Confederate division; then he made another fortune in cattle after the war, but he lost that in land speculation.

"I never knew whether I would spend the night in a tent or a mansion," Tyna Mae chuckled, "and here I am, reduced to this one room, dependent for my very survival upon the charity of my late nephew's wife. But I want you to know, Rana, girl, I wouldn't change a minute of my life with Josiah. Not one blessed minute!"

Rana lived with her mother, stepfather, and Aunt Tyna Mae in a boardinghouse that had belonged to her father. Rana's stepfather was a preacher without a church. The fact that he had no church didn't prevent him from doing what he called "God's work," though, and every day he would try to carry the message to the indigents and derelicts. His was a familiar figure along the riverfront and at the warehouses, always dressed in black and wearing a monocle. Most people accepted him as a harmless pest. Rana often wondered aloud why he wouldn't find work...or at least help her and her mother run the boardinghouse.

There was always excitement when a new paying guest moved into the boardinghouse, but when that guest was also young and handsome, Rana was doubly excited. This new guest was Gamblin McClarity, and Rana had smiled at him at the supper table once or twice and had even spoken pleasantly to him when they passed on the stairs or in the hallway. So far, however, she had gotten only the most perfunctory response from him. His aloofness both angered and intrigued her.

Rana told Aunt Tyna Mae about him.

"I don't really care that he's never noticed me. Why should I? I mean, he's handsome enough, but he's not for me. No, ma'am, he's not for me. So what do I care if he's never noticed me?"

"Of course he's noticed you," Tyna Mae said.

"He has?"

"Yes."

"How do you know?"

Tyna Mae chuckled. "He's a man, isn't he? How could he help but notice a pretty, fair-haired girl like you?"

"Because my fair hair looks just like dead grass."

"Not dead grass, dear, ripe wheat. And your eyes are as blue as a Texas sky. Don't worry, Rana. He's noticed you, you can mark my words on that."

"Well, what if he has noticed me? I certainly don't care. When I get married it's going to be to someone who is exciting, not someone who works on barges and lives in a boardinghouse."

Tyna Mae chuckled. "May I remind you that you live in a boardinghouse?"

"Yes, but I won't be here any longer than I absolutely have to be. One of these days I'm going to leave...and not only this house, but St. Louis. I'm going to Texas, Aunt Tyna Mae. I'm going to Texas and I'm going to find someone just like your Josiah Hunter Ellison."

"If you do find someone like my Josiah, I hope you have the strength to stay with him, because he'll give you quite a ride before it's all over. What's your young man's name?"

"Gamblin. Gamblin McClarity. Isn't that a silly name?"

"Silly? No, I think it's a fine, noble name," Tyna Mae said. "I'd like to meet him."

"I don't know why. He's about as exciting as one of Mama's dinner menus."

"Ask him if he would mind visiting an old lady," Tyna Mae said.

"Okay, I'll ask him. But you're going to be disappointed, Aunt Tyna Mae. He's as dull as a toad."

Tyna Mae laughed. "How do you know? I thought you'd never spoken with him."

"I just know, that's all. You can look at him and tell."

"Methinks the lady doth protest too much," Tyna Mae teased.

Rana relayed the information to Gamblin after supper that night.

"I know you probably have better things to do than visit an old lady," she said, "but my aunt would like to meet you sometime."

"How about now?" Gamblin asked.

Rana was surprised by Gamblin's quick acceptance. She had thought he would find some excuse to avoid the visit.

"You're sure you don't mind?"

"Of course I don't mind. As a matter of fact, I've been wanting to meet her anyway."

"You have? Why?"

"I heard she was from Texas," Gamblin said, smiling broadly. "I'm from Texas. I think people from Texas should stick together, especially if they find themselves in some far-off place like this."

"Okay," Rana said as they reached her aunt's room. "Wait here, just for a moment." She knocked lightly on the door, then stepped inside. A moment later she came back, smiling. "Can you believe it? She wanted to put on a bed jacket so she would look nice for you."

"Of course I can believe it. She's a Texas lady, isn't she? She has her pride, you know."

Gamblin and Aunt Tyna Mae had an instant liking for each other. It turned out that Gamblin's father had once worked for Tyna Mae's husband, and they exchanged Josiah Hunter Ellison stories for nearly an hour.

After that, Gamblin visited Tyna Mae almost as frequently as Rana did. He genuinely enjoyed the visits with Tyna Mae, but it also gave him the opportunity to visit with, and to get to know, Rana, and he enjoyed that as well. Then, on the night they finished reading Tolstoy's *Anna Karenina*, Rana followed Gamblin into his bedroom after they had told Tyna Mae good-night.

"What are you doing in here?" Gamblin asked.

"I just came to visit you," Rana said. "You don't mind, do you?"

"No, of course I don't mind. But your stepfather might."

Rana smiled and tossed her short hair coquettishly. "So what if he does? I don't care. Anyway, I don't see any difference from us being together in Aunt Tyna Mae's room," she said.

"Rana, there's a big difference and you know it," Gamblin said.

"All right," Rana pouted. "If you want want me to leave, I'll leave." She started for the door.

"No, no, I'd like for you to stay," Gamblin said. "I was just thinking about your stepfather, that's all."

"Pooh. The Reverend Mr. Wood is always looking around, peeking through his monocle, trying to find wrongdoing," Rana said. She made a circle of her thumb and forefinger, then held it over her eye in imitation of the single eyeglass her stepfather affected.

Gamblin laughed at Rana's impersonation. "The Chinese have a saying about people who wear monocles," he said. "They say that people wear monocles so they will never see more than they can understand."

Rana laughed richly. She liked to laugh and she did so often, even though she was constantly reminded by her stepfather that so much laughter was an invitation to the devil to work his ways with her.

"The devil walks the streets as a roving lion seeking

whom he may devour," Wood always said. "And excess joy is his invitation."

Rana didn't believe that. She couldn't see how anything as innocently enjoyable as laughter could be a sin.

Rana sat down on Gamblin's bed and pulled her legs up to rest her chin on her knees. The action caused her skirt to rise, which exposed a white flash of thigh above her rolled-down silk stockings. She saw that her legs didn't go unnoticed by Gamblin, and that pleased her. Rana liked it when, sometimes on a streetcar, she could feel a man looking at her. She enjoyed the expression on a man's face when she knew that he was hurting inside from wanting her. And now, to her delight, she was seeing the same expression on Gamblin's face.

"Did you like the book *Anna Karenina*?" Rana asked.

"Yes, I liked it."

"Do you think Anna is a sinner?" Rana asked.

Gamblin laughed. "What? A sinner? I don't know. What would make you ask such a question?"

"Because I want to know what you think."

"Your stepfather is the man to ask that question," Gamblin said. "He's the expert on sin, not me."

"I don't have to ask Mr. Wood," Rana said. "Anna committed adultery with Vronsky, didn't she? That means they were having sex, doesn't it?"

"I suppose so." Gamblin cleared his throat. "Don't you think it somewhat improper for us to be discussing sex in my bedroom?"

"All right. I'll talk about something else if it bothers you," Rana said. She looked around Gamblin's room. There was a framed picture on the dresser of a man and woman staring stoically at the camera. "Who are these people?" Rana asked, picking up the frame.

"My mother and father," Gamblin answered.

"Where are they now?"

"They're both dead. In fact, I don't even remember my mother. She died when I was born, and my father died when I was fifteen."

"Where did you go?"

"What do you mean?"

"Who took care of you?"

Gamblin laughed. "Nobody took care of me. I took care of myself."

"How?"

"I got a job in the oil fields. I worked there for eight years, then I had a run-in with a wildcatter, so I left the oil fields and went to sea. Now I'm here."

"A wildcatter?" Rana laughed. "What's a wildcatter?"

"Someone who searches for oil," Gamblin said. "They call them wildcatters because most of the time they're just scratching around like wildcats, trying to keep from going broke. Most of the time, they go broke anyway."

"Then why do they do it?"

"Because sometimes they find oil.... Then they wind up rich."

"Have you ever worked with a wildcatter who struck oil?"

"Yeah," Gamblin said. He smiled. "You should've been there when she came in. A huge, roaring gusher of oil blew out the bit, tore off the gin pole, the crown block, even the upper platform. It spewed a hundred feet into the air before it started raining back down. It was the most magnificent black fountain you could ever see."

Rana could see Gamblin's eyes glowing with the excitement of that moment, and his excitement excited her. She reached out and put her hand on his arm.

"Are you ever going back to Texas?"

"Someday," Gamblin said. "Yeah, someday."

"When you do go, I want you to take me with you. I'd like to see something like that," she said. "Would you take me to see one?"

Gamblin laughed. "It isn't something you just go to see, like taking in a baseball game."

"I know. You have to be there when it happens. But that's what I'm talking about. I want to be there."

Rana turned her head toward the open window, then brushed her hand through her hair. "Ah, feel that heavenly breeze coming through your window?"

"Yes," Gamblin agreed. "It's nice."

"It's too bright, though. Don't you think it's too bright? The light makes it hot in here. Turn off the light."

Gamblin turned off the overhead light, then turned on a small desk lamp. Instead of the white light of before, the room was now illuminated by a soft yellow glow.

"Is that better?" Gamblin asked.

"Much," Rana said. She lay back on his bed to let the breeze blow across her, then, suddenly and daringly, unbuttoned the top three buttons of her dress and let the material lie open, exposing her brassiere. "Don't be shocked," she said, feigning a nonchalance she didn't feel. "I'm as covered as I would be in a bathing suit."

"What makes you think I'm shocked?"

"Then why don't you come over here and lie beside me?" Rana suggested. She scooted over, closer to the window, then patted the bed beside her. "It's a shame to let such a nice breeze go unused."

"Rana, I don't like playing around like this. Things can get out of hand."

"Oh, pooh. What could happen?"

"What could happen?" Gamblin repeated. He walked over and sat on the bed. "You know damned well what could happen." He looked down at her pointedly, and his eyes started at her neck, then traveled down the smooth skin until they reached her breasts, barely constrained by the brassiere she wore.

Rana had been playing a game with Gamblin, but now she saw something in his eyes that both frightened and thrilled her. He reached for her.

"No," Rana said, rolling away. "Don't do anything. Gamblin, you're frightening me."

Gamblin sighed and pulled his hands back. "All right," he said. "If you are going to play games with me, you can forget about it. Just remember, I didn't ask you in here. You came of your own free will."

Gamblin started to get up, but Rana reached for him and, putting her arms around his neck, pulled his mouth down to hers. "Kiss me, Gamblin," she said. "Kiss me, hard."

Rana felt Gamblin's lips against hers, tender, yet with an urgency that intensified her own aching desires. She made a strange, animal sound deep in her throat and she didn't know whether she was asking him to go on or to stop. She closed her eyes and waited for him to make the next move.

Gamblin, taking advantage of the opportunity, put his hands on the material of the brassiere and pulled it down below her breasts, exposing the creamy mounds to the soft caressing breeze that was coming through the window. She felt her nipples harden, drawn into aching little buds. Gamblin ran his tongue around first one, then the other, lightly, teasingly, and Rana felt tiny electric charges coursing through her. She moaned and put her hands behind his head, pulling him to her and forcing her breast into his mouth.

For the next moment there was movement and sound as they took off their clothing while still maintaining as much bodily contact as possible. Then, when they were both nude, Gamblin got on his knees to look down at her. Rana returned his stare, feeling his hot gaze on her naked body. Her legs were spread wide and little diamonds of her desire were glistening in the bush of light-brown hair that stood up like a crown in the golden glow of the desk lamp. She could feel beads of perspiration around her lips and she slipped her tongue out once, like a serpent, then slid it back in. She held out her arms to beckon him to her.

Gamblin lay down with her and she could feel the heat of his skin and the hardness of his body. He pulled her to him, pressing her breasts flat against his chest. Her hands moved across his body, then found his testicles. She had never felt a man before and she paused for a moment to consider the textures. She felt him moving into position then, but she was ready for him. When he entered, she was only barely aware of the resistance that her virginity caused.

Afterward, they lay together for several moments, listening to the night sounds that came in through the open window. From somewhere nearby, Rana heard the loud, angry voices of the neighbors next door to the boardinghouse. They were having one of their frequent arguments. A little farther away she heard a woman's shrill laughter, and, farther away still, the sound of a train leaving St. Louis and heading for Eades Bridge.

Within the boardinghouse itself the toilet was flushed and the pipes rattled and rushed as water refilled the tank. Finally, Rana raised herself on one elbow and looked down at Gamblin.

"You didn't answer my question," she said.

"What question was that?" Gamblin replied, confused by the comment.

"Do you think Anna Karenina was a sinner?"

Gamblin laughed.

"I'm serious," Rana said. "It's very important to me."

"Why?"

"It just is. Do you think she was a sinner?"

"All right, if it's so important," Gamblin said. He raised his hand to her face and traced his finger lightly along each eyebrow. "No," he said finally. "I don't think she was a sinner."

"Why not?" Rana asked. "She was having sex with someone who wasn't her husband."

"I know," Gamblin said. "But she was in love with him. When there is love, there can be no adultery. At least, that's the way I believe."

"I'm glad you believe that," Rana said. "That's what I believe, too."

Chapter Six

It was late that same summer when Gamblin saw the hearse pass him as he was walking home from work. He was still four blocks away from the boardinghouse and he hadn't seen where it had come from, but somehow he knew that Mrs. Ellison was in that hearse. He quickened his pace.

"Gamblin! Oh, Gamblin!" Rana cried, meeting him on the front porch. She had been crying. Her eyes were red-rimmed and she was clutching a tear-stained handkerchief. "It's Aunt Tyna Mae."

"I know," Gamblin said, reaching out to comfort her.

"You know? How did you know?"

"I just had a feeling. When did it happen? I told her good-bye this morning."

"It must've been around three," Rana said. "I talked

to her just a little after two. Then, when I went back later, she was...she was..." Rana couldn't go on.

Gamblin took her into his arms and was comforting her when the Reverend Mr. Wood came to the screen door and looked outside. He stared disapprovingly at the embrace, though he said nothing about it, as if making allowances for the situation. Finally, he cleared his throat, and when Gamblin looked at him, he spoke.

"Mr. McClarity, I wonder if you would come into the living room for a moment?" he asked. "I would like to speak with you."

"Certainly, Reverend Wood," Gamblin said. He stepped through the screen door and followed Wood into the living room, which was part of the manager's apartment. It wasn't often he was in this part of the house, and he looked around at the lace doilies and the bright chintz sofa and chairs. A needlepoint sign on the wall proclaimed JESUS SAVES.

"She was a decent woman," Wood said. "It'll be a privilege for me to preach her funeral."

"When will that be?"

"The buryin's to be tomorrow," Wood said. "Nine o'clock at Potter's Cemetery."

"Isn't that awfully fast?"

"The county's buryin' her," Wood said. "They set up the schedule. All we can do is follow their rules." Wood took a handkerchief from his pocket, and Gamblin thought he was going to use it to wipe his eyes, as if crying. Instead, Wood blew his nose noisily, then put the handkerchief away.

"Anyway," Wood went on, "there ain't no one around to mourn her but us. And we can't really have a funeral, I mean in a church or a funeral home, or anything like that. All I can do is say a few words over her grave. That don't seem right, somehow, but that's the rules of the county, too."

"Didn't Mrs. Ellison leave enough money to see to her funeral?" Gamblin asked.

"None to speak of. What money she did leave has got to be used to pay some of the bills her sickness run up," Wood said.

Gamblin knew that her sickness had cost nothing. There had never been a doctor to see her, and the only medicine she had ever taken was an occasional aspirin. But he didn't challenge the reverend's statement.

"Well, I'm sure that the words you say over Mrs. Ellison's grave will be just as meaningful as if you said them in a church," Gamblin said.

"That's sort of my thinkin', too," Wood said. "By the way, she left you somethin'."

"I beg your pardon?"

"It seems Aunt Tyna Mae set quite a store by you and Rana visitin' her, and readin' to her and all. Truth is, it was a right Christian thing for you to do. Anyway, she told me, oh, two or three weeks ago, that she wanted me to give you this here envelope when she died. She musta knowed then she wasn't goin' to have too long left to live."

The Reverend Wood took a large brown envelope down from the top of a secretary and handed it to Gamblin. "Here it is," he said.

"What is it?" Gamblin asked. There were papers inside the envelope.

"They are oil leases," Wood said matter-of-factly.

"Oil leases?" Gamblin tore open the envelope and pulled out the documents. "My God, they *are* oil leases!"

"They's no need to take the Lord's name in vain,"

Wood said sharply. "I told you what they was. And they ain't all yours. Fact is, she left 'em to you and Rana together, such as it is."

"Such as it is? How can you be so nonchalant about them?" Gamblin asked. "Don't you know what these are? They grant Rana and me the exclusive right to drill for oil in..." he began leafing through the leases "...five thousand, ten thousand, twenty thousand... My God! Fifty thousand acres! These are ninety-nine-year leases to fifty thousand acres!"

"I told you, Mr. McClarity, I don't appreciate you a'takin' the Lord's name in vain like you keep on a'doin'. You ought to be more appreciative. These leases are worth a little bit of money, you know."

"They're worth more than a little bit!" Gamblin said excitedly. "They could be the key to a fortune!"

"I suppose so, if you are greedy enough to want to risk everything," Wood said. "I'm afraid Aunt Tyna Mae was that way. She could have sold them, maybe got enough money to help out a little; but, no, she hung on to them. And why? Because her worthless husband left them to her."

"Why would she want to sell them?" Gamblin asked.

"If you don't sell them, what good can they possibly be? You can't farm the land, you can't run cattle on it, you can't borrow against it, you can't even take water from it. All you can do is drill for oil, if you have the money, and if there is any oil there in the first place, which there prob'ly ain't, or it woulda been found by now."

"Not necessarily," Gamblin said. "If Mrs. Ellison held the drilling rights, no one else would have been able to look there."

"Yes, well, that's neither here nor there, now. The

thing is, what are you goin' to do about these leases?"

"What do you mean? I'm going to keep them."

"Uh-huh. Then what are you going to do about Rana's share. Half of the leases belong to her."

"I understand that."

"I don't think you fully understand, Mr. McClarity. You see, I went down to the bank to talk to a fella about these leases and he tole me that the big oil companies would pay a fella a dollar for ever' ten acres they could get hold of. That means these here leases is worth five thousand dollars. Five thousand dollars, cash money. That's near a fortune, Mr. McClarity. Imagine that ole lady havin' all that money, all this time, and not sayin' a word to anyone about it. Anyway, iffen I was you, I'd sell these and be quick about it."

"Well, you aren't me, Reverend Wood, and I have no intention of selling them."

"Then there's the question of Rana's share," Wood went on. "You see, her share comes to twenty-five hundred dollars, and we want the money. The truth is, I don't know why she left anything to you in the first place. By rights, we shoulda got it all, bein' as Aunt Tyna Mae was our kin and all. And besides that, we took care of 'er all these years. But she left it to you, so I'll be thankin' you to come up with Rana's money jes' as quick as you can."

"Don't you think I ought to have something to say about that?" Rana asked, coming into the living room then.

"Rana, this here talkin' is between Mr. McClarity and me," Wood said. "We don't need you a'puttin' in your two cents' worth."

"But half the leases are mine, aren't they?" Rana asked.

"Yes, they are, and that's jes' what I'm talkin' to Mr. McClarity about. I'm a'lookin' out for your interests."

"It seems to me more like you're looking out for your own interests," Rana said. "Do you think I don't know who would get that money?"

"I figure a fair share of it's mine, yes," Wood admitted. "After all, we took her in and treated her nice and she weren't no kin to us a'tall."

Gamblin chuckled. "Just a while ago you were saying she was kin and you couldn't understand why she left any of the leases to me."

"Well, she wasn't blood kin, but she was practical kin, bein' as she was the aunt of my wife's first husband. Nevertheless, we was out a tolerable amount of money to look after her, so I figure it's only right that we get some of it back. Now, when do you aim to sell the leases?"

"I told you, I'm not going to sell."

"Then when do you aim to pay us for our share?"

"*My* share, Mr. Wood," Rana said quickly. "And I don't want to sell either."

"What do you mean? Have you lost your head, girl? If you don't sell, what do you think will happen to your share?"

"I intend to keep my share and look for oil," Rana said. "That's what Aunt Tyna Mae must have wanted, or she wouldn't have left them to me."

"There ain't no oil there," Wood said. "So, if you're smart, you'll sell them leases to a big oil company like I said."

"If there's no oil there, why would a big company buy the leases?" Rana wanted to know.

"I don't know," Wood said. "Maybe jes' to keep

people like you from gettin' in the way out there in the oil fields."

"I think we ought to go out there and look for ourselves," Rana said.

"What?" Wood replied, gasping. "What do you mean, we? Look here, you ain't plannin' on goin' off with him, are you?"

"Why not? We own the leases together."

"But...it's not Christian!"

Rana smiled sweetly, innocently. "Don't worry, Mr. Wood," she said. "Nothing can happen that hasn't happened already."

"What? What are you talkin' about?"

"Rana," Gamblin said quietly, "Rana, I can't take you with me."

"Don't you love me, Gamblin? You told me you loved me."

"Yes, I do love you," Gamblin answered.

"Are you two sayin' you love one another?" Wood asked. "When did that all come about? What's goin' on here? Would somebody jes' please tell me what's goin' on?"

"If you do love me, then you'll take me with you," Rana said, ignoring Wood's protestations.

"I can't do that, Rana. These leases are out in West Texas, in the desert and hill country. I'll be living under the most God-awful conditions you can imagine."

"Sir, I have asked you not to take the Lord's name in vain under this roof," Wood said, "and I must insist that you honor my wishes, as this is my home."

"Anyway," Gamblin went on, "it wouldn't be possible for me to have a wife under such conditions."

"A wife? See here, there will be no marryin' without

my permission. No marryin', do you understand that?" Wood sputtered.

"I'm not asking you to marry me," Rana said to Gamblin. "I'm only asking you to take me with you. I'll put up my share of the money. My father left me five hundred dollars. You're going to have to have some money to go, aren't you? You're going to need a car. Do you have enough for a car?"

"You can't use that five hundred dollars!" Wood said. "That money is for emergencies."

"It's my money and this is my emergency," Rana said quickly. She looked at Gamblin. "What about it? Couldn't you use the extra money?"

"Yes, of course," Gamblin said. "But even with that money we wouldn't be able to afford separate accommodations. We'd have to sleep in the car, or out under the stars."

"That's all right. We can sleep together," Rana said. She walked over and hooked her arm through his. "After all, it won't be the first time we've slept together, will it?"

"Oh, shit!" Gamblin said quietly.

"Goddamn it!" Wood swore. "You!" He pointed to Rana. "You get back to your room right now!"

"I'm not going anywhere," Rana said. "I love Gamblin and I want to be with him. You can't stop me, so don't even try."

"Whore!" Wood shouted, slashing the back of his hand across Rana's cheek. "Slut! Shameless daughter of Satan, get out of my house!"

Wood hit Rana with each curse and she fell down, crying under the blows.

Before he realized what he was doing, Gamblin put his hand on Wood's shoulder and spun him around.

Then he caught him in the jaw with a short, brutal right hook. Wood went down like a sack of flour.

"Oh, shit!" Gamblin said, looking at Wood, who was sprawled out on the living room floor. "What have I done?"

"Mr. McClarity, perhaps you'd better leave before he comes to," Rana's mother said. It was only then that Gamblin realized she had come into the room in time to see the whole thing.

"Mrs. Wood, I didn't mean to —"

"I know," Mrs. Wood interrupted. "It isn't the first time he's hit Rana. There've been times when I wish I could have done just what you did. Now, go quickly."

"I'll have to get my money and clothes from my room," Gamblin said.

"Mama, I'm going with him," Rana said.

Mrs. Wood held her arms open wide and Rana ran to her. "I know you have to go, darlin'," she said. "I know you have to."

"I know where we can pick up a car for a pretty good price," Gamblin said. "We'll leave tonight."

Chapter Seven

There were two other cars sitting in front of the service station when Gamblin pulled in. Both cars were piled high with the personal belongings of the occupants; one had a rocking chair tied to the luggage carrier in the rear, and the other had an old grandfather clock lying down, lashed to the roof.

It was funny, Gamblin thought, what families decided to take with them when they moved. And now there were a lot of people on the move. The automobile had reawakened America's pioneer spirit, but instead of long trains of Conestoga wagons plodding along at ten miles per day, today's pioneers moved west on ribbons of cement, sometimes at speeds of up to fifty miles per hour.

Steam was rushing from the radiator of Gamblin's Chandler and he got out to look at it. He found a stick, and, using it to poke at the cap, he managed to turn it until air and steam gushed out. After the air and steam came the water, surging up like a geyser, then raining back down on the dirty hood of the car.

Rana had been sleeping in the back seat, but the spewing, rushing sound awakened her. She sat up and rubbed her eyes as she looked around.

"Where are we?" she asked.

Gamblin looked toward the front of the service station. It was a small, unpainted clapboard building with a hand-lettered sign hanging from the eaves of the front porch. The sign read COWBOY SERVICE STATION. The only other sign was an advertisement: SPRAY FLIT...KILLS FLIES...ON SALE HERE.

"I don't really know," Gamblin said. "The sign says Cowboy Service Station, but I don't know if that means just this service station, or if there's a town named Cowboy."

Rana laughed. "That would be a funny name for a town."

"No funnier than Cut 'n Shoot," Gamblin said. "There's a town in Texas named that."

"Uh, it's hot," Rana said. "Isn't it hot, though?"

"Yeah," Gamblin said. "But we can take the heat okay... it's the car I'm worried about."

"What's wrong with the car?"

"The thermostat keeps sticking, and the engine is overheating. If this keeps up, we're going to burn out a bearing. Then we're really in trouble."

A man came out of the building, wearing a pair of denim trousers, a yellow shirt, and a cowboy hat. He was chewing on a toothpick.

"You need gas, mister?"

"Yes," Gamblin said, "about ten gallons, please."

The man began working a handle back and forth on the gasoline pump, and the large glass cylinder at the top of the pump started filling with gasoline. The man pumped until the gas in the cylinder was even with the ten-gallon mark. Then he took the hose and stretched it to the gas cap in front of the windshield. The gas bubbled down out of the glass cylinder while fumes rose in shimmering waves from the open cap.

"Do you have cold soda pop in there, mister?" Rana asked.

"Sure do, miss," the attendant answered. "There's an ice box in the back. Just dip your hand down in there and fish out whatever you like."

"Would you like one, Gamblin? It's so hot," Rana said.

Gamblin smiled. "You're in charge of the money. Can we afford it?"

"I think so," Rana said. She handed a dime to the attendant, then skipped across the gravel parking area of the service station. As she ran, Gamblin watched her legs flash beneath the swirling skirt. He thought of the body under that dress and of the strong young back, which, when they were making love, could buck against him for an hour without getting tired. He thought of how much he loved her and how he wouldn't be able to stand it now if he lost her.

In a way, Gamblin felt guilty, as if he were a despoiler of virgins. She was so very young, not only in years, but in her ways, and she had an innocence about her that he found delightful. Despite that innocence they had made love every night, and even a couple of afternoons, since leaving St. Louis. He recalled with pleasure the two days they had spent on the bank of the White River in the Ozarks of Missouri.

Neither her innocence nor her sensuality detracted from Rana's business sense. Gamblin discovered that when they bought the Chandler. The used-car dealer was asking one hundred seventy-five dollars for the car, and Gamblin was willing to pay his price. Rana managed to get it for fifty dollars less; not by using a woman's wiles, but by good, hard trading.

She had made several other monetary suggestions over the course of the trip, as well, and Gamblin quickly came to accept her as a partner in fact as well as in name. Now, by mutual agreement, she was handling their remaining finances because he was convinced she would make the money last longer than he could.

Several people came out of the service station then and started for the other two cars. There were two men in work overalls, eight children of various ages, male and female, and two women who looked much older than he imagined they really were.

"Those folks are headed for California," the attendant said as the cars pulled away with rattling frames and clanking engines. "Seems to me like they're makin' an awful long trip for nothin'. Don't know what California's got that they can't find in Texas." The attendant looked at Gamblin through narrowed eyes. "You ain't leavin' Texas, are you?"

"No, sir," Gamblin said. "Just comin' back, that's all."

"That so? Where you been?"

"I went to sea for a while. More recently I was in St. Louis."

"That where you met your wife?"

"What?"

"Your wife," the attendant said. "I could tell soon's I heard her talk that she wasn't from Texas."

"Uh, yeah, that's where I met her," Gamblin said, figuring it would be easier to let him believe Rana was his wife.

"Let's see, you had ten gallons. That'll be a dollar fifty."

"I thought gas was supposed to be cheap in Texas," Gamblin said, handing the man the exact amount. "This is where it comes from, isn't it?"

"It may be," the attendant said, "but I gotta pay for it just like you do, mister. I don't own no wells."

"My radiator's cooled down enough now. I need to put some water in," Gamblin said.

"Help yourself, the water's free," the attendant said.

Gamblin pumped water into a bucket, then began pouring it into his radiator. The radiator hissed and snapped as the water hit the hot metal.

"Here's your pop," Rana said, coming back to the car. "They had orange pop and I know how you like it, so that's what I got for you." She handed him a bottle and the liquid gleamed orange-gold in the sunlight. It was wet and cold, and a little piece of ice stuck to its side.

"It's good and cold," Gamblin said.

"I'll say," Rana agreed. "I had to stick my arm way down in the water to get it. It was so cold that it hurt."

"Yeah?" Gamblin remarked, turning the bottle up and taking several Adam's-apple-bobbing swallows. When he took it down, he smiled at her. "I thought you were complaining of being too hot."

"I was hot," Rana said. "I'm still hot. Only my arm is cold."

"Maybe I should take you back in there and dunk you

all over," Gamblin teased, taking a step toward her. "Then you'd quit complaining about being hot."

"Gamblin, you wouldn't really, would you?" Rana asked, taking a couple of steps back, not entirely sure that he wouldn't do it.

"I might," Gamblin said.

"If you do, I'll never speak to you again," Rana warned.

"Well," Gamblin replied, laughing, "that might make it all worth it."

Rana danced away from him, putting the car between them. Gamblin laughed. Then, tiring of the game, he turned and looked out toward the highway. It was supposed to be a gravel road, but there was very little gravel left. As a result, a constant cloud of dust lay over it, lifted into the air by the passing of each car. The cloud hung there in the shimmering Texas heat, rising and falling over a series of small hills until it disappeared in the distance.

"You'll have to leave the bottles here," the station attendant said, "or else pay for 'em."

"We'll leave them here," Rana said quickly. "Fact is, we have about six bottles. Will you buy them?"

"I reckon I can," the attendant said, "if they're the kind I handle."

"They are," Rana said, getting the bottles out of the back of the car. "I looked."

While Rana was getting the deposit on the bottles, Gamblin pointed down the road. "This is the road to Texon, isn't it?"

"Texon? Yep, it's about fifteen more miles down the road. You from Texon?"

"No, but we've got business there," Gamblin said.

"Then you'll be wantin' to meet Jason Hewlitt, I

reckon."

"Jason Hewlitt? Who's he and why would I want to meet him?"

"You say you got business there, don't you?"

"Yes."

"Well, mister, they don't nobody do nothin' in that town without goin' through Jason Hewlitt first. You might say he *is* Texon."

Chapter Eight

Before Gamblin went to sea he had worked for eight years in the oil fields of East Texas. He remembered the fields as forests of ugly wooden derricks and the air as reeking with the stench of crude oil. He remembered that the natural gas, which was being flared at the wellheads, created a smoke so thick that he could imagine what hell must look like.

At first Gamblin had worked at minimum-wage, minimum-skill jobs, such as loading and unloading pipe, tools, and other equipment. But he was an exceptionally good worker and a quick learner. He soon worked himself up to being a tool dresser and, eventually, a full-fledged driller.

Despite the hard work and ugliness all around him, Gamblin had been fascinated by the business and could still recall the almost sexual excitement of watching a well come in. Sometimes, in his private dreams, he would envision himself as a wildcatter.

Gamblin definitely had what it took to be a wildcatter. He could handle pipe with any roustabout and he could read core samples as well as a geologist. He also had something that couldn't be acquired, something a person had to be born with. He had a feel for oil, for what it was, and what it would take to get it out. In fact, if ever a person was destined to become a wildcatter, it was Gamblin McClarity, and he would have become one long before now, had it not been for Clem Nester.

Clem Nester was the last oil man for whom Gamblin had worked. To finance his operation, Nester had solicited a group of Houston businessmen for backing. Oil was bringing three dollars a barrel at the wellhead, and one-thousand-barrel-per-day-producing wells were being brought in as a matter of course. Fortunes were being made, and those who were in were becoming instant millionaires.

The same primordial urges that had sent thousands of fortune hunters streaming to California for the gold rush seventy years earlier now infected twentieth-century businessmen. Investors, anxious to capitalize on the oil boom, were easy to come by. They were so easy, in fact, that some people were getting rich off the investors.

Gamblin soon discovered that Nester was doing just that. He was more interested in tapping his investors than the oil fields. As a result, Nester was making no serious effort to find oil.

Ironically, Gamblin had believed there was oil close to their drilling site, and he had tried to get Nester to punch another hole in another location. Nester had refused, so, on his own, Gamblin had installed a whipstock one thousand feet down in the hole they had already drilled. This was a beveled wedge of steel, designed to change the angle of the drill bit. So, instead of drilling straight down beneath the derrick, they were actually boring off at a rather severe angle.

When Nester found out what Gamblin was doing, he fired him and publicly accused him of trying to sabotage the operation. Nester told his backers that the high cost and the failure of his venture was due to Gamblin's incompetence. Nester was a respected wildcatter who had brought in some successful wells in the past; Gamblin was just an upstart driller who didn't do what he was told.

From then on no oil man would hire Gamblin, and he had left Texas in disgrace, swearing never to return to Texas until he could return as his own man. That was why, when he was robbed in St. Louis, he decided to stay in the city.

Now he was back. He didn't have a lot of money, but he had something even better. He had the oil rights to fifty thousand acres of Texas land.

It was about six o'clock in the evening when Gamblin and Rana drove slowly down the street of Texon, Texas, for the first time. As a town, Texon didn't appear to have much going for it. It did have two roads, one that connected it to San Angelo and Fort Stockton, and another that came down from Midland.

The San Angelo-Fort Stockton road formed the major thoroughfare of the town. The Midland road came south to join in a T with the San Angelo road, and there were a few stores and buildings along that road as well. The population of the town, according to a sign just outside the city limits, was six hundred forty.

"You hungry?" Gamblin asked Rana. He pulled into the parking lot of a combination service station-lunchroom. "We can get something to eat here."

"All right," Rana agreed. She looked at herself in the mirror, then made a face. The Chandler may have had a canvas top at one time, but it wasn't with the car when they bought it, so they had driven in an open car all the time, rain or shine. As a result, the swirling dust had covered both car and occupants with a thick layer of red dirt.

"Oh," she said, "look at me. I'm an absolute mess. I'll never come clean again."

"That's all right," Gamblin teased. "I can remember what you used to look like."

They got out of the car, and as they slammed the doors, red dirt slid off the hood and fenders. Each of the running boards held about three inches of dirt. For a moment they brushed dirt off each other. Then, after they had cleaned each other as much as they could, they started toward the little café.

The sun, which was fairly low on the western horizon, had lost much of its brilliance but little of its heat, and it blazed down on them as they crossed the lot heading for the lunchroom. A big Irish setter was lying in the lengthening shadows of the building by the front door, so secure of his position that he didn't even open an eye as they walked by. Gamblin held the door open for Rana, then followed her inside.

The café had a lunch counter with stools and about half a dozen tables. There were four men at the counter and two of the tables were filled. The place smelled of fried-meat grease and Flit. The Flit was coming from the waitress who was busy pumping the handle back and forth on a spray gun, pushing a noxious cloud of insecticide out into the room.

"Be right with you folks," she called. She followed one dazed fly over to the corner, then worked him over all the way down to the floor. "Goddamn it, Sue Ellen, you're not s'posed to have to drown 'em with that stuff," called one of the men.

"I don't care," the waitress answered, continuing to pump the handle, soaking the fly, which was now lying on the floor. "What that fly's been doin' to me all day just pure ain't Christian. I'm bound to be rid of 'im, once 'n' for all."

The waitress walked back over to the counter and put the spray gun away. Then she picked up a menu and came to Gamblin and Rana's table.

"Is there a place I can wash up a bit?" Rana asked. "We've been on the road all day."

"I know. Ain't this dirt just pure awful? The county was s'posed to oil the road last week to keep the dust down some, but the county seat's over at Big Lake, and Big Lake's all they care about. There's a washroom 'round behind the kitchen. You have to prime the pumps, but there's a can of water on the windowsill. Ought to be a piece of soap there, too."

"Thanks," Rana said. She got up and started toward the back.

"You want me to wait to take your order, honey?" the waitress called.

"He can give it," Rana said.

"We'll each have a hamburger," Gamblin said, "and a cold orange drink."

"Comin' right up," the waitress promised.

Rana came back a few moments later with at least her face and hands clean. It was obvious that she was feeling much better. Gamblin excused himself and washed up as well, so that by the time the hamburgers arrived, the spirits of both the travelers had risen considerably.

"Is there anything else I can get you?" the waitress asked as they finished eating.

"Yes," Rana said. "Is there a hotel in town?"

"There's the Hewlitt Hotel down the street, just next door to Hewlitt Hardware."

"Would that be Jason Hewlitt?" Gamblin asked.

"Yup. Know him?"

"No," Gamblin said. "I just heard the name, that's all."

"I don't wonder. He owns practically the whole town. He owns the hotel, the hardware store, the grocery store, and this here place, too. And that's just about all there is to the town."

"You're forgettin' about the Dandy Lion," one of the male customers said. It must have been an inside joke, because everyone laughed.

"The Dandy Lion? What is the Dandy Lion?"

"Well, let's put it this way, mister: iffen you got a hankerin' for a drink, I reckon that'd be the first place you'd check."

Gamblin smiled. "Well, Texon can't be all bad if a place this small has a speakeasy."

"'Course, there's some fellas hanker for a little more than a drink, and when they do, why, the Dandy Lion's the place for that, too."

"Paul Henry, that's enough of that kinda talk," the waitress said. "These folks are just passin' through our town. You want to give them a bad impression?"

"Don't worry about the impression," Gamblin said, "and we aren't passing through."

"You aren't passing through? What do you mean?"

"We're going to live here," Gamblin said.

Chapter Nine

*Aboard Texon One, approaching Washington, D.C.
— 1986*

The phone beside Rana's chair buzzed and she interrupted her story to pick it up.

"Yes?"

"Mrs. McClarity, it's the president of the United States," the flight engineer said, his voice reflecting his awe.

"Put him through."

"Yes, ma'am."

"Rana" — the president's voice came over the phone — "welcome to Washington."

"Mr. President, how good of you to call."

"Why wouldn't I call? You're one of my favorite

people," the president said. "I'm very much looking forward to our dinner this evening."

"Thank you. Oh, Mr. President, Rebel Hewlitt and my grandson, Deke, are with me. I would take it as a personal favor if you would include them in your invitation for dinner."

"Of course they are included," the president replied. "And now I have a favor to ask of you."

"What is it?"

"I wonder if you could find time to visit with me in the Oval Office before dinner tonight. I thought perhaps a personal chat, away from the crowd, so to speak, might be beneficial."

"I would be delighted, Mr. President," Rana said.

"Fine, fine. I'll see you then."

Rana hung up the phone and looked over toward Deke and Rebel.

"We're having dinner with the president tonight," she said. "I promise to finish the story as soon as I can. But first, you can't go to dinner looking like that. I want you two to get something to wear as soon as we land."

"Dinner with the president?" Rebel remarked, smiling broadly. "That sounds exciting."

"I can think of things I'd rather do," Deke suggested.

Rana looked at the two of them and chuckled. "Seems to me like you've thought of too many things to do already, or you wouldn't be so concerned about Evan's gossip."

Maria stuck her head through the door.

"We're beginning our descent now," she said. "Would everyone please buckle up?"

A fleet of cars met the airplaine when it landed, then took the passengers to their various destinations. Rana,

Maggie, Deke, and Rebel were taken to the Watergate, where Texon had offices and apartments. There, Deke and Rebel transferred from the limousine to a nondescript, two-door Plymouth, thus acquiring some anonymity for their shopping trip.

An hour later, with their purchases in the trunk of the car, Deke and Rebel stopped for coffee at a little coffee shop on Tenth Street, right across from Ford's Theatre. As she drank her coffee, Rebel watched a mother and father herd two little boys into the theater.

"I wish we could do that," she said, nodding toward the theater.

"See where Lincoln was shot? Do you want to go?"

"No," Rebel said. "That's not what I mean. I mean..." She let the sentence drop and Deke looked across the street to see the line of tourists moving into the theater. Deke saw the look in Rebel's eyes and put his hand across the table to take her hand in his.

"I think I know what you mean," he said.

"Don't you ever feel like that?" Rebel asked. "Don't you ever wish we could just be like other people — marry, have kids, and live our own life?"

"Yeah, without it turning up on the front page of one of those damned supermarket newspapers every time one of us farted," Deke added.

"Evan Hewlitt farts, Stewart Jackson's brains get blown out," Rebel teased and they both laughed.

"Listen to us," Deke said. "You know what Grandpa would say if he heard us talking like this. He'd say — " Deke leaned back and affected the low, gravelly voice of Gamblin McClarity. " — 'Boy, you'd bitch if you got hung with a new rope.'"

"I miss Gamblin," Rebel said.

"Me too," Deke said. "I never knew my father...

Grandpa was the only father I ever had."

"Deke, what's going to happen to us?"

"What do you mean?"

"What was Daddy talking about? Do you think there really is some dark secret that will prevent us from getting married?"

Deke furrowed his brow, then put his other hand on Rebel's.

"I don't know," he said. "I only know that I don't intend to lose you now. I love you, Rebel Hewlitt, and nothing anyone could possibly say will ever change that."

"Excuse me," someone said, and Deke and Rebel looked up to see a woman standing beside their table.

"Yes?" Deke asked.

The woman looked right at Rebel. "Didn't I see your picture on the cover of *Woman's World*?" she asked. "You're Rebel Hewlitt, aren't you?"

"Yes," Rebel admitted.

"Oh, I knew it!" the woman enthused. "Oh, I think you are such a beautiful woman... and you lead such a glamorous life. I can't wait until I tell all my friends that I saw you."

"Well," Rebel said self-consciously, "I hope you have a nice day." As the woman walked away from the table, Rebel stood up. "Come on, Deke," she said. "Let's get out of here before she brings her friends to meet me."

Deke left some money on the table and chuckled as they left the restaurant.

"I'm hurt," he teased. "She didn't even recognize me."

"Let's face it, Deke, you just aren't 'star' material, and I am."

"Yeah? Well, I notice that she didn't ask you for your

autograph, so you can't be that much of a celebrity."

The president had said that he wanted to speak to Rana away from the crowd, but when he greeted her in the spacious Oval Office that night, he wasn't alone. There were three men with him, including Senator Morgan Carmack and Evan Hewlitt's man, Stewart Jackson.

The president was standing in front of the three tall windows behind his desk, and behind him Rana could see the brilliant white, well-lighted shaft of the Washington Monument. Farther still, across the Tidal Basin, she could see the Jefferson Memorial, surrounded by clouds of pink from the blossoms on the Japanese cherry trees.

Rana looked around the office, at the green carpet with its official seal, the presidential banner and the American flag draped in front of the windows, and Washington's portrait over the mantel. She had been visiting presidents in their lair since Herbert Hoover held the job. She had a deep-rooted respect for the continuity of the office, but she had long since gotten over her awe of the man who happened to occupy the White House.

"Thank you, Rana, for stopping by to see me," the president said. "I believe you know these gentlemen? Stewart Jackson, one of my special advisors on energy, Senator Morgan Carmack, and the Honorable Fernando Lopez of the Latin Energy Commission."

Rana nodded at the men, then sat down in a big leather chair across from the president's desk.

"What is it, Mr. President?" she asked. "Why the sandbags?"

"Mrs. McClarity, I wouldn't want you to think of us as sandbags," Jackson said.

"You're Evan Hewlitt's man, Mr. Jackson, chorus

and verse. What should I call you?"

"You should call me someone who is concerned about the future of energy," Jackson said.

"And you certainly can't say that I'm Hewlitt's man," Senator Carmack said. "You may know that my committee is investigating Mr. Hewlitt."

"I take no pleasure in that investigation, Senator," Rana said. "Though Evan and I may not see eye to eye on the running of our company, we are at least together in wanting the company to succeed. Your investigation can only hurt Texon."

"If he is engaged in kickbacks and bribes, eliminating that kind of business practice can only help Texon," Carmack insisted.

"Mrs. McClarity, we're here to try and persuade you to change your mind, before you gut Mexico of its oil," Jackson said.

"Gut Mexico?"

"Yes," Lopez answered, speaking for the first time. "I am with the Latin Energy Commission. As you know, the LEC is vitally concerned with the status of fossil fuels, not only in Mexico, but in all of Latin America. We are disturbed by the Texon proposal to take so much oil from the Bustamante Basin. We have had experts look into this, and their findings are most disturbing. We released a report on those findings, Mrs. McClarity. Perhaps you have seen it?"

"I've read the report."

"Then you know that if you go through with your plans, it will bring about a total collapse of Mexico's energy position. The LEC suggests that by the time the Texon contract is fulfilled, over three-fourths of Mexico's oil will be gone."

"That's bullshit, Mr. Lopez, and you know it. Even

the Mexican government has dismissed that report."

"You can't just dismiss this report out of hand," Jackson suggested. "Until it has been disproven, it must be considered."

"There's something else that must be considered, Mr. Jackson," Rana said. "LEC has never been friendly to Texon. I think it should be very clear that they have a vested interest in whether or not that contract goes through."

"As one of the president's advisors on energy, I have gone on record as saying that I believe the LEC report."

"Yes, well, we all know where your loyalties are, don't we?"

"See here, are you accusing me of putting vested interests above the interests of our country?" Jackson sputtered.

"I thought I had made that clear," Rana said.

The president held up his hand in the role of peacemaker.

"Mrs. McClarity, Stewart Jackson is friendly with Evan Hewlitt, as he is with half a dozen other oil magnates. I don't believe such friendships are detrimental to his position as energy advisor; on the contrary, if he couldn't get along with any of them, he would be useless to me. I'm convinced that he is acting in the best interests of the country."

"Not if he is willing to accept the LEC report at face value," Rana challenged.

"I am aware that the LEC report has been challenged, but there are also those who are concerned about the outflow of dollars," the president went on. "We were hoping that we might persuade you to hold up on any final agreement until all of these concerns are addressed."

"We can't stop. Mr. President, you must understand

how complicated these negotiations are. We must maintain the momentum; otherwise, we may never reach this point again."

"I can force you to stop, Mrs. McClarity," Stewart Jackson said.

"Try it, sonny, and I'll crush you like the *pissant* you are," Rana retorted.

"Mr. President, I protest this —" Jackson started to say, but the president interrupted him, then chuckled aloud.

"Jackson, you knew she was a fighter when you asked for this meeting," the president said. "Just what the hell did you expect? Did you think she would roll over?"

"I thought she would listen to reason," Jackson said.

"Perhaps she would, if we had any reason to give her. I think you'd better go back to the drawing board on this one. If you can bring me definite proof that the Texon deal is detrimental to the U.S., I'll stop it; otherwise, I see no reason why she can't at least continue the negotiations."

"Thank you, Mr. President," Rana said.

"Now, gentlemen, if you'll excuse us," the president added, "Mrs. McClarity and I have a dinner to attend."

The man in the tuxedo held a cigar in one hand and a drink in the other. He waved his drink as he talked, and Rebel had to move back when some of the drink sloshed over the rim.

She'd enjoyed the dinner, the elegant surroundings, the distinguished company, and the thought of sitting at the same table as the president of the United States. The dinner had been small and controlled, but once dinner was over the number of guests had grown dramatically. There were dozens of congressmen, entertainment personalities, star athletes, and business people present. One of the businessmen had managed to maneuver Rebel and Deke into a corner.

"Yes, sir," the man went on. "I was with the Redskins organization then, and when our time came around, ole Deke here was still available. Hell, as far as I was concerned, he was the best quarterback in college football that year and no one had selected him. I told the front office to grab him, but they wouldn't do it."

"They called me," Deke said. "But you're wrong when you say no one drafted me. The U.S. Army wanted me."

"We could've gotten you out of that."

"I didn't want out. Anyway, I wasn't interested in playing pro football."

"Not interested? How can you not be interested in playing football in the pros? That's every man's dream!"

"Not mine," Deke said. "I had other things to do.... Oh, would you excuse us? I see an old friend waving at us."

"We could've made you a star," the man called to Deke as he guided Rebel through the crowded room. "We could've made you a star, but you threw it away."

"Who'd you see?" Rebel asked.

Deke laughed. "I didn't see anyone. I just wanted to get away from him. In fact, I'd like to get away from this party. What do you say?"

Now it was Rebel's turn to laugh. "I don't know," she said. "Isn't it considered a terrible breach of etiquette to walk out on a presidential function? I mean, it just isn't done."

"All the more reason why I want to do it," Deke said. "Come on, let's get out of here."

Fifteen minutes later Deke was driving the same Plymouth they had used for shopping across the Arlington Bridge onto Mount Vernon Memorial Highway.

"Where are we going?" Rebel asked. "Aren't we going back to the Watergate?"

"No," Deke said. "Unless I miss my guess, your father is there now, waiting for us. I'm not ready to deal with him just yet."

"Nor I. But where are we going?"

"I've got a friend who owns an apartment building in Alexandria," Deke said. "I thought we'd call on him."

"Who is he loyal to? Your grandmother or my father?"

Deke chuckled. "Neither. Fact is, he's not even associated with them. He's an old army buddy."

"That was a long time ago. You think he'll remember you?"

"He'll remember me," Deke said. "I'm a silent partner in the apartment building he owns."

A uniformed guard approached them at the entrance to the apartment parking garage, but a call to the upstairs soon passed them through. A few moments later they were inside the comfortably furnished apartment of Deke's friend.

"Rebel, this is Colonel Mike Rindell, U.S. Army, retired. He was my C.O. in Nam."

Rindell was a short man, shorter even than Rebel. He had thin gray hair, sparkling blue eyes, and a friendly smile.

"Hello, Colonel," Rebel said.

"Mike," Mike corrected. He shook Rebel's hand. "Well, this is a pleasant surprise, Deke. I had no idea you were coming to town."

"I didn't either," Deke admitted. "It was a spur-of-the-moment thing."

"My God, look at the way you two are dressed," Mike said, noticing for the first time that they were both formally attired. "You make me feel absolutely naked."

"Shit, Mike, if you're not worth dressing up to see, who the hell is?" Deke teased. He slipped off his shoes, tossed his jacket onto a chair, and undid his tie to let it hang open on the front of his shirt. He sprawled out on the couch and held out his hand. "Wanna put a beer in this hand?" he asked.

"How about you?" Mike asked Rebel. "Beer, or would you prefer a mixed drink?"

"Beer's fine," Rebel answered. She walked over to look through the window toward Washington. Mike's apartment was on the twentieth floor of the building, and the urban area was displayed before them like a beautiful Christmas tree of lights. "Oh, what a lovely view you have," she said.

Mike popped the tops off three cans of beer, then began pouring them into glasses.

"Yeah," he said. "Mary used to like to turn the apartment lights off and stand right there where you are to look at the city at night."

"Mary. Your wife?"

"She died fourteen months ago," Mike said, handing each of them a glass. "I still miss her."

"I'm sorry," Rebel said automatically.

"I've seen your picture in magazines and on TV a couple of times," Mike said, changing the subject. "You're even prettier in person."

"Thank you," Rebel said.

"I wouldn't want you to get carried away by his flattery," Deke warned. "Don't forget, I've seen this silver-tongued devil in action."

"I'll just bet you can be a smooth operator," Rebel said, rubbing her finger around the rim of her glass.

"Ah, my lovely, if only we could get rid of the ugly one there," Mike teased.

When Rana returned from the presidential reception that evening, she found Evan Hewlitt waiting for her in the apartment. It was not unexpected.

"Evan, it's always nice to see you."

Evan smiled. "I can tell by the enthusiastic tone in your voice how much you really enjoy it. How was your meeting with the president?"

"Oh, I'm sure you'll get a complete report from your man Jackson in the morning," Rana said.

"I suppose I will," Evan said, making no effort to deny what he knew Rana knew.

"To what do I owe the pleasure?" Rana asked.

"I understand my daughter came to Washington with you. Would you happen to know where she is?"

"You mean she isn't in her room?"

"No," Evan said. "And neither is Deke."

Rana smiled and sat down. "Well, that should tell you, then. Wherever they are, they are together."

"It pleases you that they are together?"

"Yes, of course it does," Rana said. "It's obvious to anyone who knows them that they are in love."

"You haven't told them yet?"

"Told them what?"

"That they can't be married."

Rana leaned her head back on the chair and closed her eyes for a moment.

"I know that you would like nothing better than to

"I know that you would like nothing better than to gain control of my daughter's votes," Evan went on. "But I would think that even you would put the welfare of my daughter and your grandson above any benefit you might derive from their merger." Evan twisted the word "merger" so that it came out harsh, and ugly.

"Evan, if you would excuse me now, I do have a terrible headache," Rana said. "The cigarette smoke, the champagne, the noise...I find functions at the White House to be extremely trying."

Evan looked at her for a moment, then sighed and walked over to the door. He put his hand on the doorknob, then turned to look back at Rana. For a moment the anger and challenge that had been in his face were gone, replaced by a look of genuine anxiety.

"Rana, whatever differences we have between us, you must understand that my first concern is for my daughter. I wanted to give you the opportunity to tell them because I felt it would be less painful coming from you."

"Wrong. You wanted to put me on the spot," Rana replied.

"Think what you want," Evan said. "But if you don't tell them, I will. This marriage cannot take place."

"Good night, Evan," Rana said.

Chapter Ten

Texon, Texas — 1923

When Gamblin came down to the lobby of the hotel the next morning, a man who had been sitting in one of the chairs stood up.

"Mr. McClarity?"

Gamblin was surprised to hear himself addressed by name. He didn't know anyone in Texon, and he certainly didn't know this man.

"Yes?"

The man was slightly taller than Gamblin, but somewhat on the thin side. He had brown hair and light blue eyes, and he smiled and stuck out his hand.

"My name's Jason Hewlitt," he said. "I'd like for you

and Miss Wood to have breakfast with me this morning, if you would."

"How did you know our names?" Gamblin asked. He had registered last night; it would have been fairly easy for Hewlitt to find out his name. But, in order to save money, he had registered them as man and wife, so how did Hewlitt know Rana's name?

"Oh, I've been waiting for you, Mr. McClarity. I've been waiting for quite a while."

"Waiting? What do you mean?"

"I'll explain everything to you over breakfast," he said. "Will Miss Wood be coming down?"

"Yes," Gamblin said. "She had just come from her bath when I left the room."

"Then the two of you will join me?"

"What's this all about, Mr. Hewlitt?" Gamblin asked.

"I want to discuss some business with you."

"What kind of business?"

"Oil business," Jason answered, smiling broadly.

When Rana came downstairs Gamblin introduced her to Jason Hewlitt. Jason reissued his invitation to breakfast, and when Rana accepted, he took them through the main dining room of the hotel to a smaller, private dining room at the rear. It was obvious that he had expected them to accept his invitation, because the table was already laid with three place settings of china, silver, and crystal, far more elaborate than one might expect to find in a hotel, let alone in a town as small as Texon.

"I thought a small breakfast steak might be in order," Jason said. "I hope you don't mind. I've already given the cook instructions."

"You're paying for the breakfast, aren't you?" Gamblin asked.

"Yes, yes, of course I am."

"Then anything we have is fine with me," Gamblin said.

Jason hurried around the table to pull out Rana's chair, and he held it for her until she was seated, then he sat down directly across from her. Gamblin was in the middle, with Rana to his right and Jason to his left.

"Was your room comfortable?" Jason asked as the meal was served.

"Yes, thank you," Gamblin answered.

"I really enjoyed the bathtub," Rana offered. "I feel like I washed half of Texas away last night, and the other half this morning."

"I know what you mean. The roads are really dusty," Jason said, continuing the small talk.

"Okay," Gamblin finally said, "get on with it. What do you mean you want to talk oil business? And why would you want to talk to us?"

Jason smiled and dabbed at his mouth with a table napkin. "They said you were a man who likes to come right to the point," he said.

"They? Who the hell is 'they'?"

"The people I asked about you. You are the same Gamblin McClarity who worked for Clem Nester a couple of years ago, aren't you?"

Gamblin's eyes narrowed. "So what if I am?" he said. "Whatever happened between Nester and me is my own business. It's certainly none of yours."

Jason chuckled. "That's not quite true," he said. "I mean about it being none of my business. It so happens that I lost a good deal of money then. I was one of the investors in that operation."

Gamblin pushed his chair back from the table and stood up. He tossed his napkin on his plate.

"Thanks for breakfast, Mr. Hewlitt. Rana, let's go."

"Aren't you interested in what I've got to say?" Jason asked.

"No."

"I'm interested," Rana said quietly.

"Rana?"

Gamblin had told Rana the story of his experience with Clem Nester. Why did she want Hewlitt to bring it up again? He looked at her as if she had just given him the Judas kiss.

"Please go on, Mr. Hewlitt," Rana invited.

"But not until I've left," Gamblin insisted. He shoved his chair in and turned to leave.

"Gamblin, wait," Rana called, sticking her hand out as if to hold him. "I don't think Mr. Hewlitt is upset with you about the Nester incident. I don't think that's what he wants to talk about."

Jason smiled broadly. "You are a most perceptive woman, Miss Wood. Mr. McClarity, I'm not about to condemn you for anything — quite the contrary. I want to congratulate you."

"Congratulate me? Congratulate me for what?"

"As you may know, the company formed to back Clem Nester went broke. Nester blamed you, and most of us, myself included, I'm ashamed to admit, believed him. We signed letters that were sent to every drilling operation in the state, telling them that our failure was due to your incompetence. You are aware of that, of course, as the oil business was closed to you. But I have discovered something recently that very few people know. A new corporation bought the leases to the area where you were drilling, and they've brought in six new wells. The first well they brought in was by drilling exactly where you were headed with your angle bore. You were right, Mr. McClarity. If you had been allowed to continue just a few more days I would be a much richer man than I am today."

Gamblin sat back down and looked at Jason with his eyes open in shock.

"They brought the well in?" he asked.

"They sure as hell did. It blew six months after you left Texas."

Gamblin smiled and slammed his fist into his hand. "I knew it was there," he said. "I just knew it!"

"How did you know?" Jason asked. "It wasn't over an anticline, and the surface conditions showed gypsum and rock salt. According to all the books, oil shouldn't have been there."

"This is 1923. All the books haven't been written yet. Besides, they'll never be able to write a book to explain how I knew there was oil there, because I can't even explain it. I knew oil was there because I could feel it, taste it, smell it," Gamblin said. He smiled. "I know that sounds silly, but it's like I have a compass inside me that points down when I'm over oil."

"I don't think it's silly," Jason said. "I think there are people who can find oil, just like there are people who can dowse water. Maybe you're one of them. Now, tell me, is there oil here?"

"Here?"

"Let's not play games, Mr. McClarity. I know you hold the leases to fifty thousand acres of land between here and the Middle Concho."

"How do you know that?" Rana asked.

Jason smiled. "I paid good money to find out. I tried to buy the leases, only to discover that the leases had been sold to Josiah Hunter Ellison. Of course, everyone has heard of Josiah Hunter...I mean his name is mentioned in the same breath with Shanghai Pierce, and Jinglebob John Chisum. But Josiah Hunter Ellison died twenty years ago, so I tried to get the state to declare a quit claim. That was when I was informed that his widow was still alive and still held the leases. I tried for three years to find her, but I couldn't. Then, a few days ago, one of my informants told me that a change of ownership had been filed on the leases, that they now belonged to Rana Wood and Gamblin McClarity. You, Miss Wood, I had never heard of. But Gamblin McClarity...now there was a name I recognized. I figured you'd be comin' down here soon, so I've been on the lookout, and sure enough, here you are."

"Yes," Gamblin said. "Here I am."

"I suppose you're anxious to look over your lease land," Jason said. "I've got horses — we can probably see as much from horseback as any other way. Suppose we do that, then you can get an idea as to where we should start drilling first."

"We?"

"Yes, we," Jason said. "You're going to need equipment and money. You'll have your own living expenses, plus you'll have to hire a crew. That's going to cost several thousand dollars, Mr. McClarity. Are you prepared for it? Do you have that much money?"

"I'll come up with the money," Gamblin said.

"Maybe you will and maybe you won't, Mr. McClarity. But, for half ownership, I'll put up all the money you need."

"I told you, I'll come up with the money. We'll get by without your help, thank you," Gamblin said.

"No, wait," Rana interjected. "Gamblin, we are going to need money. You know we are."

"I'll find a bank to lend us the money. Rana, we don't want to take on a partner. I've seen these operations in the past — the partner who puts up the money always winds up owning everything, while the other partner is left suckin' hind tit. Thank you, no. I'm not interested in a partnership."

"Mr. McClarity, before you make up your mind..."

"I've already made up my mind," Gamblin said firmly.

"I think you should know that all the major oil companies had their geologists scurrying all over Reagan County — the report from all of them was negative. Not one major company is willing to put down so much as a test well here. With that kind of report, do you really think you'll find a bank that will lend you the money?"

"I'll get it somewhere," Gamblin insisted.

"Mr. Hewlitt," Rana put in, "if you know all this, why are you even interested in us? Why would you be willing to put up several thousand dollars if the oil companies aren't willing to take a chance?"

Jason smiled. "Well, I'll tell you," he said, "I'm only interested in putting up the money if McClarity thinks there's oil out there."

"You'd be willing to risk that much, just on my say-so?" Gamblin asked, surprised by Jason's statement.

Jason spread jam on a piece of toast and took a bite before he answered. He smiled broadly.

"Yeah, Gamblin," he said. "I'm willing to risk that much, just on your say-so."

"Why?"

Jason laughed. "It's hard to explain, but I'll try. You

have a nose for oil. You say that, and I believe you. In fact, I would believe you even if I didn't know the full story of the Nester operation. And the reason I would believe you is that I, Mr. McClarity, have a nose for money. I look at you and I feel money — big money — and I want to be part of it."

"I see," Gamblin said. "But you only feel money if we are partners, right?"

"No," Jason admitted. "Whether we are partners or not, you are going to make big money. I do believe it will be easier if we are working together."

"If the money is really that big, then there should be more of the pie to slice, right?" Rana asked.

"What do you mean?"

"I mean we'll make you a partner, but not for half. You'll be in for a third."

"A third? Oh, I don't know," Jason said. "It's going to cost a lot of money to bring in the first well. You'd be asking a lot for a third."

"It's the only way we'll do it," Rana said. "One third for you, one third for Gamblin, and one third for me."

Jason looked at Gamblin. "Would you go along with that arrangement?" he asked.

Gamblin ran his hand through his hair and sighed. "Is this what you want?" he asked Rana.

"Do you know any better way to get the money?" she asked.

"No."

"Then this is what I want."

"All right," Gamblin agreed. "It's a deal."

"I'll get papers drawn up, forming a corporation," Jason said. "We'll need a president."

"I'll be the president," Rana volunteered.

"I don't know, maybe..." Jason started.

"Look, there's no way Gamblin is going to be happy if you are the president," Rana said. "And I don't see you putting up all this money with Gamblin as the president. That leaves only me."

Jason laughed. "I guess you have a point," he said. "Is that all right with you, Gamblin?"

Gamblin laughed. "Do we have a choice?"

"What will we call this company?" Gamblin asked. Both men looked at Rana.

"You're the president, Rana. Come up with a name," Jason said.

"How about Texon Petroleum?" she suggested.

"Texon Petroleum it is," Jason agreed. "We'll be in business by this afternoon." Jason extended his hand, and Rana and Gamblin took it, forming a three-pointed star with their arms.

Rana raised the dust as she swept the floor of the little two-room building. It had once served as a doctor's office, but the doctor had returned to Big Lake, leaving the building empty. Now it sported a big sign above the door out front, making the grandiose claim that this was headquarters for the TEXON PETROLEUM CORPORATION.

The sound of a klaxon horn caused Rana to look up and she saw Gamblin waving at her from behind the steering wheel of a new truck. He was smiling broadly.

"Come out!" Gamblin called. "Come out and look at her! Isn't she a beauty?"

Rana leaned the broom against the desk and hurried out front. The truck was a Reo, and the name of the company, Texon Petroleum, had already been painted on the doors.

"Oh, Gamblin, I do believe this is the most beautiful

thing I have ever seen," Rana said excitedly. She put her hand on the hood, rubbing it gingerly against the smooth, gleaming paint. The metal work around the grille was silver and shining.

"It'll be even prettier when it's all covered with mud and dirt," Gamblin said.

Rana laughed. "Why do you say that?"

"Because that means it's working."

"When are you going to go out into the field?"

"Today!" Gamblin answered excitedly. "I'm going up to San Angelo to pick up a few supplies. Then I'm going out to find oil."

This was the moment Rana had been waiting for, but now that it had arrived, she realized that she and Gamblin were going to be separated, possibly for a long time.

"How long will you be gone?" she asked in a soft voice.

"Quite a while," Gamblin answered. "From two to four weeks for sure."

"That means I won't see you for a month."

"Could be," Gamblin agreed.

Rana looked back at the little office building, then around at the tiny town, its weathered buildings fronting the dirt street. The prospect of spending a month alone in this town chilled her.

"Oh, Gamblin, are you sure you don't want me to come with you?"

"I'd rather work alone," Gamblin said. "Besides, I need someone back here that I can trust, someone to look out for the money, make sure the equipment I order comes in — that sort of thing. And I sure don't trust Jason Hewlitt."

"I think you are wrong about him. Jason is our partner," Rana said. "I'm sure he wouldn't do anything to hurt the company. Why should he?"

"What do you mean, why should he? So he can take over for himself, that's why," Gamblin said.

Rana shook her head. "No. He wouldn't do that. Gamblin, I wish you would make an effort to get along with Jason. He's certainly gone out of his way to be nice to us."

"You mean be nice to you, don't you?"

"To us," Rana insisted. "And I don't want to hear any more about it. There are three of us in this company, all equal partners, and my biggest job is to keep the peace between you two. If you can't get along with him now, before we even start, then this whole thing is doomed from the beginning. Now, you have to promise me that you'll try and get along with him. After all, he has put up all the money, hasn't he?"

"Oh, I'm sure he won't let us forget that," Gamblin said.

"Why do you say that? Has he balked on a cent we have asked for?"

"No," Gamblin admitted grudgingly.

"And has he questioned anything you spend the money on?"

"No," Gamblin admitted. "I guess he hasn't."

"Then why do you have such an attitude about him?"

"I don't know. I guess I just hadn't planned on anyone else coming in on our deal, that's all."

"We wouldn't be this far if we didn't have him, would we?"

"No."

"Then I say I'm glad we ran across him. Promise me you'll try to get along with him."

Gamblin smiled and ran his hand through Rana's hair.

"Yeah, okay," he said. "Hell, what's there to getting along? I'll be in the field and he'll be here."

"Right," Rana said. She put her arms around his neck, then raised her lips to his. "The only problem is, I'll be here, too. I want you to know what you're going to be missing." She kissed him and pressed her body against his.

"Woman!" Gamblin said, pulling away from her. "We're standing right in the middle of the goddamned street!"

Rana laughed. "Are we, now? And did I embarrass you, Mr. McClarity?"

"No. I mean yes. Well, Goddamn it, that isn't exactly the kind of kiss you give a man in the middle of the street, you know."

"I just wanted you to miss me, that's all."

Gamblin smiled. "Don't you worry about that. I'm going to miss you. I'm going to miss you plenty." He walked back out to the truck, then stepped around front and jerked the crank through. The truck started on the first turn. With a big smile, he hopped in behind the wheel, then looked over at Rana.

"Wish me luck!" he called as he moved the truck into gear.

"Good luck!"

The truck rolled down the main street, then turned north toward San Angelo. Rana stood on the porch until she could no longer see him, until the sighing wind carried away the last sound of the engine. Then she went back inside to finish sweeping, feeling a sense of excitement she could barely control.

The first pink fingers of dawn fanned up from the eastern horizon; the light was soft and the air was cool.

Gamblin liked the prairie best early in the morning. He was camped in a dry wash and he looked toward the last morning star, now a bright pinpoint of light in the graying dawn.

The coals from his campfire of the night before were still glowing. He threw on chunks of wood and stirred the fire into crackling flames that danced merrily against the bottom of the suspended coffeepot. He made himself a cup of coffee and sat down to enjoy it. It was black and steaming and he had to blow on it before he could suck it through his lips. He watched the sun climb full disc above the horizon, then stream brightly down onto the prairie floor.

Gamblin thought of Rana. It had been five weeks since he left Texon, and his last view of her was her standing in front of the office, waving at him. He had missed her much more than he thought he would.

Gamblin was used to being alone. The circumstances of his youth had made him a loner, and he had remained that way by choice when he worked in the oil fields. He had made no fast friends while in the merchant marine and actually enjoyed the solitude of the long, silent watches at sea.

Rana had changed all that. In the time they had been together, she had become so much a part of his existence that he could no longer imagine a life without her. He missed her laugh, her conversation, and her warm body next to his at night. He should have brought her out here with him. Dammit! He should have brought her.

Gamblin stood up and stretched to work out the kinks from spending the night on the ground, then tossed out the dregs of his third cup of coffee. He cleaned up his breakfast dishes and then went over to the dust-covered pickup truck to take out the tripod, pulley, and lengths of pipe he was using in his exploration.

Fifteen minutes later he had his contraption set up and he began methodically to pull the rope, winching the pipe up, then letting it fall. He did that over and over again until the pipe began working its way into the ground, picking new dirt up at the bottom, forcing the old through the top. Every so often he would grab a handful of dirt from the bottom end of the pipe and roll it through his hands, feeling it, sniffing it... sometimes even tasting it.

He knew this method of searching for oil would make sense to no one else. Geologists would laugh, bankers would blanch, and the average person would think he was crazy. Let them think what they wanted. When he was over a pool of oil he would know. He couldn't explain it to anyone... but he would know.

Rana moved into the office from the hotel room they'd had since they came to town. It was a simple thing to do; she just brought a bed over and moved it into the back room. A small dining table and a tiny stove completed the appointments and she was home.

As Rana lived and worked in the same building, the line between working and not working grew indistinct. Often she found herself still going over the books late at night.

It was after nine o'clock and the rain that had been threatening all day had finally made good on its promise. It drummed onto the tin roof of the little house and blew against the windows. It felt good to be inside.

Rana was startled by the sound of tapping at the window of the front door. When she walked over to peer through the curtain, she saw Jason Hewlitt standing on the front porch with his collar turned up, carrying a basket of some sort. She opened the door to let him in.

"Good heavens!" she said. "What are you doing out in weather like this?"

"Thank you for having pity on a poor wet wretch," Jason said, stepping into the room. He took his hat off and shook the water from it, then slipped out of his raincoat. He set the basket on the floor.

"Well, if you don't have enough sense to get in out of the rain, someone has to have mercy on you," Rana said.

Jason looked over toward the desk and saw the open books and papers full of Rana's figures.

"Do you work twenty-four hours a day?" he asked.

"Not really," Rana answered. She smiled. "Sometimes it just seems like it."

"I've been waiting for you to come into the restaurant at the hotel," Jason said. "For three days I've been waiting, but you haven't shown up."

"Why were you waiting for me?"

"I was hoping we could have dinner together. Or have you given up eating?"

Rana laughed and ran her hand through her hair.

"Not entirely," she said. "I guess I just didn't realize it was so late. I'll fix myself a sandwich later on."

"Uh-uh," Jason said. "I brought supper for us."

"You what?"

"Well, you know what they say — if Mohammed won't go to the mountain, the mountain will go to Mohammed. You won't come to the restaurant, so I'm bringing it to you. At least, the best they have to offer. It's in the basket."

"I can't believe this." Rana laughed.

"Believe it. You're my partner, aren't you?"

"One of them, anyway," Rana said.

"The prettiest one," Jason replied. "Get the desk cleared off. We need a place to eat."

"Oh, I've got a table in the back room," Rana invited. "Bring it back there."

Jason picked up the picnic basket and followed Rana into the back room. There, in addition to the bed and table, was a small dresser, a couple of chairs, and a trunk. Curtains had been hung on the windows and a brightly colored oilcloth was spread on the table.

"This is the first time I've been back here," Jason said. "I must admit, you've made the place almost homey."

"The biggest thing was just getting it cleaned up," Rana said.

"Let's see what's in here, shall we?" Jason asked as he began unloading the basket, spreading out the food on the table. The basket contained cold sliced roast beef and ham, fresh baked bread, potato salad, olives, pickles, and a bottle of wine.

"I hope you appreciate the wine. It's the genuine stuff. I bought it from a bootlegger in San Angelo."

"Heavens, you've brought enough for an army!" Rana exclaimed after he finished unloading the hamper.

"Maybe, but I didn't know how long it'd been since you'd eaten," Jason quipped. "I thought I would be ready for anything."

Rana pinched off a piece of the roast beef and tasted it.

"Mmm," she said. "Positively delicious."

Jason uncorked the wine bottle, then poured each of them a glass. He handed a glass to Rana.

"For you, my dear," he said.

"Thank you," Rana replied. She started to drink, but Jason put his hand on hers to stop her.

"Wait," he said. "Shouldn't we propose a toast?"

"Oh, yes," Rana enthused. She held her glass out toward his. "To Texon Petroleum."

"May it be successful," Jason concluded.

Rana drank the wine. "Mmm, my compliments to the bootlegger," she teased. "This is good."

Jason made a sandwich and handed it to Rana, then took one for himself.

"Are you going to marry Gamblin?" he asked.

"That's a bit personal, isn't it?"

"I guess so. But we're partners. Seems to me like we have a right to know a little something about each other. I know about Gamblin; I've made it a point to find out. I don't know anything about you."

"Not much to know. My great-aunt had these oil leases. When she died she left joint ownership of them to Gamblin and me."

Jason smiled. "So, it's circumstances that have brought you together and not something more personal."

"You might say that," Rana responded. Almost as soon as she spoke the words, she felt a sense of guilt, as if she were somehow denying Gamblin.

"Do you love him?"

"Of course I love him," Rana answered. "That doesn't necessarily mean I'm in love with him." Again, she felt that by dodging the issue, she was denying Gamblin.

She looked at Jason. He was a handsome enough man; she certainly had to give him credit for that. She thought his lips were a bit too full for a man, but even that seemed to make him more sensual. He was a polished man, a man who seemed to give off an aura of confidence. Rana inherently knew that he was a man of great experience around women, and that knowledge both frightened and intrigued her.

Oh, God, was she sexually attracted to him?

Jason smiled broadly. "Then perhaps it isn't too late for me to put in my bid?"

"Your bid for what?" she asked coyly.

"For your attention," Jason said easily. "Gamblin's been gone for nearly two months now, and I've kept my distance from you. But, if you tell me that you aren't engaged to be married, perhaps I've been too cautious. Perhaps I could start seeing you?"

Rana laughed, but it was a weak laugh. This conversation was getting on dangerous ground.

"Don't be silly. You see me every day."

"I don't mean that," Jason said. He put his hand on Rana's cheek and she felt an incredible heat in his fingers. Her heartbeat increased and she felt flushed.

"Jason, I don't want you to get the wrong idea," Rana said.

"Tell me right now that you belong to Gamblin. Tell me and I'll walk away."

"I...I don't see why I have to belong to anyone," Rana said in a husky voice. "I'm old enough to be my own person."

Why did she answer that way? All she had to do was say she belonged to Gamblin and this difficult moment would pass. Could it be that she didn't want it to pass?

Rana suddenly realized that she had just denied Gamblin for the third time, and the Gospel account of Peter denying Jesus came to mind. She grew frightened and confused and tears welled in her eyes.

"Please, Jason," she said. "Please, go away now."

Jason caught one of her sliding teardrops with the tip of his finger. He raised the teardrop to his lips and kissed it.

"I don't think you want me to go away," he said. "Not really."

Rana was quiet.

"Do you want me to go, Rana? Or do you want me to stay?"

Rana had never been more confused in her life. She had given Gamblin her innocence, explored the range of her passion with him. But now she was feeling sexually attracted to another man, and in this little cabin, pounded by rain, she felt their souls touching.

"I... I want you to stay," she muttered.

Rana's heart was racing. She couldn't believe what she was feeling and saying. It was as if she were suspended above herself, watching this go on. She looked into Jason's blue eyes and hoped that he knew some of what she was feeling.

There was a flicker of understanding in Jason's eyes as he put his arms around her. His breath was suddenly warm against her mouth, hovering there for just an instant before he kissed her. The touch of his lips was a searing heat. A hot, languorous passion enveloped her, slowly consuming her until she was pliant and willing and completely trusting.

Jason turned off the light. A lamp still burned in the front room, and a bar of light splashed through the door so that, though it was darker, they could still see each other.

Jason took Rana's hand in his and guided her over to the bed. They sat on the bed and he reached for the top button of her blouse.

"No," Rana whispered breathily.

"I thought you wanted to."

"I do," Rana said. "But I want to take off my own clothes. I don't want you to take me. I want to give myself to you."

Rana began to remove her clothes, and for just a moment Jason was mesmerized by her beauty. Her breasts were round and upturned, her skin smooth and white as ermine.

Rana climbed slowly into the bed and looked up at Jason as he undressed. She could tell that he was ready for her, and when he climbed into bed, she knew instinctively that he would be slow, patient, and understanding with her. She knew that he would be her tender teacher and she opened herself to him, enjoying the sensuality of the moment.

Jason didn't rush. Though this was their first time together, he seemed to know everything about her... what she desired and needed and more. He knew how to give what she dared not ask for. He lay against her, pressing his body against hers, caressing her breasts, kissing her all over. His tongue was both gentle and rough, tentative and demanding, enticing and frightening, and she sought it eagerly, lost in the sensations that were overcoming her.

Outside, Rana could hear the rain. It was like music, perfectly orchestrated with rhythmic percussion, harmonic bass notes from the larger drops, and delicate trills and melodious tinkling from the water that ran off the roof. The music built and swelled, joining the sweet refrain of the music of her own racing blood.

The connection their bodies made shot through her like a bolt of lightning. Jason pushed into her, moving her from ecstasy to ecstasy, thrusting himself in her again and again, jolting her flesh with sharp, almost painful sensations. Once more he thrust himself in her and she felt her body leap in its final, shattering, white-hot explosion and then she knew she was falling, falling away, through endless corridors of space.

Afterward, they lay hushed together on the bed, listening to the rain pelt against the window. Rana's clothes lay on the floor beside the bed. Jason had already pulled on his pants and now he sat there looking down at her.

"I...I hope you don't think my sole purpose for coming over here tonight was to seduce you," he said. "I wouldn't want you to think I took advantage of you."

Rana looked at Jason and smiled, a slow, almost sad smile, still coasting down from the tremendous heat of moments ago.

"I'm a big girl, Jason," she said. Then she added, "And I suppose the stars are still in their heavens."

"You're not like the others," Jason said, turning away a little, deep in his own thoughts. "The other girls I have...known. You're different, Rana. You're very different."

Rana smiled again. Then she sat up and leaned over to kiss him. As she did so, her breasts swung forward, brushing lightly against his cheek, sending one last small charge of sensation through her body. She could smell her own musk and she almost wished Jason could be reawakened as easily as she. He couldn't, of course, and that was really all right. It was over now and the clock was speeding the event further and further away with every tick, so that already it was only a whisper in time.

For the moment she didn't even think of Gamblin, somewhere on the prairie, riding out the storm. For the moment, at least, he didn't even exist.

Chapter Eleven

Several nights later, Rana was sound asleep when a knocking on the front door finally seeped through to her senses. At first, the knocking seemed to be part of her dream, and she didn't wake up. But it continued beyond the dream and finally she realized that someone was at the front door.

Rana sat up, fully awake now, and heard the knocking, loud and insistent. She reached for her robe.

"Just a minute," she called. "I'll be there in just a minute."

Rana walked boldly to the front door. It never occurred to her that a woman living alone might be well advised to exercise caution when answering an unexpected knock in the middle of the night.

She opened the door and there, standing on her front porch, illuminated only by the soft, silver light of the moon, was Gamblin McClarity.

"Oh, Gamblin!" Rana said with a happy shout. She threw her arms around his neck. "What...what are you doing here in the middle of the night?"

"I've found it, Rana!" Gamblin said excitedly. "I've found the place I want to drill. There's oil there, girl, I know it."

"Oh, come in, come in!" Rana said. She dragged him inside, then turned on a small table lamp. In the dim light of the room, she looked at him. There was a glow of excitement in his eyes that was undeniable.

"I came upon it late yesterday afternoon," Gamblin said, slipping out of his jacket and sitting in a chair by the table. "I could smell it in the air... taste it in the dirt. I was going to poke around some more this morning, but I was too excited to sleep, so I decided to come in and tell you."

"Oh, Gamblin, I'm so happy you did," Rana said. "Listen, are you hungry? You want something to eat? Some coffee, maybe?"

"I'll tell you what I'd really like," Gamblin said, wiping his hand across the stubble of his chin. "I'd really like to shave and take a bath...if that isn't too much trouble."

"No trouble at all," Rana said. "I can heat some water and fill the tub. Have you got any clean clothes to put on?"

Gamblin grinned at her. "Well, to tell the truth," he said, "I'm not going to be in that much of a hurry to get back into clothes, if you know what I mean. I've missed you, Rana. I've missed you something awful."

Gamblin reached for Rana, but she moved out of his

way, doing it with such subtlety that Gamblin wasn't sure she had done it at all.

"I've missed you, too, Gamblin," Rana said. She went over to the little hot-water heater and started a fire. "It's good to have you back."

"Did you miss me enough to scrub my back?" Gamblin asked.

Rana chuckled. "Yes," she said. "I missed you enough to scrub your back."

Gamblin smiled. "That's all I wanted to know."

Half an hour later Gamblin was sitting in the bathtub with a cigar elevated at a jaunty angle from his freshly shaven face. Rana was washing his back.

"I'm going to make you rich, Rana," Gamblin said. "Rich as old King Midas."

"Rich enough that I won't have to be on my hands and knees, scrubbing your back?" Rana answered.

"Ha!" Gamblin said. "Rich enough that I can afford six lovely young maids to do that for me."

"And six handsome young men to wash my back, I suppose?" Rana teased.

"Ow, what are you telling me, woman? That you would like such a thing? Have you turned into a hussy these past six weeks?"

Rana thought of the night she had spent with Jason and she gasped when Gamblin made his innocent remark. The sponge she was holding popped out of her hand and bounced across the floor.

"Here, now," Gamblin said apologetically. "I was just teasing you, Rana. I meant nothing by it."

Rana's heart was screaming at her to tell him...to confess to him that she had given herself to Jason. And yet her mind put up a block and no words came.

"Are you all right?" Gamblin asked.

"Yes," Rana said. "I...I just dropped the sponge, that's all."

"That's okay," Gamblin said. "I'm finished anyway." He suddenly stood up, naked, dripping water from his well-muscled body. He pointed to a towel on a nearby chair. "Hand me the towel, will you?"

Gamblin began drying, and as he did, he looked into Rana's eyes. He saw something in them that puzzled him, and the puzzlement reflected in his own eyes.

"Rana, is something wrong?"

"Wrong? No," Rana said quickly. "What makes you think something is wrong?"

"I don't know. I can't put my finger on it...it's just that..."

Rana interrupted him by stepping up to him and kissing him full on the lips. She pressed her body against his naked skin, mashing her breasts against him, grinding her pelvis into him until he started reacting instinctively.

"I've missed you," Rana said.

Whatever doubt or confusion Gamblin may have been experiencing vanished at that moment. He returned her kiss eagerly, happily, and his kiss burned through to her very core, making her grow dizzy from the sensations it evoked. Gamblin's tongue forced its way past her lips, then inside, and she felt its sweet thrilling pressure in her mouth.

Rana felt every muscle in her body grow weak and she recalled all the other times with Gamblin. She thought of her mother's boardinghouse in St. Louis, the lovemaking on the road during their trip to Texas, and in the hotel before Gamblin left for the field. Why had she ever betrayed him, even for a moment?

Finally, the kiss ended and Gamblin pulled his lips

away. He continued to hold her, though, and her body trembled in his embrace.

"Rana, girl, I've been nearly mad with want for you every moment we were apart. The times we've been together are the nearest I've ever come to heaven, and the time we were apart the closest I've been to hell. I won't let you get away from me again. I won't."

Gamblin picked Rana up and carried her back into the little bedroom. Rana, making no effort to resist him, put her arms around his neck and kissed him as he carried her to bed.

Somehow, some way, Rana's robe and nightgown disappeared and she lay on the bed, moving her body eagerly to allow Gamblin to continue his supplications to her desire. She tingled as his fingers trailed lightly across her nipples, then moved down the smooth skin of her stomach and into the soft down at the juncture of her legs. She welcomed Gamblin back with her heart and her body and she cried from the sheer joy of the moment, urging him to go on and on and on. No sense of guilt, no feeling of shame could extinguish the fires she felt raging within.

Rana pulled Gamblin to her, not surrendering to, but embracing the moment. There was a commingling of passion and emotion that made them as one, until finally a burst of pleasure, which exceeded all other pleasure, swept over her in wave after wave. Rana's whole body seemed to dissolve under the intensity of the sensation. The waves of ecstasy rippled through her body in such rapid succession that it was as if there were one long, sustained period of rapture. The feeling of pleasure was greatly multiplied by the waves of delectation, one after the other. Even when it was all over and they lay together side by side, Rana could still feel tiny tinglings of excitation as her inflamed senses slowly returned to normal.

Rana and Gamblin had just sat down to breakfast the next morning when Jason showed up. He came in without bothering to knock.

"I saw you were back," he said. "Have you found anything?" He went to the cupboard and took out a cup, then poured himself a cup of coffee.

"Too early to say," Gamblin said.

"He has," Rana said, excited. "Oh, Jason, he found the place for us to sink our first well."

"You did?" Jason asked.

Gamblin warmed to the subject, his skepticism evaporating. "I think so, yes," he said.

"Where?"

"I'll show you on the map," Gamblin offered. "Rana, hand me the county map there."

Rana handed the map to Gamblin, who cleared the table, then spread out the map, holding down the corners with coffee cups and plates.

"Over here in the eastern part of the county, at the junction of South Mustang Draw and North Mustang Draw," Gamblin said, punching a finger down to the map.

"No roads out to there," Jason observed.

"We'll make one," Gamblin replied. "It's easy enough country, flat plateaus, grass-covered prairies, low hills, and draws. Hell, we don't even need one to get started. I drove right across country."

Jason sat down and looked at Gamblin and Rana. He had a big smile on his face and he hit his fist into his hand.

"Damn!" he exclaimed. "Damn, damn, damn! I

knew it! I knew I was smart to back you in this!"

"You're not a genious yet," Gamblin warned him. "I told you, I just feel oil there; I still can't show anything."

Jason stood up and took Gamblin's hand in his. "Partner, if you feel it, that's enough for me," Jason said. "I'll put every cent I've got into proving this well."

"Thanks, Jason," Gamblin said. "And I don't mean thanks just for the money. I mean thanks for the confidence."

As Rana watched the seeds of genuine friendship being sown between the two men, she suddenly realized the complexity of her own situation. Both men were now her lovers. She could very easily be the wedge that could destroy this partnership, or she could be the glue to keep it together. She had to keep them together no matter what it took.

The place Gamblin had chosen to sink his first well was located in the eastern part of Reagan County. Though no road went directly to it, the trucks and wagons that began bringing material to the site soon cut a trail to the property so that a road was formed.

Gamblin hired a crew of roughnecks, riggers, tool dressers, and a foreman. Within two weeks, the place was transformed. A small stream running through North Mustang Draw was dammed up to provide water, and a bunkhouse and cook shack were built. A steam engine was hauled in by wagon to provide power for the drilling tools, draw works, pumps, and generator.

Gamblin selected the place for the derrick and the men went to work. Soon four timber legs stood upright, tapering from base to crown block, held together with a network of wooden cross braces. The derrick stood a little over eighty feet high, a black finger reaching to the sky.

For the entire two weeks of construction, Gamblin stayed in the field with the men, sleeping in the bed of the truck until the bunkhouse was built. Now everything was ready for the spudding operation that would mark the actual beginning of drilling.

There was an excitement in the air this morning as Gamblin stood by the front of the truck, eating his breakfast off the hood. Bevo Francis, his foreman, stood beside him drinking coffee. Gamblin knew Bevo from the days he had worked in the fields before he went to sea.

"We're ready to start any time you give the word, boss," Bevo said.

"Rana and Jason are supposed to come out here today," Gamblin said. "I promised them I wouldn't start until they arrived."

"Okay by me. I'll make sure all the loose ends are tied up."

Gamblin walked over to look at the machinery: the power drill, the bit, the pipe extensions. So far there was at least eight thousand dollars invested in equipment, all funded by Jason Hewlitt, but Jason had never complained about or questioned the slightest expenditure.

"Hey, boss, here comes someone!" one of the men shouted, and Gamblin stepped down off the base to meet the car as it arrived.

Jason and Rana were in the car, as he had expected, but there were two other men in the car as well. One was a short, fat man, the other lean and weathered, like a man who spent time outdoors. Gamblin felt a little twinge of alarm. Who were these people? Why had Jason brought them out here?

"Gamblin, this is Harry Malloy, my banker," Jason said of the fat man. "And I forget this other man's name."

"Decatur. Claude Decatur," the lean man said. "I'm a geologist."

"A geologist?" Gamblin replied. "Jason, we don't need a geologist."

"He's not my idea, Gamblin, I assure you," Jason said.

"Then what's he doing out here?"

"Mr. McClarity, the bank has loaned Mr. Hewlitt a great deal of money on this operation, and he is asking for more," the banker said. "I thought — that is, the bank feels — that the report of a geologist might be helpful in arranging the loan."

"Tell me, Mr. McClarity," Decatur said as he looked over toward the derrick, "just what made you decide to start here?"

"Because this is where the oil is," Gamblin said.

"I see. And how did you determine that?"

"Creekology," Gamblin answered.

"Creekology? You are risking all this money on creekology?"

"I don't understand," Rana said. "What is creekology?"

"It's a term for a skill, most unscientific and very unsubstantiated," Decatur explained, "which some men are said to have for finding oil. A hunch."

"See here, Mr. McClarity," Malloy said. "Are you saying that you risked the bank's money on a hunch?"

"Wait a minute," Jason spoke up quickly. "I thought this was my money."

"You are responsible for the loan, yes," Malloy said. "But we need a reasonable assurance we will get the money back."

"And you think a geologist can give you that assurance?" Gamblin asked. "You make fun of creekology, but there is no scientific method known for finding oil. Am I right, Decatur?"

"Well, while it is true that we have enjoyed only limited success in finding oil, we are pretty good at ruling out places."

"How do you know? Because when you rule out a place no oil is found? That's because no one has the courage to look. Well, I'm telling you there is oil here."

"And I'm saying that in this whole unlikely county, this is the least likely spot," Decatur replied.

"Mr. Decatur, are you saying that it is not a good risk to drill here?" Malloy asked.

"That's exactly what I'm saying."

"That's all the bank needs to know," Malloy said. "I'm sorry, Mr. Hewlitt, but unless you can find some way to secure the loans we have already made you, the bank is going to call your note."

"Harry, let me talk this over with my partners for a few moments, will you?" Jason asked.

"Of course," Malloy said. "Take your time."

Jason, Gamblin, and Rana walked over to stand just outside the cook shack. The men on the drilling team, realizing that they might soon be out of work, stood quietly under the derrick.

"You heard him," Jason said.

"What happens if he calls in the loan?" Gamblin wanted to know.

"I'll have to sell everything in order to pay it. The truck, the drilling equipment, everything."

"Jason, you won't do that?" Rana queried. "Surely, after coming this far, you won't back out now?"

Jason ran his hand through his hair and looked at Gamblin.

"Creekology?" he said. He smiled.

"Creekology," Gamblin answered.

"What do you think?" Jason asked Rana.

"You know what I think," Rana answered. "The question is: What do you think? Right now, it's all in your hands."

Jason sighed. "All right, I'm going to put up everything I have to secure the note — my hotel, my store, my service station, my house. I'm going to put up everything and raise as much money as I can, because I think we are going to need more before we are finished, and if I don't get everything I can now, we aren't going to have a way of raising any more."

"You won't need to," Gamblin said. "This well is going to come in, Jason. I promise you."

"It damned well better," Jason said. "Or all three of us are going to wind up pecking shit with the chickens. All right, let's get this done."

The three partners returned to the car where Malloy and Decatur were still standing.

"Harry," Jason said, "you and your geologist take this car back to town. You might as well — I'm putting it up, along with everything else I own, to raise money for this well."

"Jason, as your friend as well as your banker, I strongly advise against that," Harry protested.

"I'm not asking for the bank's advice, or yours," Jason replied. "All I want is money, as much as I can raise on my holdings. Now, you get on back to town and take care of that for me. My partners and I are busy."

"All right, men, let's drop the spud!" Gamblin

shouted, and Bevo and the others gave a cheer.

Malloy and Decatur drove away while the men began their work.

"Oh," Rana said, her eyes glowing brightly, "this is all so exciting! What happens first?"

"First, we have to bore a hole sixty feet deep so a full string of drilling tools can be suspended from the rig's walking beam," Gamblin explained. We do that by using something we call a spudding bit. It's just a bit and a jerk line suspended from the crown block. We raise the bit and drop it, raise it and drop it again, until it reaches sixty feet. Then we can attach the drilling tools."

"Mr. McClarity, Mr. Hewlitt, Miss Wood, you wanna drop the bit?" Bevo asked.

"Oh, yes," Rana said. "Let's do."

The three partners moved over to stand beside the derrick and were handed a rope's end by Bevo.

"What do we do?" Rana asked.

"We've already got the bit hoisted to the crown block. All you have to do is let go of the rope."

"Wait a minute," one of the workers called.

"What's wrong?"

"Nothing's wrong. It's just we ain't got a name for this oil well yet. It's bad luck to start drillin' before the well has a name."

"How about Texon Oil Well Number One?" Gamblin suggested.

"That's so dull-sounding," Rana complained. "We ought to have a better name than that. It ought to be something glamorous."

"Would you like to hear the name we come up with?" the worker asked.

"What?"

"Santa Rana Number One."

"Yes," Gamblin and Jason said simultaneously.

"Oh, no, I don't think so," Rana said.

"Miss Wood, you want to hurt the men's feelings?" Bevo asked. "This is the name they chose."

"No, of course I don't want to hurt their feelings."

"Then let them have their name," Bevo said.

"Besides," Gamblin added, "Jason and I have both agreed, so you are outvoted."

Rana looked at the derrick, then laughed.

"Okay," she said. "I just hope I bring it luck."

"Ready to drop? Let's do it on three," Gamblin said, and he counted for them.

The bit fell true and took a deep, satisfying bite from the earth. Drilling had begun on Santa Rana Number One.

Chapter Twelve

Houston — 1986

Maggie St. John turned on the television set, then called to Rana.

"He's about to come on."

"I'll be there in a minute," Rana answered. "Would you like coffee?"

"Yes, that would be nice. Oh, I think Angela has already gone upstairs, though. Would you like me to get it?"

"I already have it," Rana said, coming into the room carrying a tray. "That's where I was."

Rana set the tray down, then poured two cups of coffee, handing one to Maggie. She settled into a big brown leather chair and looked toward the TV. Above the TV, a large portrait of Gamblin stared back at them. On the screen the network logo flashed. Then there was intro music for the program they were about to watch. A handsome, silver-haired man stared into the camera.

"Good evening, and welcome to 'Hot Seat,' where each evening our panel interrogates a name in the news. I am the moderator, Marcus Lane. With me on the panel are Carl Dean and Sylvia Collins."

Carl Dean was short, nearly bald, and wore glasses. Sylvia Collins was an attractive blond woman in her early forties.

"Texon Oil is currently engaged in controversial multibillion-dollar negotiations with Mexico for the rights to extract oil from the Bustamante Basin. Why is this controversial? There are some who claim that while this will be good for the balance of trade with Mexico, it will have an adverse effect on the overall outflow of U.S. dollars. Others are afraid that the operation will completely gut Mexico of all its oil, leaving that already poor country in an even poorer condition. And there are even some who fear that a revolution could take over the Mexican oil fields, perhaps for Communist forces. Our man in the hot seat tonight is Deke McClarity, grandson of one of the founders of Texon Oil and senior vice-president of operations for that company. Mr. McClarity, welcome to 'Hot Seat.'"

"Thank you," Deke said. He smiled disarmingly and brushed his hand through his hair. "On second thought, maybe I had better withhold my thanks until I see how this all comes out."

The panel members laughed diplomatically.

"Mr. McClarity, Evan Hewlitt is very much opposed to this project, isn't he?" the moderator asked.

"Yes," Deke answered. "I believe he is."

"He is a major stockholder, is he not?"

"Next to my grandmother, he is the company's biggest stockholder."

"Then don't you think if a major stockholder — by your own admission, the second biggest stockholder — is opposed to the transaction, his views ought to be seriously considered?"

"I assure you, Mr. Lane, his views have been considered," Deke said. "Evan Hewlitt has a voice on our board, a very big voice. His views have been given every possible consideration."

"But you are still going through with it?"

"Yes."

Carl Dean had been tapping his teeth with his pencil. Now he brought it down and leaned forward to ask a question.

"If Evan Hewlitt was concerned about the questions being raised, why haven't the rest of you paid any attention? If these fears are realized, it could cause serious consequences."

"Mr. Dean, Evan Hewlitt didn't respond to those questions, he raised them. He is using these questions to support his position, when, in fact, he doesn't believe them any more than I do."

"Are you saying they are not valid questions?"

"Yes, that's exactly what I'm saying."

"Mr. McClarity, Stewart Jackson, one of the president's own advisors, is known to be against this transaction. Even the president is studying it," Sylvia Collins said.

"The president should study it," Deke said. "If he does, he will realize all of these fears are groundless."

"Would you care to address each of them in turn?" Marcus Lane asked. "How would you address the question of balance of payments, for example?"

"There is already a great imbalance between the U.S. and Mexico, in favor of the U.S. The purchase of additional Mexican crude by U.S. dollars would go a long way toward easing that problem for the Republic of Mexico. And as far as the overall balance is concerned, the Bustamante fields will give us the opportunity to export refined oil again for the first time in several years. The oil that we export to nonproducing countries will improve our balance of trade."

"And the possibility of a revolution taking over the oil fields?" Dean asked.

"Look, a country that is economically strong, that can provide jobs for its people, social services, public projects, and is traditionally a democracy besides, will not have a revolution. We spend money supporting unpopular regimes with weapons and military advisors, when the truth is, all we would have to do is help the countries solve their internal problems and there would be no revolution. The Bustamante Basin will go a long way toward making Mexico one of the strongest countries in the Western Hemisphere."

"What about the charge of taking all Mexico's oil, leaving them helpless?" Sylvia Collins asked.

"Right now we are guaranteeing the Mexican government that we will pay one-eighth royalties of twenty-four-dollar-per-barrel crude for the first five hundred million barels. Do you know what the price of crude is right now?"

"No, sir, I do not."

"As of this morning it was under thriteen dollars a barrel," Deke said. "Fourteen years ago, when the big energy crunch hit, oil was selling at three dollars and seventy-five cents a barrel. Then it shot up to as high as forty, and, with the recent glut, it has drifted all the way back down to its present level. In point of fact, energy has reversed itself from being the cause of runaway inflation to being the factor that has stabilized America's economy."

"All the more reason Mexico should hang on to their oil," Dean said. "Perhaps they should hold on to it as a hedge against the future."

"It could be, Mr. Dean, that if they don't get some badly needed money, they won't even have a future. Besides, the current low price isn't going to hurt them. I told you, our offer is locked in. Even if oil drops to ten dollars a barrel, we'll still pay royalties on twenty-four-dollar oil. That means a sizable bonus for the Mexican government."

"Why would you do that, Mr. McClarity? Surely Texon Oil is not a charitable operation."

Deke laughed. "No, sir, we aren't. But neither are we out to make windfall profits on the inflation of assets. Believe me when I tell you that we can still make money even if the cost of crude drops to ten. My grandfather got rich when it was a lot lower than that."

"Mr. McClarity, I'd like to change the subject here if I may. Your grandmother is one of the original founders of Texon Oil; in fact, isn't the first oil field named after her?"

"That would be the Santa Rana field in Reagan County, Texas — yes," Deke said.

"There were two others: Gamblin McClarity, who was your grandfather, and Jason Hewlitt, who was Evan Hewlitt's father. The three were said to be not only business partners, but very good friends. Why is it, then, that Evan Hewlitt and your grandmother seem to hate each other so? What is the cause of this feud?"

"Why did they ask him that?" Maggie demanded. "They had no right to ask him about something like that. I thought the briefing papers said they would talk only about the deal with Mexico."

"Don't worry about it," Rana answered easily. "Deke will be able to handle it."

Maggie chuckled. "Do you remember when we were watching the Texas-Arkansas game in Deke's last year of school? Texas was losing and they were down to their last play. You were so worried about it and Gamblin said those same words... 'Deke will be able to handle it.'"

Rana smiled. "And as I recall he did handle it, didn't he? He threw a long pass that got them close enough for a field goal and Texas won the game."

"I wish he had a football in his hands now. There are rules in a football game. I'm not sure these people follow any rules at all."

"Evan Hewlitt and my grandmother have a mutuality of interests in several things," Deke answered. "They both want what is good for Texon, and, ultimately, what is good for our country. They have long histories of exemplary service to the nation. It is only natural that occasional differences will arise as to the best way to achieve that mutual goal. But those are internal differences. When the chips are down, they will be together, as they always have."

"Evan Hewlitt was quite a playboy in his day," Sylvia Collins remarked. "A handsome bon vivant whose picture was on the cover of all the magazines. He was a race-car driver, a polo player, an international yachtsman. And yet it is reported that he once said he would be opposed to any marriage between you and his daughter because you have that same reputation. Don't you think that's unfair?"

"That's a little like asking a man if he's stopped beating his wife," Deke answered with a smile. "No matter how I answer that question, it's going to look bad, so I'm sure you'll understand if I just step aside and ask that we return to more substantive issues."

"If you and Rebel Hewlitt marry, it is a substantive issue," Dean countered. "After all, you would be bringing the two largest shareholding families together in one marriage. What about it? Are there wedding bells in your future? And, if so, what chance will you have for this marriage to be any more successful than your last? As you must know, Carol McClarity has made the charge that your marriage was destroyed by the fact that you had to live your life in the fishbowl."

"I'm sure you can appreciate that some things are considered private, even to those of us who must live our lives in a fishbowl," Deke replied. "I'd rather not get into that subject."

"Gentlemen, I'm afraid I'll have to interrupt at this point for a commercial break. Our guest in the hot seat is Deke McClarity, senior vice-president of operations for Texon Oil. We'll be right back."

"Ooh!" Maggie said. "Why did they have to bring up that awful woman's name? Isn't she getting rich enough off the McClarity name as it is? You can't go into a grocery store now without seeing something about her in one of those awful newspapers."

When the show resumed, the panel's interest returned to the real issues at hand. Deke handled the questions very well, but that was to be expected. He had a great deal of experience dealing with hostile questions. He had been a guest on dozens of television and radio shows and the target of some particularly barbed questions by reporters from the print media.

It had begun during his collegiate football days, when a nationally syndicated gossip columnist suggested that Deke's starting position as quarterback was bought by his family's money. That charge was answered by an article in *Sports Illustrated:*

> Mr. Jensen, who wrote the article attacking Texas quarterback Deke McClarity, obviously isn't a sports fan and knows very little about the University of Texas.
>
> In the first place, the University of Texas owns the Santa Rita oil fields and thus has a continuing source of income that far outstrips any endowment a family might make just for a guaranteed starting position on a football team.
>
> In the second place, no major university anywhere would jeopardize its football program by playing less than its best people.
>
> And, in the third place, Deke McClarity's credentials are such that he is being mentioned along with O. J. Simpson and Leroy Keyes as a candidate for the Heisman Trophy. Miami in the AFL and Washington in the NFL are both said to be looking at him as a possible number-one draft pick.
>
> Deke McClarity's starting position was bought for him? Notre Dame should be so lucky.

Deke walked around New York for a long time after the taping of the show. He wasn't walking to any particular place, but he soon found himself approaching Times Square. He passed a pretzel vendor and a young man who stood on a corner handing out leaflets, asking the world to repent before it was too late. A young woman in a tight red dress, spiked high heels, heavy makeup, and empty eyes stepped toward him, then stepped back out of his way when she realized he wasn't a potential customer.

On the corner of Forty-second Street, someone pressed a leaflet into his hand. He looked at it. The copy read:

SULTAN'S PLEASURE
Ten Beautiful Girls
Enjoy a Champagne Massage

He smiled and wondered just what a champagne massage was as he thrust the paper in the nearest trash receptacle.

He passed a sidewalk newsstand then and saw a nearly nude picture of Carol smiling at him from the cover of a magazine.

The headline on the magazine read:

I TAUGHT DEKE MCCLARITY
EVERYTHING HE KNOWS ABOUT SEX!

Despite himself, Deke chuckled. Of all the claims Carol Masters McClarity had made since their divorce, this one was the closest to the truth. Deke picked up the magazine and looked at it. The photo spread inside contained more nude pictures of Carol with another woman, but it wasn't the same woman she was with in the *Playhouse* spread.

The picture of Carol brought him back to the Christmas of 1968 and the First Field Hospital in Saigon, where he met Nurse Captain Carol Masters. He was lying in the officers' ward with his right leg elevated and bandaged, a hole in his thigh where the V.C. bullet had been dug out. He was an infantry platoon leader and he had been in Vietnam for nine months when he was hit. Nine months of fire fights and combat assaults without so much as a scratch, then he was hit by a sniper while his platoon was providing security for the recovery of a downed helicopter. It was supposed to be a cushion assignment, a "pussy" job earned by his platoon for having taken point on the last three assaults.

The wound wasn't that critical, but any wound, even a cut on one's hand from a C-ration can, provided an opening for one of many virulent staph infections; and that was what had happened to Deke's leg. It throbbed painfully and there was a constant discharge from the wound. About the only time his leg didn't hurt was when he slept, and he did that as often as he could.

"Hey, asshole, wake up, Goddamn it! Your country isn't paying you to come over here and sleep while the Commies run amok in the countryside."

Deke opened his eyes, then smiled broadly.

"Bubba!"

Bubba was Bubba Baker, a large black man who had played offensive tackle for the Longhorns.

"How you doin', Deke?" Bubba asked.

"Not very well. Where the hell were you when I needed you?"

"What the hell you talkin' about?" Bubba asked. "Man, that wasn't no linebacker hit you, that was one of them speedin' bullets like the kind Superman is faster than... but not ole Bubba."

"Yeah, well, as I recall, you didn't always stop the linebackers either," Deke said.

Bubba smiled. "I let a few through ever' now 'n' again jus' so's you'd know how important it was to keep ole Bubba aroun'. Tell me, my man, is this a goin'-home wound, or what?"

Deke smiled. "Yeah. It wouldn't be, but by the time I'm out of the hospital my time will be over. I'm rotating in about four more weeks."

"I'm sorry, Specialist, but you'll have to go now," a voice said. The nurse, who had just come in, was a strikingly beautiful, tawny-haired woman who walked with an unselfconscious easy gait as sensual as a teenager's.

"Carol, this is Bubba Baker," Deke said by way of introduction. "Bubba was in my offensive line."

Carol smiled at Bubba. "Offensive line? Does that mean you were one of the guys who protected Deke?"

"You got that right, Cap'n," Bubba said.

"Well, then I got you to thank for keeping his face so handsome for me, don't I?"

Bubba smiled broadly, then looked at Deke. "Goddamn, man, you 'n' this nurse got somethin' on?"

"It beats lying here reading old magazines," Deke retorted.

Bubba laughed. "Sheeeit, man, I'm gonna get myself shot." He was still laughing as he left the ward floor.

"It's time for your treatment," Carol said as she pulled the curtain frames around the bed. Then, smiling seductively, she began to unbutton the top of her uniform until she could free one of her breasts. She leaned over and stuck a nipple in Deke's mouth. "Come to mama," she said.

Deke began sucking with sweet, smacking sounds.

Carol groaned once, then stuck her hand under the sheet.

"You know what I like about these hospital gowns?" she said.

"What?" Deke asked, his query muffled by the breast in his mouth.

"You wear nothing underneath." Carol wrapped her fingers around him and his penis began to grow, leaping to her touch. It was hot, so incredibly hot.

"Yes," Deke said. "That's it."

"Don't talk," Carol said. "Just lie back."

Carol began moving her hand up and down and Deke felt her long, cool fingers on the hot, smooth skin. She moved her hand skillfully and, in a very real way, lovingly. Deke began to breathe in labored gasps and he felt the muscles in his stomach tense and strain, then grow unbelievably hard.

"Go ahead," Carol whispered into his ear. "Go ahead, let it happen." She increased her efforts, working with quick, sensual strokes, gentle, yet demanding.

Deke grunted and groaned with each hot spurt. Carol continued to work her hand as the hot wetness cascaded down over her fingers until, finally, the spurting stopped. She held on for a moment longer, squeezing gently but firmly until the last twitching movement stopped and Deke began to relax, to grow flaccid in her tender grasp. When she finally released him, Carol used the washbasin and cloth beside the bed to clean him tenderly and with concern.

"Remember, love, that's just a preview," Carol said. "When your leg gets better I have more to show you. A whole lot more."

Deke chuckled as he recalled that promise. Carol had made good on it. She had more to show him than he ever could have imagined. The problem was, she showed not only Deke, but half the population of Houston as well. She was the only totally nondiscriminating sex machine Deke had ever known. She would have sex anytime, anywhere, with anyone, male or female, black or white, old or young.

"You gonna buy that magazine, mister, or just get a cheap thrill by lookin' at the pictures? I gotta make a livin', you know," the newsstand man said.

Deke handed the man a five-dollar bill.

"Here, keep the change and the magazine." He put the magazine back in the rack and walked toward the nearest bar. He felt the need for a good bourbon-and-branch.

Chapter Thirteen

Texon, Texas — 1923

It was fascinating to be around Santa Rana One once the actual drilling got under way. Cars, trucks, and wagons came and went on a daily basis so that sometimes there was a regular traffic jam around the site. There were at least a dozen men on the job and they worked barechested, browning under the hot Texas summer sun.

There was a constant noise, a fever-pitch buzz, that added to the overall excitement. The sounds came from the chugging donkey engine, the creak and rattle of the walking beam and drive chain, and even from the wind, which whistled through the derrick. On top of that were the shouts, whistles, and songs of the men themselves.

Though Rana's office was still in town, she often

came out to the drill site just to stand around and watch so she could feel more a part of what was going on. Sometimes she would pack a lunch and put cold orange drinks in a tub of ice and bring her bounty out to the site. She had done that today, and though she and Gamblin were finished with their lunch, they were still drinking orange soda, leaning against the front of the car and talking.

Rana loved driving...she loved the freedom of having a car and being able to go where she wanted, when she wanted. Because she drove so much, Gamblin had traded the old Chandler for a newer Dodge. Jason went along with it, because neither one of them wanted to take the chance of Rana's breaking down in the middle of nowhere.

Rana watched the walking beam, a long horizontal bar that formed a "T" across the top of a vertical post. The contraption was on the drilling platform beneath the derrick and it was rocking up and down. She pointed to it.

"I've been coming out here watching this thing ever since we first started," she said, "but I still don't have any idea how it works."

"Don't worry about it. It isn't a woman's business to know."

Rana put her hands on her hips and faced Gamblin with fire in her eyes. "Not a woman's business? I'm a full partner in this operation, Gamblin McClarity. And anything I want to know is my business. If you won't tell me how this thing works, I'll damned sure find someone who will."

"All right, all right, if it means so much to you," Gamblin said. He finished his drink and set the bottle on the hood of the car. "You see that long cable hanging down from the end of the walking beam, going down into the hole?"

"Yes."

"That's called the tool string, and way down at the bottom of that tool string is the bit. The tool string is connected to the walking beam, which works off a crank on the band wheel. The donkey engine, which is what we call our steam engine, turns the band wheel, which causes the walking beam to seesaw back and forth. You see, it's pivoted right there on an upright post, a Samson post. Each time it rocks up, it pulls the bit up. Each time it goes down, it drops the bit back into the rock and earth down at the bottom of the hole. The bit and tool string together weigh just over a ton. It's a little like banging into the ground with a long chisel and a big hammer. Now, do you know any more than you did before you asked?"

"Yes," Rana said. "Thanks."

"Hey, Gamblin!" Bevo called. "Gamblin, you want to come over here and take a look at this?"

"Yeah," Gamblin answered. "I'll be right there." He looked at Rana and smiled. "Thanks for comin' out here today, Rana. I get to missing you if I don't see you ever' day or so."

"Oh? You mean you don't think a woman's place is back in town?" Rana teased.

"Listen, you're not gonna hold that woman's business thing against me, are you?" Gamblin asked. "I guess I was a little out of line."

"I guess you were," Rana said. She smiled. "But I won't hold it against you...this time."

"Gamblin, you comin'?" Bevo called again.

"Yeah, be right there!" Gamblin yelled back. He looked back at Rana. "There won't be a next time," he promised. He kissed her lightly, then, with a smile and wave, walked over to see what Bevo wanted.

Rana loaded the picnic basket back into the car. She left the tub of ice on the site because there were two cases of soft drinks down in the cold water and she figured the men would enjoy them.

Rana opened the door to get in the car, then suddenly and unexpectedly felt a wave of dizziness and nausea wash over her. She held on to the door for a moment. Then, when it passed, she slipped in behind the wheel.

Unlike the old Chandler they had driven out from Missouri, the Dodge she was driving now had an electric starter. She was glad. She didn't feel up to twisting a crank.

The nausea came on her again the next morning, and the morning after that. Then about a week later she was in the café when it was so strong that she had to get up from the table and go into the bathroom to throw up.

"Are you all right, honey?" Sue Ellen asked when Rana came back from the bathroom and sat at the table looking pale.

"Yes," Rana said. She dipped a napkin into a glass of water and patted her forehead. "I... I don't know what's gotten into me."

"Maybe it's a touch of something," Sue Ellen suggested. "Do you have a fever or headache?"

"No," Rana said. "It's the same thing every morning. The least little thing, the smells of certain foods, for example, and I get so nauseous and dizzy I can hardly stand up."

Sue Ellen looked at Rana with a curious expression on her face. "What do you mean, certain foods?" she asked.

"Well, the smell of frying bacon, for example," Rana answered. "You know I have a little stove over in my office, and I used to cook breakfast. Now, I find that I can't stand the smell of cooking bacon."

Sue Ellen put her hand on Rana's forehead.

"Uh-huh," she said. "And how long has this been going on?"

"About two weeks, I'd say," Rana answered. "Why? Do you know what it is?"

Sue Ellen looked out over the café. There was only one other customer in the place and he had already eaten. He was sitting there drinking coffee and reading the paper.

"Sue Ellen, how 'bout another cup of coffee?" he called when he saw Sue Ellen glance his way.

"It'll be about ten minutes, Harry," Sue Ellen replied. "I'll have to make some fresh."

"Oh, never mind, then," Harry answered. He stood up and left a couple of coins on the table. "Thanks, but I'd better get going."

"You come back now, you hear?" Sue Ellen called as the customer stepped through the door.

"I'm sorry to be such a sourpuss this morning," Rana said.

"Don't you worry about it," Sue Ellen said. "You want a cup of coffee? I just made some."

Rana looked at Sue Ellen in surprise. "You just told Harry — "

"I know what I told Harry," Sue Ellen interrupted. "I wanted him to leave so we could be alone."

"Be alone? Why?"

"I figure we got some girl talk to do," Sue Ellen said. She walked over behind the counter and poured two cups of coffee, then brought them back to the table. She sat down across from Rana. "Can you drink coffee?" she asked.

"Sure. Why not?" Rana answered.

"Because sometimes when a girl gets in your condition funny things happen to her tastes. She starts liking things she never liked before, and she stops liking things she's always liked."

"My condition? Sue Ellen, what on earth are you talking about?"

"I'm talkin' about havin' babies," Sue Ellen said. "And I know what I'm talkin' about because I've had two of my own."

"Having babies? What on earth..." Rana started to say. Then she gasped and put her hand to her mouth. "Oh, my God!" she exclaimed.

"That is what's wrong with you, isn't it? Aren't you pregnant?"

"No!" Rana insisted.

"Are you sure? You have all the symptoms. Now remember, Rana, this is just girl talk," Sue Ellen went on. "But is it possible?"

"It... it might be possible," Rana agreed reluctantly.

"When was the last time you had your period?"

Rana thought for a moment. Then she groaned and put her hand to her forehead. "My God, Sue Ellen!" she said. "I *am* pregnant."

"Uh-huh," Sue Ellen said. She took a drink of her coffee and studied Rana over the rim of the cup.

"Oh, Sue Ellen, what am I going to do?" Rana moaned. "I can't have this baby. Not now, not with everything that's going on."

Sue Ellen chuckled. "I've got news for you, honey. There's no such thing as a little pregnant. Once it starts, it keeps going."

"Oh, this is awful," Rana said. Tears welled from her eyes and slid down her cheeks. "Oh, what am I going to do?"

Sue Ellen looked at Rana for a long moment. Then she took a deep breath. "You've only got two choices," she said.

"Two?" Rana asked in confusion. "What two? What are you talking about?"

"Well, you either have the baby, or you don't have it."

"What do you mean, don't have it? Like you say, there's no such thing as a little pregnant."

"Maybe not," Sue Ellen said. "I know a couple of the girls over at the Dandy Lion. I know they've found themselves in this condition a couple of times and they... uh... had it taken care of."

"Taken care of?"

"Abortion," Sue Ellen said simply.

"Oh," Rana said in a small, quiet voice.

"I could probably get a name for you, maybe find someone in Houston or Dallas who would do it."

"Oh, Sue Ellen, would you?" Rana asked.

"Is that what you want?"

"I...I don't know," Rana said. "I know that I don't want to have the baby now. Not now...it would ruin everything."

"You sit there for a few minutes," Sue Ellen said. "I'm going to step next door to the Dandy Lion and get Julie over here to talk to you."

"Is Julie one of the... uh..."

"Whores?"

"Well, I didn't want to come right out and say it."

Sue Ellen laughed. "Oh, we used to call ourselves soiled doves, or pleasure girls. But those were just words. We knew who and what we were."

"We?" Rana asked in a surprised voice.

"Yeah, honey, we," Sue Ellen said. "I got two kids, and I got both of them while I was on the line. I...I couldn't go through with an abortion, so I decided to have them. I went back to work after the first one, but after the second one I got to thinkin', shit, I'm so damned fertile I'll singlehandedly raise the population of Texas by a dozen if I don't quit."

Rana laughed.

"I was workin' down in Houston," she said. "Not many folks up here know about that, so I'd just as soon you not say anything about it."

"Oh, no, of course not," Rana said. "I won't say anything, I swear."

Sue Ellen smiled. "Didn't really think you would. 'Course now, the girls at the Dandy Lion, they already know. But they're not the type to gossip about it. Wait here. I'll bring Julie over."

Rana watched Sue Ellen leave and she sat at the table and thought about her condition, which certainly did give her a lot to think about. Now, she'd have to do more than think about it. She was going to have to meet the issue head on.

The door opened and Sue Ellen came back, followed by a very young girl whose pageboy haircut and Cleopatra eyes made her look like a little girl dressing and making up like a grown woman.

"Rana, this is Julie. Julie, Rana. Don't need last names," she added. "Would you like a cup of coffee, Julie?"

"Yes, thank you, with lots of cream and sugar,' Julie answered. She sat down at the table with Rana. "Got yourself in a fix, have you, honey?" she asked.

Up close the girl looked older. In fact, when Rana looked into her eyes, she looked very old.

"What?" Rana asked. It wasn't that she didn't understand. It was just that she had been studying the girl so hard that she didn't hear the question.

"Pregnant," Julie said. "Sue Ellen says you're pregnant and you want an abortion."

"Uh...yes," Rana said.

Sue Ellen came back to the table with Julie's coffee and joined them. "Tell her about it, Julie," Sue Ellen invited.

"You know how to get one?" Rana asked.

"Yeah, sure, I know," Julie said. "I got one just last month, down in Houston."

"Do you know the doctor's name?"

Julie laughed. "Doctor?"

"Yes, the man who performed the operation."

Julie laughed again. "You don't know a lot about this, do you?"

"No, no, of course not."

"I didn't think so," Julie said. She pulled a pack of cigarettes from the pocket of her dress and offered one to Rana. When Rana declined, she pulled one out for herself, lit it, and let out a long blue stream of smoke before she spoke again.

"It ain't a doctor that does it, honey."

"It isn't? Well, who does perform the operation?"

"A midwife. Only, instead of this midwife helpin' with the birthin', she helps you get rid of it."

"Where does she do it? In her office?"

"Oh, honey, this ain't somethin' you set up shop and advertise with a sign and all," Julie said. "It's illegal and she could go to prison if they found out. She ain't got no office. What she's got is a bag of tools."

"I don't understand. Where does it happen?"

"It's up to you to rent a hotel room somewhere and she'll meet you there and take care of it. The midwife gets rid of the baby, you give her fifty bucks, then she leaves. It's as simple as that."

"You mean... it all takes place in a hotel room?" Rana asked.

"Yeah, only it's really more of a flop house than a hotel. You see, the nice hotels can't take a chance on lettin' somethin' like this happen, so the dumps cash in. They charge as much for a room as the plushest hotel in Houston, and they know there's nothin' you can do about it. After all, you have to have someplace to go."

"What happens next?"

"Next, you stay in bed for a few hours. If you haven't started hemorrhaging, you can get up and go home."

"What if you have started — to hemorrhage, I mean?"

"Then you have two choices," Julie said. "One is to hope it stops by itself. The other is to call a doctor... only if you call a doctor, you're gonna wind up in prison."

"How... how was it for you?"

"Quick, cold, impersonal," Julie said. "I didn't hemorrhage. But a couple of days later I discovered a bonus to the operation."

"What sort of bonus?"

"I got an infection," Julie said. "A real bad infection. I almost died from it. That happens sometimes when they don't use sterile tools. I guess it's pretty hard to carry sterilized tools around in one of those little bags."

"I wouldn't call an infection a bonus," Rana said.

"Oh, that ain't the bonus I'm talkin' about," Julie

said. "You see, I can't have kids now. Not ever again. In my profession, you might consider that a bonus, don't you think?"

"I...I guess so," Rana said. She felt sick to her stomach, but it wasn't the same type of nausea she had been feeling for the last few days. This was a new type of nausea, one that came from deep down inside. She leaned her head on her hands and stayed that way, with her eyes closed, for quite a while.

"You okay, honey?" Sue Ellen asked.

"Yes," Rana answered quietly. "Yes, I'm fine."

"What about it?" Julie asked. "You want the name?"

"No," Rana said finally. Her mind was made up. She was going to have the baby. "No, thank you. You've been very kind."

"Okay, have it your way," Julie said. She stood up and started to leave. Then she looked back toward Rana. "Only I think I ought to tell you, honey, if you're goin' to have an abortion, it's best not to wait too long. The longer you wait, the more dangerous it becomes. If you're gonna do it, do it now."

"Thank you," Rana said. "If I change my mind, I'll get in touch with you."

"Thanks for coming over, Julie," Sue Ellen called as Julie left.

The two women were quiet for a long moment, then Rana spoke.

"You knew I wouldn't go through with it after I listened to her, didn't you?"

"Yes," Sue Ellen admitted.

Rana smiled and put her hand on Sue Ellen's. "Thanks," she said. "I guess I needed a little straightening out."

"Honey, I know you're goin' through a hard thing

right now," Sue Ellen said. "Like I said, I been there myself. I got two kids, neither one of them know their daddy."

"Maybe they don't know their daddy," Rana said, "but they sure have a good mama."

"Which brings us up to something else to think about," Sue Ellen said.

"What's that?"

"I didn't know who was the daddy of either of my kids, but I was a whore. Sometimes I'd have as many as fifteen or twenty men in a single night. I don't figure you have that problem. So what about the baby's father? Don't you think you ought to tell him?"

"No," Rana said. "No, I can't do that."

"Why not? Don't you think he'd like to know? Maybe he'd do the right thing by you."

"Sue Ellen, you don't understand. That's the most difficult thing about this whole business."

"What do you mean? Rana, you... you do know who the baby's father is, don't you?"

Rana took a drink of her coffee, then was silent for a long moment.

"Rana?" Sue Ellen asked again.

Rana sighed. "The father could be either Gamblin or Jason," she said.

"My God," Sue Ellen said. "Well, do you know which one?"

"Yes," Rana said. "I know which one. But I can't let them know."

"I don't understand," Jason said. The three of them — Jason, Rana, and Gamblin — were in the office. It was late at night, and though it wasn't raining, there was a hard wind blowing and the little office shook and rattled in the stiff breeze. "You called us in here to say that you are pregnant?"

"Yes," Rana said.

"And you know who the father is?"

"Yes."

"But you won't tell."

"No."

"Goddamn it, Rana!" Gamblin said. He had been particularly hurt to discover that there was even a possibility that the baby could be Jason's. "Goddamn it! It's bad enough I find out that you and Jason have... have been together. Now you tell me you're pregnant and it could be mine, or it could be his, but you won't even say."

"Gamblin, suppose I told you the baby was Jason's."

"Is it my baby?" Jason asked hopefully.

"I'm not saying," Rana replied. "I'm just posing this question. Gamblin, if the baby is Jason's, what would you do?"

"I... I don't know," Gamblin said. He ran his fingers through his hair and sighed. "Yes, I do know. I would leave."

"You'd just pull up stakes and go, with the well half finished and Jason in hock up to his elbows."

"If it's Jason's baby, I don't give one little damn about how much in hock he is," Gamblin growled. "As far as I'm concerned, he crawled into my bed; now he can sleep in it."

"Your bed? What do you mean, your bed?"

"You know what I mean, Rana," Gamblin said. "You were my woman and he..."

"Let's get this straight, Gamblin McClarity. I was not, and I am not, your woman."

"Tough luck, old man," Jason said.

"And I'm not your woman either, Jason Hewlitt!"

Rana said, lashing out at him as severely as she had at Gamblin.

"What are you saying? That you don't care for either one of us?" Jason asked.

"No, I'm not saying that. But I don't belong to either one of you. I am my own woman! So you, Gamblin, cannot say that Jason crawled into your bed. He crawled into mine and he did it because I let him in, just as I let you in."

"Yeah," Gamblin said. "Well, in answer to your question, if I thought this was Jason's baby, I'd pull up stakes right now."

"What if it were your baby?"

"That's different," Gamblin said. "If the baby was mine, I'd stay."

"I see. And you, Jason? What if I told you this was Gamblin's baby? Be honest with me. What would you do?"

"I don't know," Jason said. He looked at Gamblin. "I guess I'd salvage what I could from the operation and pull out."

"And if the baby was yours?"

"Well, of course, if he was mine, I'd stay with job until it was done," Jason said.

"Do you see now why I won't tell who the father is?" Rana asked. "I love both of you and I don't want to lose either one of you. The way I figure it, this baby could be the thing that breaks us up once and for all, or it could be the glue that holds us together. Gamblin, if you think it's your baby, you'll stay around. And Jason, if you think it's your baby, you'll see the deal through to the end. Well, as far as the two of you are concerned, it is your baby. It could belong to either one of you, so I want you to consider it yours."

"That's crazy," Gamblin growled.

"No," Jason said, stroking his chin with his hand as he looked at Rana. "No, my friend, that isn't crazy at all. That's brilliant."

"Brilliant? For her to stand there and tell me the baby might be yours?" Gamblin demanded.

"Or yours," Jason replied. "You may have loved her longer than I have, Gamblin. But you can't love her any more deeply than I do. I'm just as hurt at the thought that it might be your baby as you are that it might be mine. But I am also determined that I'm not going to abandon this child as long as there is a possibility that it might be mine. We're partners in everthing else; you may as well get used to the fact that we're going to be partners in this as well."

"Gamblin?" Rana asked.

Gamblin looked at the two of them for a long moment. Then he chuckled and put out his hand to take hers. Rana signaled for Jason, who added his hand to theirs, forming a three-armed star.

"This is the goddamnedest thing I ever heard of," Gamblin said. "But I don't see any other way around it than the way you've got figured."

"There's one thing," Jason said.

"What's that?"

Jason took a deep breath, then let it out. "Rana, before the baby is born, I want you to marry one of us."

"Which one?" Gamblin asked quickly.

Jason held up his hand, as if saying he didn't want to get into a fight.

"I figure she ought to marry whichever one of us she wants," Jason said. "But I want my baby to have a name, even if that name's McClarity."

"Gamblin?" Rana asked. "What if the name I give the

baby is Hewlitt? Do you agree with Jason?"

Gamblin sighed. "Yeah," he said, "I agree."

"All right," Rana said. "I'll choose one of you to marry. But let me say right now that if I choose one of you, that doesn't necessarily mean the one I choose is the father."

"What does it mean?" Jason asked.

"It just means that you are the one I chose," Rana said simply.

Chapter Fourteen

The Hewlitt Hotel was the biggest hotel in Texon. In fact, if one didn't count the widow Johnson's house, which she converted into a small rooming house after her husband died, the Hewlitt Hotel was the only hotel in Texon. It was three stories high, with fifteen rooms on each of the top two floors and a restaurant and community room on the ground floor.

Every Saturday night during the summer, the community room was taken over by the Reagan County Social Club for a dance. The dance was free to all comers and was the biggest — in fact, the only — social event in Texon.

Excitement would begin to build Saturday morning, when the bus would arrive with the band. The children of the town would start gathering around the bus depot about half an hour before the bus was due, laughing, pulling one another's hair, sometimes breaking into a dance of their own. The young boys would pretend to be the band, strumming imaginary guitars and playing phantom fiddles and accordions, while the girls would dance to the make-believe music.

A few of the young men of the county would drift by casually, as if they had other business to attend to and just happened to be in the area. The young women would drop into the store next door to the bus station where they would buy brightly colored ribbons or notions, pretending an innocence of the fact that this was the day of the dance. On many such mornings last-minute adjustments to dance cards were arranged by these "chance" meetings.

The arrival of the bus would first be announced by the grinding clack of gears as the bus downshifted to pull up Hewlitt's Hill. Next would come the honking of the klaxon horn to alert potential passengers that the bus was arriving. By the time the long motorized stage rolled down Main Street, children would be running alongside and everyone in town would know that it had arrived.

Rana stood in the window of the Texon Petroleum Corporation office, watching as the bus stopped and the four men of the band climbed out, then began taking their instruments from the large baggage hold. They realized they were the center of much attention and they moved importantly, engrossed in the work of unloading, seeming to taking no notice of the excitement caused by their arrival.

"How do they look?" Jason asked. He was sitting at Rana's desk balancing his checkbook.

"How does who look?" Rana asked.

Jason laughed. "The band, of course. Aren't they what you're studying so intently?"

Rana smiled and came away from the window. She sat down in a chair across the desk from Jason. "They look like a fine band," she said.

"I hope so. If I'm going to dance with the prettiest girl in the county tonight, then I want a fine band to provide the music."

"Jason," Rana said, taking a deep breath, "I'm going to have to get married soon. I'm beginning to show."

"Good. That's what we've been waiting on."

"You know I can only marry one of you."

"Yes, I know. The law is funny that way," Jason said. "I guess the next question is whether you've made your decision."

"Yes, I have."

"Who is it?"

"I've come to you first because..."

Jason grinned broadly and stood up. "Me?" he asked, happily interrupting her. "Rana, you've chosen me?"

Rana closed her eyes tightly, but despite her efforts, a tear slid down her cheek. She was quiet for a long moment.

"Please," she said. "Try to understand."

The smile left Jason's face. He sat back down, then let out a long, suffering sigh.

"It isn't me, is it?"

"I'm going to marry Gamblin."

Jason was silent for a long moment, but he looked at Rana with eyes that were open all the way to his soul. She could see the pain of loss etched deep inside and she reached out to touch him.

"Oh, I wish it were different," she said. "I wish I could be two people...or that I had never met you, or never met Gamblin. Jason, please try to understand...my heart is torn to pieces over this. But I don't know what to do. I just don't know what to do."

"Do you love him more than you do me?" Jason asked.

"I don't know," Rana answered with a sob. "I suppose...I suppose I must. I've been agonizing over this from the moment I learned I was pregnant. I knew I would have to choose one of you, and I've been dreading the decision. And after all that, I have decided on Gamblin. Maybe that means I love him more...maybe it just means that I have loved him longer. But it doesn't mean that I don't love you...only that I can't have you."

Jason walked over to Rana and put his arms around her. He stroked her hair gently.

"I guess when you come right down to it, Gamblin and I have been pretty selfish," Jason said. "Here each of us has been wanting you to choose us, thinking only about our own hurt. We never stopped to think that you would be hurt, no matter how it came out."

"I'm glad you understand," Rana said. She let him hold her close for a long moment. Then she felt an unmistakable reaction in the front of his pants. For an instant she leaned into it, pressing herself against him, feeling with every fiber in her body that she wanted to give herself to him. Then, with a little cry, she pulled away and walked to the other side of the room. "No!"

"I'm sorry," Jason said.

Rana looked out on the street at the band and its admirers. She was silent for a moment, as if composing her thoughts, or perhaps chastising herself.

"We must be more careful from now on," she said finally.

"I'm afraid I can't control how I feel... or what happens to me when I feel that way."

"But we have to control it, don't you see?"

"It's not that simple," Jason said. "I can't just forget the touch of you, the smell, the taste. You're asking me to pretend none of that ever happened."

"No, I'm not asking you to forget, I could never do that. Memories are all we do have now. Jason, there will always be a part of you in my heart, in a secret chamber that will be yours alone. You'll have to be satisfied with that. Once I tell Gamblin that I'm going to marry him, I intend to be true to him, in spirit as well as in fact."

Jason smiled. "I know," he said. "And if I had been the lucky one, I would have hoped for and expected the same thing." He held up his hands. "You'll get no more trouble from me, I promise."

"I want more than a promise of no trouble," Rana said.

"More? What more could you possibly want?"

"I want your support. Jason, I'm going to marry Gamblin, but I don't want you to close yourself out of our lives. We're a team and I want us to stay a team. Remember, I might be carrying your baby."

"Since you've been so honest in all other things, how about a little honesty now? Is it my baby?"

"I won't say," Rana answered. She brushed the hair back from her face. "Jason, given the choice of believing that it might be your baby, or knowing for certain that it isn't, which would you take?"

Jason smiled sadly. "I believe I would like to think there is a chance the baby is mine," he said. "That thought sustains me."

"Then don't make me kill that for you or for Gamblin. "Let it be."

"All right," Jason agreed. "And, Rana? Whether you believe it or not...I wish you and Gamblin nothing but happiness."

By dusk, the excitement that had been growing for the entire day in Texon was full-blown. The sound of the practicing musicians could be heard all up and down Main Street. Children gathered around the glowing yellow windows and peered inside. The dance floor was cleared of all tables and chairs, and musicians had been installed on the platform at the front of the room.

Cars, pickup trucks, and buckboards filled every parking spot on Main Street. Men and women streamed toward the hotel, the women in colorful satin dresses, the men in clean blue jeans and brightly decorated vests.

Gamblin arrived at the office promptly at seven. He, like most of the other men, was wearing jeans and a vest. He had cleaned up at the drill site before coming into town. He smiled at Rana, who was wearing a bright blue dress, trimmed with white fringe. A wide red sash was around her waist, covering the slight bulge of her early pregnancy. Gamblin took in a sharp breath when he saw her.

"My God!" he said. "You are the most beautiful creature I've ever seen."

"Why, thank you," Rana answered, her eyes sparkling at the compliment.

Gamblin looked around the office.

"Where's Jason? I thought he was going to the dance with us."

"Jason thought it would be nice if we went alone tonight," Rana said.

Gamblin grinned broadly. "Well, now, I'd say that's

damned nice of Jason. Yes, sir, damned nice of him." He held out his arm. "Come on, what do you say we take advantage of his generosity?"

As Rana had shared Jason's sense of hurt over the news she told him, she was now feeling a sense of excitement over what she would tell Gamblin. She knew she had made the right decision. She loved Gamblin, and being with him now reinforced that feeling.

Rana strolled alongside Gamblin as they walked to the hotel. Even before they arrived they were able to feel some of the excitement, for the hotel was aglow with light and bubbling over with conversation and laughter. The high skirling of the fiddle could be heard from a block away.

Inside, the excitement was all it promised to be. Girls in colorful dresses and men in denim and leather laughed and talked. To one side of the dance floor there was a large punch bowl on a table. Rana watched as one of the men walked over to the punch bowl and, unobtrusively, poured whiskey into the punch from a bottle he had concealed beneath his vest. A moment later another man did the same thing. There seemed to be no limit to the amount of liquor present, despite the law of national prohibition.

The music was playing, but as yet no one was dancing. Then the music stopped and one of the players lifted a megaphone.

"Choose up your squares!" the caller shouted.

The music began, with the fiddles loud and clear, the guitars carrying the rhythm, the accordion providing the counterpoint, and the dobro singing over everything. The caller began to shout and he clapped his hands and stomped his feet and danced around on the platform in compliance with his own calls, bowing and whirling as if he had a girl and was in one of the squares himself. The dancers moved and swirled to the caller's commands.

Rana danced three sets, then pleaded exhaustion and asked Gamblin to sit out the next few.

"We're just getting started," Gamblin protested.

"You forget it's a little more work for me now," Rana teased.

"Oh, yes, the baby," Gamblin said. "My God! How could I forget that? Listen, you want some punch? How about a nice cup of punch?"

Rana laughed and made a face. "Are you kidding? One swallow of that stuff and there's no telling what might happen to me. Have you seen what they've been putting in it?"

"Oh, yeah," Gamblin said. He looked around. "What do you want to do?"

"How about if we take a walk outside and get a breath of air?"

"Okay," Gamblin agreed.

A moment later they were walking across the street from the hotel toward the café and service station. The café was closed, and the round glass tops of the gas pumps stood silent vigil over the darkened service station. From behind them they heard a woman squeal and a man laugh. Overhead, stars winked down on them, bright in the dark sky.

"You're right," Gamblin said. He wiped the sweat from his face with a red handkerchief. "It is nicer out here."

They walked across the street, then sat on a wooden bench in front of the dark café.

"How is it going on the site?"

"I saw a rainbow on the mud today," Gamblin said.

"A rainbow on the mud? What does that mean?"

"It means oil," Gamblin said. "Already it's beginning to creep up and make a film. That's what's causing the rainbow."

"You think it'll be much longer?"

"No, not long. Pay sand is just below us now, I know it."

"I hope so," Rana said. "Jason hasn't said anything, but he's worried."

"About what?"

"Gamblin, everything he has is tied up in this drilling. He's hocked his store, his hotel, even this café and service station. If we don't hit soon, the banks are going to foreclose and we're all going to be out on our ear."

"We'll hit soon," Gamblin said. "I promise."

"I hope so," Rana said. She looked up at him and smiled. "Otherwise, how are you going to support a wife and baby?"

"How am I going to..." Gamblin started to say. Then he stopped and stared at Rana. "See here, girl, what are you saying to me?"

"I'm saying I want to marry you," Rana said. "That is, if you'll have me."

Gamblin stood up and walked over to one of the gas pumps. He turned and looked back at Rana, his face a contrast of silver and black from the moon and shadow. "Are you serious?"

"Yes, of course I'm serious."

Gamblin broke into a big smile. He just stood there for a moment. Then he stabbed his arm into the air and let out a loud *ya-hoo!*

Across the street from the closed café, Jason was sitting alone in the darkened front room of his apartment.

He heard Gamblin's shout of joy, even above the music of the dance. He raised his glass and drank, offering a silent toast to the two people who had come to mean more to him than anyone else in the world.

Rana Wood and Gamblin McClarity were married three days later in a small civil ceremony that took place in the community room of the hotel. Sue Ellen was matron of honor; Jason acted as Gamblin's best man.

The wedding took place at nine in the morning and was followed immediately by a wedding breakfast, attended by as many of the workers from the site as Gamblin felt could be spared. Several of the citizens of the town were there as well, because even though no oil had yet been found, Texon Petroleum was already the town's biggest business.

Later, when the oil workers had returned to the field, Sue Ellen had left to open her café, and the townspeople had gone to their own places of employment, only Rana, Gamblin, and Jason remained around the big table. The plates on the table showed the remains of breakfast, a few cold, scrambled eggs on some, greasy bits of bacon on others. Unconsumed grits hardened and dried, some of which had been profaned by ground-out cigarette butts. Other cigarette butts floated in half-full cups of cold coffee. Very few, it seemed, made it to the crystal ashtrays that were in abundance.

"I want to say a few words," Jason said.

Rana and Gamblin looked up at him.

"Things are getting hard now. The banks are starting to put the squeeze on me. My little empire, such as it was, is crumbling around me."

Gamblin started to speak, but Jason held up his hand to stop him.

"Let me finish," Jason said. "I'm telling you this not to frighten you, but merely to illustrate how much I am still committed to our operation. Gamblin, I told you when I first met you that I could smell money. I know we are going to hit it, and I want you to concentrate solely on bringing in this well. Don't worry about anything else...you let me handle the banks and the lawyers and the sheriff's deputies with their foreclosures."

"That's asking an awful lot of you," Gamblin said. "Maybe we could sell off some of the equipment and..."

"I assume we need everything we have, right? Or we wouldn't have bought it in the first place."

"That's right," Gamblin agreed.

"Then we'll sell nothing. The drilling must go forward at full speed. Don't you see? Right now, that's our only chance out of this."

"All right," Gamblin said.

Jason smiled. "Gamblin, my friend, you married the girl both of us love. She's carrying our baby. Someday I'll find a woman of my own and I'll fall in love with her and I'll marry her. Our lives will begin to take different paths. For one thing, we are going to have money...more money than any of us ever dreamed. But when that time comes...when I am married to another and have a family of my own, when we are among the wealthiest people in the world...I don't want us ever to forget this moment."

Jason put his hand out and Gamblin and Rana joined their hands to his, forming the three-armed star that had come to symbolize their unique union. They held that for a while. Then Gamblin cleared his throat.

"I know it's a hell of a thing to do to you on our wed

din' day, darlin'," he said. "But I've got to get back to the drill site."

"I understand," Rana said. She kissed him. "You go ahead. I'll be all right."

Gamblin looked at Jason and smiled. "I know," he said. "I couldn't leave you in better hands."

Rana walked out to Gamblin's truck with him, kissed him again, then waved good-bye as he drove off, spewing a rooster tail of dust behind him. She watched until his truck was out of sight. Then she went back into the hotel. Jason was sitting at the table smoking a cigarette.

"Some honeymoon," Rana said. Tears welled in her eyes and she wiped them away with a finger.

"You've got a good man, Rana," Jason said. "The rest of your life will be a honeymoon."

"Oh, Jason, he is a good man, isn't he? Are you happy for us?"

"Do you think I would have gone to such lengths to have such a fancy wedding for you if you were marrying anyone else?" Jason asked. He waved his hand across the table. "Look, scrambled eggs, grits, bacon, sausages, biscuits, gravy — nothing but the best for my friends."

Rana laughed. "You're a nut," she said. She walked over to him and put her arms around him. "There is something to be said for the Mormon custom of marrying more than one person."

"Wouldn't help," Jason said. "Mormon men could have more than one wife, but the wives could have only one husband."

"Then I guess I've done the only thing I could do," Rana said, smiling at him through her tears. "I married one of you, but I love you both."

Chapter Fifteen

Houston, Texas — 1986

Rebel drove her little Mercedes under the portico of the home of Mr. and Mrs. Geoffrey Endicott. A uniformed valet met her as she came to a stop by the door, then slid in behind the wheel to park the car for her.

There were at least half a dozen young men and women waiting to greet and park the arriving cars. One of the girl workers had been a sophomore at the university when Rebel was a senior, and when Rebel looked her way, she smiled.

"Hi, Rebel," she greeted her. "Where's your Jeep?"

"Kathy, hi," Rebel replied. The girl's smile broadened at being recognized. "I don't think it would be quite the thing for something like this, do you?"

"I guess not," Kathy agreed. "Boy, this must be some fancy do. Just about everyone is here tonight."

"Yeah, well, believe me, I wouldn't be here if it weren't for my dad. He's over in the Middle East somewhere and he asked me to attend this thing for him."

"Kathy," one of the boys interrupted. He was holding a phone on his shoulder. "Anything you don't like on your pizza?"

"I don't like anchovies."

"Who the hell does?" the young man replied, and those around him laughed.

"How's school?" Rebel asked.

"Oh, it's just fine," Kathy replied. "I'll graduate in one more semester."

"Good for you! What's your major?"

"Petroleum engineering."

Rebel laughed. "That would make a hit with my father. I'm afraid my liberal arts degree didn't do much for him."

A Cadillac arrived and Kathy was next to take it.

"I have to go to work now," Kathy called back over her shoulder as she started toward the car. "Have fun."

"You too," Rebel replied. Rebel looked at the young men and women, laughing and joking among themselves as the expensive cars glided to a quiet stop under the portico. In a little while they'd be eating pizza and making a party of their part-time job. Rebel wondered if any of them realized just how much she would rather be out here with them than inside with all the stuffed shirts.

Rebel smoothed her hair, then started toward the door. It was opened for her and she stepped into the great foyer under a huge, glistening chandelier.

The Endicotts were patrons of the arts and they were hosting a reception to raise money for a new fine arts museum. For tonight's affair they had arranged to borrow paintings from private and public collections all over the world. Rebel had heard that more than fifty million dollars' worth of paintings would be on display, and that rumor was substantiated by the sight of armed guards all over the place. They were standing discreetly behind potted plants, in quiet corners, along the walls, away from the guests, but obviously present. Their eyes saw everything and they talked quietly to one another over their little hand-held radios.

For a two-hundred-fifty-dollar donation, anyone could come view the paintings. Many would come, Rebel knew, who had no desire to see the paintings at all, but would merely take this opportunity to see the inside of one of Houston's most elegant homes.

Two hours before the show was open to the public, a private dinner was being given for those people who had donated ten thousand dollars or more. Evan Hewlitt had donated fifty thousand dollars, thus bringing about Rebel's presence.

For dinner the guests were served lamb chops and curried rice, handled by enough help to have one servant for every two diners. The waiters were dressed in tuxedos and each of them was schooled in the European fashion of manipulating spoons and forks so that the serving of food became an art in itself.

After dinner the guests were free to wander through the ten downstairs rooms where the art was on display. Rebel excused herself and stepped into the library, while behind her the servants began to clean up from the dinner party. China and glassware were loaded onto rolling carts, ashtrays were emptied, centerpieces were disassembled, and vacuums were brought out to clean the Persian carpet. It was all very efficient, and Rebel knew that within ten minutes paintings would be moved back into the dining room. When the public arrived later, there would be absolutely no sign that guests had just eaten.

In the library one painting in particular caught Rebel's eye and she stepped up closer to it. There was a little card beneath the canvas.

> Loaned by the Art Institute of Chicago
> from the collection of
> Mr. and Mrs. Martin A. Ryerson
> OLD SAINT-LAZARE STATION
> PARIS 1877
> Oil on canvas by Claude Monet,
> 1840-1926
> 23 1/2 by 31 1/2 inches
> (59.6 by 80.2 cm)

In this picture, Monet has conveyed a very real sense of the interior of the train shed with the open space beyond, suffused by a soft, diffuse light. The sense of time and space is achieved through the rendering of steam from the locomotives as it rises to block the view of the world around.

Rebel moved around to look at the painting from several perspectives. Though it wasn't a photographic representation, it took very little imagination to hear the sound of escaping steam, the excited babble of voices, and shrill whistle of the locomotives.

"Well, now, look who we have here. Little Rebel Hewlitt, I believe. Darling, I never knew you were such a patron of the arts."

The low, sarcastic tone of voice was familiar to

Rebel, and she turned to see Carol McClarity standing behind her. Carol was smoking a cigarette, holding it in a long bone-colored cigarette holder. She was dressed in a white sheath with a neckline that plunged so dramatically that it looked as if every move had to be planned to keep everything in place.

"Carol, I thought you were in New York," Rebel replied.

"Whatever gave you that idea?"

"Isn't that where the magazine said you and your new girl friend were living?"

Carol laughed. "Don't be catty, dear, it doesn't become your innocent virgin image. But of course you and I know that is only an image anyway, don't we? Tell me, was my husband fucking you when he was still married to me? You were what... fifteen, sixteen, then?"

"What difference does it make to you?" Rebel answered. "You were gainfully occupied, I believe."

"So I was," Carol answered easily. "Is Deke here with you?"

"No."

"What a shame. I would have liked to see him."

"I'm not sure he would particularly want to see you," Rebel said.

Carol took a puff through the long holder, then let the smoke out with a little laugh.

"Darling, don't tell me you are jealous?" Carol put her hand to her chest. "You've no idea how flattering that sounds. You're such a child, and I'm..." Carol paused and laughed again. "Well, never mind how old I am. But I'm much older than you are, so you can see how flattering it is that you are jealous of me."

"Don't get too carried away with the flattery," Rebel said. "Jealousy has nothing to do with it. I just don't think Deke would care to see you, that's all."

"I do wish he wouldn't be so hurt by everything he hears and reads," Carol said. "We're both adults; we've each gone our own way."

"That's not quite true, is it?" Rebel asked.

"What do you mean?"

"I can't help but notice how much advantage you are taking of the McClarity name. Why are you keeping it? You have no children."

"Why shouldn't I keep it?" Carol replied. "After all, it is legally my name. And, I admit, it has opened certain doors for me."

"Yes, but to what?" Rebel asked. "Sleazy newspapers and porn magazines? The wonder is that you have the...the..." Rebel laughed. "I almost said 'balls.' In your case, I suppose that wouldn't be too far out of line, would it? That you have the balls to appear at a place like this. Don't tell me you made a ten-thousand-dollar donation to the Endicott Art Fund."

"Of course I didn't, dear," Carol said. "But Deke did, and when I called and introduced myself as Mrs. Deke McClarity, I was sent an invitation."

"Why in heaven's name would you want to come?" Rebel asked.

Carol pinched the cigarette from her holder, ground it out in a crystal ashtray nearby, then dropped the holder into her pearl-studded purse.

"One never knows what sort of opportunity one might encounter at such a place," she said.

"Yes," Rebel said. "If you will excuse me, I want to see the other paintings. I'll leave you to your... opportunities." Rebel let the last word slide out sarcastically.

"Do give my best to Deke the next time you see him, won't you?" Carol called after her.

Just as Rebel was leaving the library, an older woman, dripping with fur and jewels, stepped into the room. Rebel smiled sweetly at the older woman.

"Good evening, Mrs. Mortman," she said. "Are you having a nice time?"

"Why, good evening, Rebel. Yes, dear, I'm having a perfectly lovely time. And you?" Mrs. Mortman replied.

"Oh, a wonderful time. If you'll excuse me, Mrs. Mortman?" Rebel said. She turned back toward Carol. "Carol?" she called in the same voice she had used for Mrs. Mortman.

"Yes?"

"Fuck you."

Tan Amien, Nybibia

Evan Hewlitt looked out the window of the Bell Jet Ranger while the helicopter descended, blades popping as they spilled air. The pad on which they were landing was a huge square, marked with a circle H, positioned on a barge that was anchored in Tan Amien Bay. A long hose, used to transfer crude oil from storage tanks on the shore, snaked through the water toward the barge. From the barge more hoses passed through the bright blue bay to a Texon tanker anchored about one hundred yards away. Waiting patiently behind the ship being loaded were three more tankers, all bearing the blue-and-white colors and the three-pointed star of Texon. Their crews, bare-backed against the sun, stood along the rails or lazed on the deck, drawing time-and-a-half pay for every day they had to wait.

Large, multicolored patches of oil dotted the water

where the crude was leaking from joints and couplings. Here and there the beaches were soiled with great black gobs of the stuff, washed ashore by the tide.

Evan knew that in the United States the environmentalists would have long since shut down the operation. All across the nation TV viewers would be seeing pictures of birds getting trapped in the goo. But that wasn't the case in Nybibia. King Hafadiez was so happy to be moving his crude at thirty dollars a barrel that he wasn't about to let a little thing like oil spills or beach pollution get in the way.

The helicopter settled lightly on the pad. Then the pilot killed the engine. Evan slid the door open and walked away, hearing the swishing sound of the rotor blades as they spun down overhead.

"Mr. Hewlitt, it's a pleasure, sir," George Peabody said, running out to meet Evan. George, a plump, bald-headed man, was Texon's highest-ranking officer in Nybibia.

"Where can we go to talk?" Evan growled.

"The barge master has an office aft," George replied. "It isn't much, but it's private.

"Lead the way."

The two men picked their way across the barge, stepping over hoses and lines, around oil smears, and alongside wheezing, throbbing pumps and engines, to reach the afterdeck. A dozen men were working on the barge, monitoring pumps, adjusting engines, shouting, sweating, and browning in the sun. They worked long, hard hours and were unaware that to a stranger their body odors were nearly as strong as the heavy phosphorous smell of the oil.

Just the little walk from the helicopter to the afterdeck office made Evan break out in a heavy sweat and he dabbed at his face as they stepped inside. A little oscillating fan sat on a cluttered desk and George turned it on.

"This may help a little," he said. From the chair he brushed away a pile of *Playboy* and *Penthouse* magazines and one of them fell open on a smooth-skinned, full-breasted young woman whose frontal nude picture graced two pages. "Have a seat," he invited. "I must say, this is a pleasant surprise, Mr. Hewlitt. What brings you out here?"

"Are you aware of the cost of North Sea crude as of this morning?" Evan asked as he sat down.

"No," George said. "I haven't been following it."

"Well, perhaps you should," Evan suggested. "It's selling for thirteen-fifty. Thirteen dollars and fifty cents a barrel, Goddamn it! And we're paying royalties on thirty dollars a barrel for this shit."

George whistled softly. "Son-of-a-bitch. We're paying more than twice the market!"

"By the time this contract is finished, it's going to cost us one hundred fifty million dollars more than it should," Evan complained.

"Well, Mr. Hewlitt, you shouldn't blame yourself. At the time you negotiated the contract, oil was selling for thirty-eight dollars a barrel. You made a good deal."

"I know. It cost me two and a half million dollars under the table to get the deal set up. This is one of the things that bastard Carmack is looking for. But none of that makes any difference now. I want out of this operation."

"How?" George asked. He pointed to the tanker taking on oil. "We'll have *Pride of Houston* pumped full by four this afternoon and ready to start on the next load."

"I want to invoke the 'interrupted service' clause of the contract," Evan said.

"What is that? I don't understand what you're talking about."

Evan smiled. "It's something King Hafadiez insisted we put in. With America the target of so many terrorists, he was afraid something might happen to our facilities, like a bomb or something, which would stop the loading. If the service is interrupted for thirty days or longer, the contract must be renegotiated."

"And you say Hafadiez put that in?"

"Yes," Evan said. He chuckled. "Remember that was back in the days of OPEC's glory. Hafadiez and everyone else thought the price of oil would keep going up. He put this in to protect himself, only it just might turn out to be our salvation."

"How are we going to interrupt service?"

"Suppose something were to happen to this barge?" Evan ventured. "Is there a replacement pump anywhere in Nybibia?"

"Not one that could handle this job," George said.

"Anywhere else in the Middle East?"

"If there is, it's already being used," George said. "Lose this pump and we'd be out of business for at least..." George stopped and smiled. "...thirty days," he finished.

"You don't say?" Evan stroked his chin. "It would be awful if something happened to this barge some night, wouldn't it?"

"We'd have to be careful," George warned. "I'm sure that if the Nybibians suspect us of sabotaging our own barge, the interrupted-service clause could be invalidated."

"Then be careful," Evan said. He got up and started toward the door.

"Mr. Hewlitt?"

Evan stopped and looked back at George, who had a puzzled expression of his face.

"Yes?"

"Are you... are you telling me to destroy this barge?"

"Haven't you been listening? That's exactly what I'm telling you."

"But I wouldn't know where to start. I don't have the first idea about how to go about doing such a thing — especially how to do it in a way that won't be obvious. I'm a petroleum engineer, Mr. Hewlitt. For a job like this, you would need someone like an ex-military man or something..."

"No, that's exactly what I don't need. Don't you see? The more people who are aware of what we are doing, the more chance there is of something going wrong."

"But I'm not sure I can do what you want done."

"George, when I hired you as chief of operations for Nybibia, I was told that you were the best troubleshooter in the business."

"Well, I appreciate the compliment," George said. "But — "

"But what?" Evan interrupted. "Goddamn it! A troubleshooter's job is to solve problems, is it not? We've got a problem. I've identified it, I've told you what needs to be done about it. And I damned well expect you to get it done."

"Yes, sir," George said.

"I've got to get back to the airport," Evan said. "Your job is to get us out of this old contract. My job is to keep Rana from getting us into a new one."

"Don't worry about a thing here, Mr. Hewlitt," George said. "It'll all be taken care of."

Houston, Texas

"Please inform the oil minister that the Texon guarantee of twenty-four dollars per barrel is good only until the end of this week," Rana said. "After that it drops to twenty dollars, and if we still haven't come to an agreement by the end of two more weeks, it will go down to sixteen dollars."

Jose Mendoza was sitting across the desk from Rana, and he jerked upright when he heard her words.

"No, *señora*, you cannot do that," he insisted. "We have agreed. We have agreed on twenty-four dollars."

"Yes, and so it shall be — if the contract is signed this week." Rana said.

"But surely you understand there are complications...difficulties to overcome. Even you are facing such difficulties, are you not?"

"Señor Mendoza, the only difficulty I'm facing right now is getting this contract signed. Once it's signed I can get my people into the Bustamante Basin and start getting the oil out."

"But we cannot sign unless we have the permission of our foreign office. And right now, that permission is not forthcoming," Mendoza complained.

"That's your problem, not mine," Rana said. "But the longer you delay, the cheaper the oil. You might remind your foreign minister that if he waits until next week to sign the agreement, Mexico stands to lose three and a half billion dollars in revenue. And another three and a half billion for every two weeks after that. Given Mexico's international debt and appeal to the World Bank for fifty billion in credits, do you really think you can afford such a loss?"

"No, *señora*, we cannot," Mendoza admitted.

"Then I suggest you get back to Mexico City and try to talk some sense into the officials there."

"*Sí, señora,*" Mendoza said. He stood and made a small but gracious bow, then withdrew. A moment later Maggie St. John came into the office, carrying a little piece of paper.

"I think perhaps you should see this," Maggie said, handing the paper to Rana. "Our loading barge at Tan Amien Bay just exploded and sank."

"What? My God! Was anyone hurt?"

"No, I don't think so," Maggie said. "This just came across our intercompany Telex. I'm afraid it's all the news we have on it for the moment."

Rana read the report. Then, inexplicably, she smiled.

"Why, that sly old dog," Rana said. "I must confess, I didn't know Evan had it in him."

"What are you talking about? The Nybibia field is one of Evan's deals," Maggie said.

"Yes, it is, isn't it? It's been losing money for us for two years. But I believe Evan has just taken care of the leak."

Chapter Sixteen

Texon, Texas — 1924

Drilling was going on twenty-four hours a day now. By day, rain or shine, the men were at work. At night a battery of spotlights shone on the drill platform, washing out all shadows, creating a world of harsh black and stark white.

The twenty-four-hour drilling was necessary because the bank had given Texon three more days. After that, all operations would stop and the bank would seize every piece of the equipment.

With each passing day the men on the site grew more anxious. Actually, they had run into no exceptional difficulties and were drilling at a very rapid rate. The rate was even more remarkable when one considered the difficult underground formations they had encountered and the water seeps that had caused them to suspend drilling while they installed casing.

Despite that, progress was frustratingly slow compared to the rapidly approaching deadline that had been fixed by the bank. The frustrations were made all the more agonizing each time the bailer was run out to show good sign. Ever since Gamblin had first noticed a rainbow of oil on the mud, the cuttings had shouted the news that oil was somewhere below.

The question on everyone's lips was: How deep was the oil? Would they reach it before the deadline?

In the last week before the deadline, Rana closed the office in town and moved out to the site. She and Gamblin were sleeping in the drill shack. Jason, who now had no business interests left in town, had also moved out to the site and was sleeping in the tent with the men.

At about ten o'clock one night, Rana took coffee out to the workers, who didn't have time to break for anything. For a while she stayed outside in the dark and the noise watching the operation, but her back started hurting so she went into the drill shack to give it a rest.

Inside the shack she stood at the workbench and watched through the window, all the while holding her hands on her back. No one had ever told her that being pregnant was so hard on a person's back.

The morning sickness had been nothing. It was long over with now, but even when she had been suffering from it, it lasted only an hour or so every day. The back pains were constant. At least, she told herself, they couldn't go on much longer. The baby was due in less than two weeks.

Rana glanced at the drilling log. The entry for noon

that day read: "9,875 feet...good sign."

The door opened and Gamblin came in.

"How you feelin'?" he asked.

Rana smiled at him. "I'm fine," she said.

"You sure? I saw you come in."

"My back is hurting, that's all."

"I wish I had time to rub it for you."

"Mmm, I do, too," Rana said, raising his hand to her cheek and rubbing it gently. Suddenly, the thumping sound of the pump stopped. "What is it?" Rana asked, looking around. "Why did the machine stop?"

"The bit's gone dull," Gamblin explained. "I told them to pull the string so we can change it."

"Gamblin, we are close, aren't we?" Rana asked.

"Honey, we're so close I believe I could dig the rest of it by hand if I could get down there. It's just on the other side of the bottom, I know it is. And when it comes in... oh, baby, when it comes in, we're gonna be richer than you ever imagined."

"I'm going to come out and watch you change the bit," Rana said.

"I thought your back was hurting?"

"It is, but it's hurting just as much in here. Watching at least gets my mind off my back for a while."

Rana followed Gamblin back outside, then leaned against the front of the car to watch as Bevo fed power to the bull wheel. The wheel started winding up the cable, pulling the tool string up to the surface.

It took twenty minutes of winding before the drilling tools — the rope socket, the sinker, the jars, auger stem, and finally the drilling bit itself, almost six feet long — appeared at the head of the bore hole.

As the tool string worked its way up, pulverized rock and slimy mud spread across the derrick floor, then spilled over the edges like a mud waterfall. When the tools were clear of the hole, they hung, dripping, several feet above the casing head.

It took nearly an hour from the time they started drawing out the cable until the bit was changed. Once that was done, Gamblin personally worked the controls that lowered the tool string back down into the bore hole. He let in the clutch on the chain drive operating the band wheel. The walking beam started its seesaw action and drilling was under way again.

Rana watched for a little while longer, then suddenly felt a sharp pain unlike anything she had experienced before. At first she thought it was just a different manifestation of her back pain, but it was much more intense than any of the others. Besides, she couldn't say that it was in her back, exactly. It seemed a little lower than the others. Rana gasped. She suddenly realized she was having a labor pain!

"Gamblin?" she called in a hesitant, almost plaintive voice.

"Yes?"

"Gamblin, I think I'm..."

"Gamblin, you better get over here and listen to this," Bevo called, interrupting Rana.

"I'll be right there," Gamblin answered. He looked at Rana. "Anything wrong?"

"No," Rana said. She smiled at him. What if there was nothing to it? After all, the baby wasn't due for two more weeks, and she knew that Gamblin had a lot more to worry about right now than her complaints. "No, nothing is wrong. I just think I'm going to go on in and lie down now, that's all."

"Honey, I don't know why you've stayed out here this

long," Gamblin said. "Hell, it's after eleven."

"I think I'll go on to bed."

"Gamblin, are you comin'?" Bevo called again.

"Yes, just a minute," Gamblin replied. He kissed Rana. "Good night, darlin'. I'll probably be in before too much longer. We've got the bit changed. Nothing much more for me to do now."

"Okay," Rana said.

Rana walked back toward the shack. She saw Jason sitting on a keg and she smiled at him.

"What are you doing out here?" she asked.

"Nothing important," Jason answered. "I've shot my wad now. I have nothing left to offer except crossed fingers. That makes me pretty worthless around here, I guess."

"Nonsense. Look around you, Jason. Everything you see exists because you raised the money. How can you deny the importance of that?"

"Yeah, but I didn't raise enough," Jason lamented. "The whole thing's going to be closed up in three days and there's nothing I can do about it."

"You've done your part. Now let Gamblin and the others do theirs."

"Yeah, I tell myself that all I can do now is wait. But I've found that it's easier to wait if I can at least watch what's going on."

"I know what you mean," Rana said. She patted her stomach. "But this little devil in here doesn't want me to watch anymore, so I guess I'm off to bed."

"I'll come get you if anything exciting happens," Jason promised.

Rana suddenly winced and the expression of pain in her face was so intense that Jason jumped up from the keg and grabbed her.

"Rana! What is it? Are you okay?" he asked.

"Yes," Rana assured him. She laughed weakly. "I'm all right, but my back is killing me. I've got to lie down."

"Here, let me help you."

"Don't be silly," Rana said.

"I insist."

Jason put his arm around her and Rana, gratefully, leaned into him as they went into the shack.

It was dark inside, though enough light filtered in from the rig lights to allow them to see their way. Jason helped her over to the bed, where she lay down heavily.

"Are you sure you're going to be okay?" Jason asked anxiously.

"I'm sure," Rana said. She let out a contented sigh. "You've no idea how much better I feel just by lying down."

"Call me if you need me," Jason ordered.

"I will," Rana said. "I promise."

"There, hear it?" Bevo asked. That was what he had called Gamblin over for. "That's oil music sure as gun is iron."

Oil music was what the old hands called the sounds deep in the earth just before a well came in.

Gamblin cocked his ear and this time he heard it — the deep, harmonic resonance of the steel casing.

"My God!" Gamblin exclaimed. "That's gas escaping! Bevo, this is it! We've done it!"

"We sure as hell have," Bevo agreed happily.

There was a long tooting sound, like a far-off horn, then a rattling noise.

"Get the string up!" Gamblin shouted. "Get the string up, quick!"

"You heard the man!" Bevo shouted to the bull wheel operator. "Get it up! Full speed!"

The wooden floor began to shake and tremble. Gamblin felt his heart pounding against his ribs. He knew now that he had hit it big. The bit had broken through and plunged into an oil stratum. The oil was trapped under tremendous natural gas pressure, and now the gas was bursting free.

"Jason! Jason!" Gamblin shouted. "It's about to blow! It's about to come in!"

"Son-of-a-bitch!" Jason shouted happily. "Oh, son-of-a-bitch!"

"Blow, you bastard, blow!" Gamblin shouted.

Jason thought of Rana and he hurried into the shack to tell her.

"Rana, it's coming! The well is coming in! Come on, you need to..."

Jason stopped in mid-sentence. Rana was flat on her back with her knees drawn up, her dress pulled up to her waist, her blood-and water-soaked panties on the floor.

"My God! Rana! What?"

"The baby!" Rana gasped. "The baby's coming now!"

"No," Jason said. "The doctor! I'll go get — "

"There's no time!" Rana interrupted frantically. She let out a long, wheezing sigh of pain. "Help me, Jason! Help me."

"I've never done...I mean, I don't..."

"Oh, Jason, for God's sake, just do what comes natural! Don't you understand? The baby's coming now!"

"Oh, Jesus!" Jason said. "Oh, sweet Jesus!" He hurried over to the bed and looked at her. "I can see its head. Oh, Rana, I can see the top of its head!"

Rana grabbed Jason's hand and squeezed it so tightly it hurt.

Out on the rig, cable was being shot up through the bore hole faster than the bull wheel could take up the slack. Excess wire rope was looping and slashing about on the derrick floor.

"Faster!" Bevo shouted. "Take it up faster, the line's fouling!"

"It won't go no faster, Bevo! Hell, the throttle's lashed full open now!" the operator shouted back.

The cable was looping and leaping about the floor, spewing out of the hole now at an unbelievable rate.

"Boss, we better clear this rig!" Bevo shouted. "This sumbitch is gonna be spittin' out the tools pretty soon, and they gonna come out like cannonballs."

"You're right," Gamblin answered. He cupped his hand to his mouth. "Clear the rig!" he shouted. "Everyone get back! She's comin' in!"

When Gamblin was certain that everyone else had cleared the rig, he leaped from the platform and started running. He was still running when, seconds later, there was a roar as loud as a cannon shot. The heavy tools and newly installed drill bit shot up from the hole like a mortar round. The string broke apart, sending projectiles through the crown block and smashing into the crossbeams before coming back down with earth-shaking crashes.

The ejected tools were followed by a hissing spew of gas. Then, like an immense geyser, a huge column of oil burst up from the hole.

Gamblin looked at it. The column of oil was so strong and so big that the derrick was completely blotted out. Oil shot a hundred feet into the air, then fanned out to rain down in great black drops. Within seconds Gamblin and everyone around him were drenched with oil.

"Look at that sumbitch! Look at it!" Gamblin shouted.

Gamblin stood under the oil shower and spread his arms, whooping for joy.

"She'll go eight to ten thousand barrels a day or there ain't a cow in Texas!" Bevo shouted. He leaped around in a wild dance. "I ain't ever seen a gusher like that one!"

"We gotta get her capped!" Gamblin said, suddenly coming to his senses. "We gotta get her capped! Goddamn it, Bevo! That's my money we're wastin'!" he shouted happily.

"Just a little more!" Jason pleaded. He was drenched in sweat as he knelt between Rana's legs, helping to guide the baby out. "Push!" he said. "Push!"

Rana gave one last, straining cry, then heaved a mighty sigh of relief as the baby slipped out into Jason's hands.

"It's a boy, Rana! You've had a boy!" Jason shouted with excitement.

Jason had never been in on the delivery of a baby, but he had certainly helped with the birthing of calves. He knew to cut the umbilical cord and tie it off.

"Is he...is he all right?" Rana gasped.

Jason jerked the baby up by his heels and slapped its bare rump. The baby filled its lungs and let out a cry at the same instant the oil well blew outside.

"He's perfect," Jason said. He saw a washbasin on the nightstand and he filled it with water from a large porcelain vase. Gently, he cleaned the baby, while outside men were whooping and shouting excitedly.

"I want to see him," Rana said weakly. "Please, Jason, let me see him."

"I'll do better than that," Jason said. He crossed over to the bed and lay the baby down beside her. "I'll give him to you."

Rana looked down at the baby's tiny red face. She touched its head, felt the fine hair under her fingers.

"Oh," she said. "Oh, Jason, he is the most beautiful thing I have ever seen."

Jason sat on the bed beside her and reached out to touch the baby. "Rana, never again am I going to wonder who this baby's father is. For the first few moments of his life he belonged to me. That's all I'll ever need."

"Would you like to name him?" Rana asked.

Jason looked at her in surprise. "What? Are you serious? I can name the baby?"

"I think you've earned that right tonight," Rana said. "Do you want to call him Jason?"

"No," Jason said. He laughed. "I'm not sure how Gamblin would take that, and to tell the truth, I've never really been that fond of the name anyway." Jason rubbed a finger against the baby's face. His fingernail was as big as the baby's cheek.

"Well, you must have some name that you like."

"Yeah," Jason said. "My pa once rode for Mr. Charles Goodnight. Do you know who he was?"

"No, I can't say that I do," Rana said.

"Mr. Charles Goodnight was the finest cattleman Texas ever had. My pa always insisted that no one ever really tasted a steak before Charles Goodnight got into the business. I think I'd like you to call him Charles Goodnight McClarity. Anyway, I think it's a very proper name, since he was born on such a good night."

Rana laughed. "Then Charles Goodnight McClarity it will be. But that's a pretty big handle for such a little boy. I'll call him C.G. C.G., meet your godfather."

There was another excited whoop from outside and Rana looked around in confusion. "What is it, Jason? What's going on out there?"

"Oh, my God!" Jason cried, slapping his hand against his forehead. "I almost forgot! The well's come in, Rana! That's why I came in here!"

"The well! Jason, we've struck oil, and you forgot?"

Jason chuckled. "You have to admit, you kept me pretty busy."

"I guess I did at that," Rana said.

There was another whoop and Jason looked through the window.

"Go on out there," Rana said. "There's no sense in both of us missing all the excitement."

"Are you sure you're okay, now?"

"Yes, I'm perfectly all right," Rana said. "Really I am. Besides, don't you think it's time Gamblin knew?"

Jason grinned sheepishly. "Yeah," he said. "I guess it is."

"Get that gate valve over here!" Gamblin shouted.

Two men hurried over with the large valve and the three of them managed to force it down over the rush of oil. For the time being the valve was open, allowing the oil to pass through. If it hadn't been open they wouldn't have been able to overcome the pressure of the escaping fluid.

The valve was put down over the casing head. Then the holes were lined up with the studs, which were in place just for this purpose. Quickly, nuts were put on the studs, then tightened, until finally the valve was in place.

"Okay!" Gamblin shouted. "Shut her off!"

Bevo and another rigger twisted the two big wheels, closing the gate. The gush of oil grew less and less powerful until finally the gate was closed and the oil was contained.

"Hooray!" the men shouted.

"We're gonna have to hook up pipe and start diverting it pretty soon," Bevo said, "else it could blow through the head. Trouble is, we don't have anything big enough to contain everything she's gonna gush out until we can get more tanks."

"What about the dry lake bed?" Gamblin suggested.

"Yeah," Bevo answered, smiling broadly. By now his face, like everyone else's, was so black that his teeth and eyes were the only features visible. "That sumbitch will hold fifty, sixty thousand barrels easy. By that time we'll have shipping and holding tanks in here."

"Gamblin?" Jason called.

Gamblin looked around at Jason and, seeing that his was the only clean face in sight, knew that he hadn't seen the gusher.

"Jason, my God, man, you missed it! Where were you? It's the biggest goddamned gusher I ever saw in my life! The son-of-a-bitch must've been a hundred feet high."

"I've got news for you," Jason said.

Gamblin laughed. "You've got news for me? What the hell do you think this is?" He pointed to the well. "Do you realize, my friend, that by this time tomorrow night we will have earned thirty thousand dollars? And in just a little over a month it'll be a million. We're rich, Jason! We're rich!"

"I know," Jason said. He smiled broadly and shook Gamblin's hand. "I want you to know I never doubted you. Not for one minute did I ever doubt you."

"You're gonna get your hand dirty," Gamblin said. He laughed, then smeared some oil on Jason's face. "Hand, hell! Come on, man, bathe in this shit. It's oil, Jason. Black gold!"

"Rana had her baby," Jason said.

"Rana! Does she know? Did you..." Gamblin stopped in mid-sentence. "What did you say?"

"I said Rana had her baby."

"My God! When? Where? Is she all right?"

"She's fine," Jason said quickly. "She and the baby are both doing well."

"Rana!" Gamblin shouted as he ran toward the drill shack. He stopped just inside the door and looked over toward the bed. "Rana, are you all right?"

"Of course I am," Rana said. "Come over here, Gamblin, I want you to meet your son."

"I'm all dirty," Gamblin said. "I'm covered in oil."

"Might as well let C.G. get exposed to it," Rana said. "I have a feeling he's going to be around it all his life."

"C.G., is it?" Gamblin said. "What's that stand for?"

"Jason delivered him, so I let him name him. He named him Charles Goodnight."

"Yes," Gamblin said. "I know of Mr. Goodnight. That's a good name." Gamblin walked over and looked down at the baby, clearly visible in the splash of outside light. "Yes, sir, that's a fine name for the little fella." Gamblin started to touch the baby. Then he pulled his hand back.

"He won't bite."

"I want to clean up a little first," Gamblin said.

"Okay, if you insist."

"Rana, how did all this happen? I mean, I thought the baby wasn't coming for two more weeks."

"Babies don't always keep to the schedule people set for them," she said. "I guess C.G. just wanted to come into the world on the same night his daddy brought in the first well."

"Oh, Rana, I'm so sorry," Gamblin said. "When you needed me most I wasn't here."

"Hush. You were exactly where you had to be. Would Jason have been of help to you out there?"

"No," Gamblin said. "When things start happening fast, you have to have people who know that they are doing. Jason wouldn't have known whether to shit or wind his watch."

"Believe me, he knew what he was doing in here, so everything worked out for the best."

"Yeah," Gamblin said. "Yeah, I guess so." Gamblin was quiet for a moment longer. "Rana?"

"Yes?"

"I guess this really does give him a share of the baby, doesn't it?"

"Are you jealous?"

"No," Gamblin said. "I guess maybe I should be, but I'm not. I'm too happy to be jealous. This is the happiest night of my life...and I don't mean just the well and the baby. It's everything...it's...us, all of us, if you know what I mean.

"Yes, darling," Rana said. "I know what you mean."

Chapter Seventeen

Within two months after the well came in, Texon Petroleum moved out of the old doctor's office and into what had been the Cattlemen's Association building. But even this was to be temporary until the new headquarters could be built. The building, a ten-story structure, was to be constructed on a piece of property Jason already owned.

Texon had almost doubled in size since the first well came in, and all indications were that it would soon surpass Big Lake as the largest town in the county. Some farsighted dreamers saw it growing past San Angelo and Midland, maybe someday even challenging some of the bigger cities in the state.

There was, however, a problem with the location. The city owned an easement that would prevent a road from being built, a problem that normally would be easily solved by action of the city council. But the city council of Texon was totally dominated by the mayor, Luke Monroe, and Luke had been a longtime personal enemy of Jason's. He now carried that enmity over to Texon Petroleum and, by association, to Gamblin as well.

Gamblin didn't realize the depth of the problem until he appeared before the council, urging its members to change the easement. Luke Monroe called for a vote before Gamblin could even present his argument. The vote was no.

"I don't understand," Gamblin said, puzzled by the reaction of the council. "We're good for business. You have to be glad we're here."

"You and Jason may be wealthy men, Mr. McClarity," Luke Monroe said. "But I think you're going to find that we can't be bought."

Gamblin held papers in his hand that supported his request. The papers detailed the advantages the city would derive from the growth of Texon Petroleum. He rolled them up and unrolled them as he listened to the mayor.

"Texon Petroleum has already made its share of enemies," the mayor continued. "Some ranchers have been ruined because they are no longer able to get access to grazing land. Your oil field has completely taken over. Also, we are losing ranchhands. No one wants to cowboy anymore; they all want to work for you. The rest are looking for oil on their own. Everyone has a plan to get rich quick, and nothing is the way it used to be. People hold you responsible for it, so in deference to their wishes we decided against your request."

"Times are changing," Gamblin said. "If the people

want to work for us, who should blame them? The working conditions are good and we pay better wages than the ranchers could ever pay."

"That's just what I'm talking about," the mayor said. "How can anyone hope to compete with you?"

"They can't," Gamblin agreed.

"Well, here's one man who can," the mayor said, pointing to himself. "And as long as I'm mayor of Texon, I'll run the town."

"Then, Mr. Mayor, I suggest you start looking for another job, because you won't be mayor for very long," Gamblin said bitterly.

Monroe laughed. "This is my town. Not even President Coolidge could unseat me. Who are you planning on running against me?"

"I'll run against you," Gamblin said defiantly.

"You?" Monroe laughed. "Why, you young pup, I'll cut you to ribbons at the polls."

"We'll see about that!" Gamblin shouted, slamming the door to Monroe's office as he left. The mayor's laughter followed Gamblin all the way down the stairs and into the street.

Gamblin returned to the Texon building and pulled out a tablet. He began mapping out his strategy and the whole project suddenly took on the aspects of a game to him. He soon found himself getting involved with the many details, and it wasn't until after Jason stuck his head into Gamblin's office later that evening that Gamblin realized he'd spent the entire afternoon planning his strategy.

"I heard what happened at the council meeting today," Jason said. "Luke Monroe doesn't like me, but I know most of the men on the council, and they're not all bad. Maybe I can talk them into changing their minds."

Gamblin looked up from his desk with his eyes gleaming in excitement. "Jason, I'm going into politics. I'm going to be mayor of Texon."

Jason came into the office and settled onto the brown leather couch with a sigh. "Gamblin, you don't need to do this. It was just a gesture by the council. They'll come around. They just wanted to put up a show, that's all. We're moving too fast for them. They need to feel like they're still a part of things."

"Look," Gamblin said, holding up a sheet of paper. "What do you think of this as a campaign slogan? COME OUT OF THE PAST . . . MOVE FORWARD WITH McCLARITY."

"Didn't you hear what I said?" Jason asked. "You don't need to do all this."

"I thought I'd get some sound trucks from Houston, maybe even hire an airplane to do some of that writing in the sky. You know, they do it with smoke or something."

"Gamblin, listen to me!" Jason shouted, slamming his hand on the table.

Gamblin looked up in surprise.

"I said all this isn't necessary. We can get what we want without it."

"No," Gamblin said quietly. "It *is* necessary. I'll spend one hundred thousand dollars on this election if I have to, but I intend to have that bastard's job."

"Gamblin, don't you understand?" Jason said. "You could spend one million dollars and still lose the election. Monroe might be an ass, but he's a politician — and a smart one. If you want to beat him, find another ground. He's like a shark. Out of water he's helpless, but in the water he's unbeatable. Luke Monroe, in Texon politics, is a shark in the water."

"I'll have his job," Gamblin said doggedly.

Jason shook his head sadly and left the room, pulling

the door quietly closed, leaving Gamblin crouched over his desk plotting the campaign under the dim glow of his office lights.

No one had ever seen anything like it before. Gamblin held a picnic on the park grounds every Sunday afternoon, and the entire city was invited. He brought in bands, sometimes three or four at a time, so that the people could take their choice of the kind of dancing they wanted to do, or just stand around and listen to the music. He paid all the ice-cream vendors in town to give free cones to any kid who wore a McClarity button. The town itself was literally swamped with posters, pamphlets, and cards.

Gamblin chose the campaign colors of blue and white to correspond with the colors of Texon Petroleum, and soon the entire town was festooned in blue and white. The man in the street wore a McClarity button almost as a part of his clothing. The newspaper, buoyed along economically by a two-page spread on McClarity's behalf every day until the election, came out with an editorial that strongly supported Gamblin McClarity.

On the eve of the election, Gamblin held a large barbecue and invited the whole city to attend. Half a dozen speakers rose to talk on behalf of Gamblin. They spoke of what a wonderful force he had been for the economy of Texon and for the state. They praised him as if he was running for the United States Senate.

Gamblin wandered through the crowd and saw Mayor Luke Monroe with several of his friends standing together under a tree, eating barbecue and laughing.

"Well," Gamblin said, "I notice you attended my rally."

"Everyone did," Monroe said, smiling. "It's the only place I can find enough people to do any politicking."

Gamblin swept his hand over the crowd of people, all of whom were wearing his campaign buttons. "You expect to get any votes out of these people?"

Monroe laughed and a piece of barbecue fell on his chin. He pulled out a silk handkerchief and dabbed at it.

"Mr. McClarity, how many buttons did you have made?"

"I don't know," Gamblin replied. "Why?"

"A conservative estimate. One thousand? Five thousand? Maybe ten thousand?"

"It looks like ten thousand, doesn't it?" Gamblin asked proudly. He gestured toward the crowd. "Seems like just about everyone here is wearing one."

Monroe laughed. "There are only twelve hundred fourteen registered voters in Texon. I need only six hundred eight of them to win."

Everyone who was with the mayor laughed, and Gamblin looked at them in confusion. "Why are you laughing?"

"Mr. McClarity, hasn't it occurred to you that I haven't been campaigning?"

"Yeah, I noticed that," Gamblin said rather shortly.

"Didn't you ever wonder why?"

"I thought you'd given up," Gamblin said.

Luke Monroe reached over to a nearby table and took another piece of barbecue. He offered some to Gamblin. "This is really excellent," he said. "I must congratulate you on it."

"All right, why in hell haven't you campaigned?" Gamblin asked angrily.

"Mr. McClarity, I've already got my six hundred eight," Monroe replied, and the entire group laughed uproariously. Their laughter followed Gamblin as he stormed away in a rage.

"I'm sorry, Gamblin," Jason said as Gamblin walked by him. Jason had been watching the whole thing. "But I tried to warn you, he's a shark in the water."

Gamblin looked back at Luke Monroe, who was still laughing. "All right," Gamblin said quietly. "If I can't get the shark out of the water, I'll take the water away from the shark."

Two days later the citizens of Texon, still congratulating themselves over the results of the election, in which they showed the high-and-mighty Gamblin McClarity a thing or two, opened the newspaper to find a full-page advertisement purchased by Gamblin McClarity. They read it, at first casually, thinking it to be the normal political statement of thanks to the supporters, and pledging cooperation with the man who won. But they were surprised at what they read:

Citizens of Texon: Because of the humiliation I suffered at your hands in last Tuesday's election, I have decided that Texon no longer presents me with the environment I need to conduct my business. Therefore, in consultation with my two business partners, we have decided to close all operations in Texon and move to Houston.

We are withdrawing all funds from the bank, severing all accounts, and will no longer make purchases of goods or services.

In keeping with this policy, we are herewith notifying all Texon employees that residence in Texon after the first of the month shall be cause for their dismissal. Employees who do not reside in

Texon will be requested to boycott the businesses of that town, and failure on their part to do so will be construed as an act of disloyalty and sufficient cause for termination of their employment.

I am also pleased to announce that in order to facilitate shipment of oil by rail from the fields, we have agreed to underwrite half the expense of a new spur line that will connect the refinery directly to Midland, bypassing Texon. In conjunction with this spur line, we are underwriting new holding pens, feeder lots, and cattle-loading facilities in Midland to accommodate the ranchers. This will save them the necessity of coming into Texon for any reason.

Our economic advisors have informed us that Texon will be economically untenable within one year. You are therefore urged to leave the city and establish yourself elsewhere.

Texon Petroleum will provide relocation assistance for all its employees who wish to leave the city. More information will be available at a later date.

Texon died on April 15, 1926, when the remaining members of the City Council voted to withdraw incorporation status from the state of Texas. Most of the voting members of the council had their cars parked on the street out front, laden with trunks and bundles. Their families sat in the shade on the deserted sidewalk while they waited for the men to take care of the final city business so they, too, could leave the town.

Luke Monroe followed the council members out of City Hall and said good-bye to them.

"Luke, there ain't much sense in you stayin' on here

alone," one of them said as he stood by his car with the door open. His wife was sitting in the front seat nursing one baby, while two more children looked through the back window.

"I'm mayor of this town," Luke said. "And I'm stayin'."

"Ain't much need of a mayor of a town without people," the man in the car said.

"They'll be back," Luke promised, looking out across the street with eyes that were actually looking into the past. A dust devil skittered through the town and a wooden shutter banged against the window of what had been the bank.

The man's wife pulled her nipple from the baby's mouth and leaned across the front seat of the car. Her breast hung through the open blouse unashamedly and she tugged impatiently on her husband's arm.

"I'll be right there, honey," he said. Then, to Luke, he replied, "Yeah, Luke, I'm sure they'll get homesick wherever they are goin' now and they'll be back. Then they'll want you for mayor again. Hell, they elected you, didn't they? You showed McClarity and Hewlitt and that whole bunch a thing or two."

A tear glistened in the corner of Luke's eye for a second, then slid down his cheek.

"The son-of-a-bitch murdered my town," Luke said quietly, so quietly that the words were barely audible.

The man looked away, embarrassed over seeing Luke's tears. The last of the other cars left and his wife tugged on his arm again.

"I've got to be goin', Luke," the man said. "Listen, uh, if you need anything, well, you know where my brother lives. I'll be there until I can get a job somewhere. Good-bye, Luke."

The man slid in behind the wheel and drove off. Luke stood on the sidewalk until the sound of the engine was completely gone. Now there was only the banging of the shutter across the street and the singing of the wind through the dead wires.

Luke turned and walked heavily up the stairs to the door of his office. He stood there for a second and read the sign: LUKE MONROE, MAYOR OF TEXON, TEXAS.

Luke walked inside and sat on the swivel chair behind his desk. He looked at the bare spot on the desk where the phone had been removed. He looked up at the chandelier, which was still full of light bulbs, but which no longer had electricity to light them. Then he slid the middle drawer of his desk open, pulled out a .45-caliber revolver, put the barrel in his mouth, and pulled the trigger.

It was two more weeks before his body was found.

Chapter Eighteen

Washington — 1986

Stewart Jackson put in an urgent request for Evan Hewlitt to meet him for lunch. They met at a Holiday Inn in Alexandria, taking a booth located far to the back, beyond earshot of any of the other diners.

Families making a summer pilgrimage to Washington, businessmen, and the lunchroom's regulars filed through the buffet line, little realizing that they were dining in the same room as one of the world's wealthiest men.

"I was sorry to hear about the trouble you had in Nybibia," Stewart said.

"Trouble?" Evan replied. "What trouble?"

"You know, the barge blowing up? What do you think

it was, terrorists? I could have State put a little pressure on Hafadiez, insist that he provide you with more security."

"No, it wasn't terrorists," Evan answered. He twisted the pepper mill over his salad. "My chief engineer tells me it was just an accident, pure and simple. We had a blockage in one of the lines, the fuel pooled up, then exploded."

"How long will you be down?"

"Thirty, forty-five days," Evan answered.

"Too bad. Is it causing any problems?"

"None that we can't handle," Evan said smoothly.

Stewart began dumping sugar into his coffee, putting in five spoonsful before he spoke again.

"I'm glad that's okay," Stewart said, "because I'm afraid there's a problem with the Mexican deal."

"And what sort of problem would that be, Mr. Jackson?"

"It concerns the Mexican minister of petroleum."

"I thought I came up with a million reasons why he wouldn't cause us problems," Evan said.

Stewart ran his hand through his hair. "Yeah, well, it isn't working out like that," he said. "The world oil market... it's going crazy. I mean, who would've thought oil would ever go below thirteen dollars?"

"What does that have to do with the Mexican situation? I understand our offer is twenty-four per barrel."

"Yes, but while you were gone, Mrs. McClarity pulled the rug out from under us. The offer goes down to twenty next week, then sixteen two weeks after that."

Evan chuckled.

"What are you laughing about?"

"I told you not to underestimate the old gal. She's a class act, Stew."

"I don't know why you're admirin' her so," Stewart said. "I'm tellin' you, Mr. Hewlitt, she's got the whole Mexican government shook up. They've got a chance to lock in oil at twice the going rate if they sign right away. And they know they're going to blow a good deal if they don't act soon. The way it is now, there's nothing our man can do about it. Hell, if he opposes them too much, they'll just fire him."

"Then we are obviously going to have to think of another way to deal with the situation," Evan said.

"Yes, sir. Well, I've been thinking about that. You remember the Emergency Energy Act, passed during the Ford administration? Highway speed at fifty-five, public building thermostats set at sixty-eight in the winter, seventy-eight in the summer — that sort of thing?"

"I remember."

"Well, in addition to those things, it had a lot of other language, some of it pretty broad."

"As I recall, we were in a national energy crisis then," Evan said. "The Emergency Energy Act was designed to give the illusion of fighting it. The fifty-five speed limit is still around, but most of the other requirements have been withdrawn."

"Not withdrawn, just not enforced," Stewart reminded him. "They're still on the books."

"What has that got to do with our situation?"

Stewart grinned broadly. "I found one that was designed just for us." He took a piece of paper from his briefcase and handed it across the table to Evan. Evan started to read it, then handed it back.

"How about cutting through this bureaucratic language and telling me what it says?"

"Sure," Stewart replied. "It says that if the national energy advisor deems it appropriate, he may, with just cause, amend or suspend any contract entered into between wholly owned American energy companies and a company whose principal base of operation is outside the United States. As the presidential energy advisor, I am also the national energy advisor. If Rana McClarity signs the contract, all I have to do is suspend it."

"With just cause," Evan said.

"Yes, of course."

"What is our just cause?" Evan asked. "Every issue we have raised so far has been refuted by enough people that it isn't clear-cut. And the business about depleting Mexico's oil reserves would have no bearing here, because this act is clearly a protectionist act designed to save our own resources."

"And achieve energy independence," Stewart added quickly. "Remember, Nixon, Ford, Carter — all of them were harping on getting America totally self-sufficient in energy. Shale oil, tar sands, oil from coal, grain alcohol — remember those things?"

"Go on," Evan said, beginning to see where Stewart was heading.

"Most companies have suspended their exploration into these alternate energy areas. Why?"

"When oil was forty dollars a barrel there was a possibility those programs could be made feasible. With oil under twenty dollars, it simply isn't cost effective to try and extract oil from tar sands."

"That's right," Stewart replied, holding up his finger. "But Texon is willing to spend twenty-eight dollars a barrel for foreign oil. In my position as national energy advisor, I deem that a squandering of energy resources. If Texon can pay almost twice the market for oil, they can spend an equal amount of money in developing and exploring these other areas. If they refuse to do so, then

I can negate their Mexican contract under the Emergency Energy Act.

"Can you make it stick?"

"I have the authority to invoke the powers of the act today," Stewart said. "As to whether or not it will stick...well, I suppose that will be up to the courts to decide. That could take several months."

"I can live with that," Evan said. "Now, tell me what you've found out about Senator Carmack — is he vulnerable?"

"The only thing I can find is his appetite for women," Stewart said. "And his wife knows about that. They have a rather unique relationship. She likes being a senator's wife, so she doesn't care about his extracurricular activities."

"Does he have one mistress? Perhaps we can do something through her."

"No, he likes to play the field. He has someone on his staff, supposedly a research assistant, whose job it is to supply him with girls."

"Can we get to this guy?"

"The research assistant? From what I understand, he's a greedy son-of-a-bitch who'd pimp for his own mother for the right price. Yes, I believe we can get to him. Why, do you have an idea?"

"Yeah, I got an idea."

Terri looked into the mirror to check her lipstick, then back at Evan.

"You know what to do?"

"Bring him into this hotel room," Terri said, as if reciting from memory. "Make sure I maneuver him to the front of the mirror, because the camera is on the other side."

"Right. And make sure you're both identifiable."

"I don't know," Terri said. "It certainly goes against my principles to be seen with an ugly slob like that."

"Five thousand dollars seems like a good enough price for you to forget your principles."

Terry laughed. "You're right about that. How's my hair?"

"It's beautiful," Evan said. "You look beautiful. I'm tempted myself."

Terri gave Evan a dazzling smile and fluttered her eyelashes. "Don't get fresh, big boy."

There was a knock at the door.

"Just a minute," Terri called. Evan hurried through the door that connected this room with the one adjacent. Terri locked the door behind him, then walked over to let in the visitor.

"You got enough light to get everything?" Evan asked the camera operator in his room.

"You kiddin'? This baby can see in the dark," the operator said. "Look on the monitor there, you can see everything."

The video camera, which was filming through the mirror into Terri's room, was hooked up to a large-screen TV monitor in the room. Evan opened a can of beer and sat down to watch the screen.

"Shit!" he giggled. "This beats the hell out of watching 'Dallas.'"

He could see Terri open the door and Senator Carmack step into the room.

"Well," Terri said, "I was told my visitor would be someone important. I didn't know it would be as important as all this. A United States senator. I'm impressed. I'm really impressed."

"Arnie outdid himself tonight," Carmack said. "You're beautiful."

"Thank you. May I take your hat and coat?"

Carmack handed over his hat and coat and gave Terri a quick kiss on the lips.

"Oh, you do like to get down to business, don't you?" Terri giggled.

"Honey, when you get to be my age, you want to take advantage of every opportunity there is. I don't want to let any of them get by me."

Terri laughed. "My, you are ambitious, aren't you? No wonder you're a senator."

"Did Arnie tell you the rules?" Carmack asked anxiously.

"Arnie said I was to give you a good time, ask no questions, and say nothing to anyone about my visitor."

"Arnie's a good boy."

"Arnie also said you would pay me two hundred fifty dollars."

"The deal was one hundred fifty."

"I raised the ante," Terri said. Terri reached down to the front of Carmack's pants and touched the bulge there. "I'm worth it, honey. Believe me, I'm worth it."

Carmack sucked in his breath, then put his hand on Terri's shoulder.

"You... you better be," he said.

"I'll give your money back if I'm not," Terri said sweetly.

Carmack pulled the money from his billfold and started to hand it to Terri. Terri motioned that Carmack should put the money on the dresser, then, with a smile and a crooked finger, beckoned Carmack over to the bed.

"Why don't you let this thing out for a little air?" Terri said, opening Carmack's pants. "Oh, yes, doesn't it feel better now that it's free?"

Terri leaned down and licked the purple head of the enlarged phallus, then raised up to kiss Carmack. The kiss was long and grinding and Carmack seemed to melt into a mass of jelly, completely subservient to Terri's will. After a moment, Terri pulled away.

"Get out of your clothes, honey," Terri said. "I want you naked."

"Yes," Carmack wheezed, and he sat on the edge of the bed and began undressing while Terri did a slow, sensuous striptease before him. Then she delicately removed his clothes until Carmack was completely nude, lying back on the bed with his throbbing penis stabbing toward the ceiling.

Still in panties and bra, Terri lay down on him and kissed him a second time, then raised up to slip out of the panties and bra.

Beneath the bra there was nothing... beneath the panties, a stiff penis.

For a second Carmack was so shocked that he didn't realize what had just happened. When he did, he sat up with a gasp.

"What the hell's going on?" he asked.

Evan pushed open the door that separated the two rooms and walked into Carmack's room, laughing.

"Oh, you should have seen yourself," Evan said. "But, of course, I have it all on tape, so you'll be able to see it any time you want."

"Hewlitt? What's all this about?"

"Oh, meet Terri Banks. He's a female impersonator. They say he's one of the best in the business. I wouldn't know about that... I guess you'd have more of an opinion than I would."

Carmack backed all the way across the room and looked in horror at Evan and Terri. He wiped his hand across his mouth several times, then spat on the floor.

"Oh, now, Senator, hasn't anyone ever told you about spitting?" Evan asked. "It's very unhealthy, you know. You could have AIDS now, for all I know. I mean, this is how people get it."

"I don't think that's very funny," Terri said. Terri was standing in front of the mirror now. He had taken off his wig and was now wiping off the makeup. The change in his appearance was phenomenal.

"No, I guess it's a poor joke," Evan said. "Like the senator's career is... if he doesn't stop this crusade against me."

"You... you can't get away with this!" Carmack sputtered.

"Oh, I think I can," Evan said. "In fact, I think I can reasonably say that your ass belongs to me."

"Oh, what a shame," Terri said, turning to look back toward them. "And I thought it was mine."

Chapter Nineteen

Across the river from Alexandria, in the Washington Manor Motel, Carol McClarity pulled the razor gently across her smooth mons veneris. When she did her first nude photo layout, she was asked to shave herself. The request surprised her, but she wanted to do the layout, so she did what they asked.

She was afraid it would be a turnoff, but it had just the opposite effect on the men and women with whom she had sex. As a result of their reaction, Carol now kept herself cleanly shaved all the time. At first she thought it would be a pain to shave each day, but she found the experience strangely erotic. By the time she was through shaving, she was boiling in her own juices.

Just as Carol washed off the last of the cream, she heard someone knocking on the door. She wrapped a towel around her wet body and walked out into the room.

"Who it it?"

"Room service, ma'am. You ordered a half pint of bourbon?"

Carol opened the door and the uniformed bellhop started in. He was young, in his early twenties, and when he saw Carol he stopped in his tracks.

"Oh, I beg your pardon, ma'am," he said. "I'll come back."

"Nonsense," Carol said easily. She pushed the door closed behind him, then smiled. "Don't people take baths in Washington?"

"Yes, of course, but..."

"No buts to it. I ordered room service, you delivered it. It's as simple as that. Just a moment, let me pay you."

Carol walked over to the dresser and started through her purse. As she did so, the towel slipped down, just a little, but enough to allow one nipple to peek through. Carol continued to search through her purse as if unmindful of the slipping towel.

"Ah, here's my billfold," she announced triumphantly. At the same time she made her announcement, the towel came loose and fell to the floor, so that Carol was standing nude before the bellboy. His eyes opened wide, then even wider when he saw that she was cleanly shaven.

Carol reached down and picked up the towel, then held it in front, barely concealing herself.

"Oops, sorry 'bout that," she said easily. She smiled again. "At least you didn't look away."

"No, ma'am. I wouldn't look away, ma'am," the bellboy said.

"Good. I would consider that an insult, especially

after I went to all the trouble of shaving my little ol' pussy." She put a twenty-dollar bill in the young man's shaking hand. "Will this take care of it?"

"Yes."

Carol dropped the towel. "And here is your tip," she said.

The bellboy's eyes grew wider.

"I'm afraid that's all you get this time," she went on. Gently, she began maneuvering him toward the door. "I'm sorry I can't invite you to stay, but I have a date with a very jealous man."

"Okay," the bellboy said. He had been in a state of near shock from the moment she opened the door, and now he left without the slightest bit of trouble. Carol leaned back against the door after he left, feeling the tinglings and the fire in her loins.

Carol knew that she played dangerously when she did such things. One of these days she was going to encounter someone who couldn't be maneuvered, and when that happened the situation could get difficult. It could even get dangerous.

It was this potential for danger that drove Carol to do such things in the first place. The dangerous, the forbidden, the shocking... these were powerful aphrodisiacs to Carol.

It had been the possibility of discovery that heightened the pleasure Carol derived from masturbating the wounded soldiers in the hospital in Vietnam. Deke hadn't been her first... he wasn't even her last. But Deke had fallen in love with her... and, for a while, she thought she loved him as well.

Carol's lesbian affairs were another manifestation of her attraction to forbidden fruit. She had never really been attracted to other women and wasn't particularly attracted to them now. But the very act of having sex with another woman was so blatantly shocking to society that she found she could enjoy the experience immensely. That was what contributed to her seduction by an older woman when she was a fourteen-year-old girl.

Carol had been a high-school gymnast, and a good one. Though only a freshman, she had just won her conference title and was working late one night preparing for the state meet. After her workout she took her shower, then lay for a while on the treatment table. Except for a towel that was draped loosely across her body, she was nude.

"You weren't lifting your leg high enough on the pirouette," Miss Fall said from the door of the treatment room.

Miss Fall was Carol's coach. She was a small, graceful, twenty-four-year-old blonde. She had been a member of the U.S. Olympics team when she was fifteen. She was very good and very pretty and Carol idolized her.

Carol looked around in surprise.

"Oh, Miss Fall, I thought you'd already gone home."

"Really?" Miss Fall replied. The coach stepped into the room. "You don't think I'd leave before my star athlete, do you? I wouldn't feel right about leaving you here alone."

"I'm not afraid," Carol said.

Miss Fall chuckled, then came over to the table. She put her hands on Carol's leg.

"No, I guess not," Miss Fall agreed. "You're not afraid of anything, are you?"

Miss Fall squeezed Carol's leg as she spoke, but the squeeze was so gentle, the pressure so delicate, that Carol couldn't be certain she had actually done it.

Carol felt strange. She didn't know why she felt that way. She had spent many hours with Miss Fall and they were very close. Despite that, there was something — a tingling, a little voice inside — that alerted Carol to the fact that this experience was, somehow, different from all the others.

Carol raised her head and looked at Miss Fall. There was something about Miss Fall's eyes that she had never noticed before...a depth, a hunger, a light, way at the bottom. Tiny beads of perspiration broke out on Miss Fall's forehead and the coach licked her lips.

"Is... is anything wrong?" Carol asked. She couldn't shake the feeling she had. It wasn't exactly an uneasy feeling; it was more of an anxiousness, an anxiousness tinged with excitement.

"Nothing," Miss Fall replied. "I just wanted to tell you that you aren't lifting this leg high enough."

"It hurts."

"Where?"

"Up here, in my thigh."

"Let me see." Miss Fall drew the towel to one side, exposing Carol's nudity. Embarrassed, Carol started to pull the towel back.

"Oh, don't be silly, Carol," Miss Fall said impatiently, and she tossed the towel to the floor. "You'd think I'd never seen you nude before. Now, lift this leg."

Carol did as she was directed and Miss Fall began massaging it. "How's this? Does this feel better?"

"Yes," Carol admitted. It really did feel better. Miss Fall's fingers worked magic as they moved up and down the smooth skin of Carol's leg, bunching the muscle, then working the soreness out. Once or twice her fingers seemed to come up too high and they rubbed, accidentally, against Carol's slit. Each time it was just a quick flit, a brush. The the fingers would return to the leg as if nothing had happened. Each time, however, Carol jumped.

"Will you relax?" Miss Fall scolded. "How am I going to work this out if you keep jumping on me?"

"I only jump when you..." Carol started to say. Then she stopped.

"When I what?" Miss Fall asked.

"When you touch my pussy," Carol answered quietly.

Miss Fall chuckled and put her hand there again. "You mean like this?"

Carol drew in a short breath. "Yes," she answered.

"Now what makes you think I want to touch your little pussy?" Miss Fall asked. There was something in Miss Fall's voice, a huskiness Carol had never heard before. She moved her hand slightly and her fingers slipped into the slit to touch the clitoris. Carol shivered.

"I...I notice you haven't taken your hand away," Carol said. For some reason she found it difficult to talk.

"So I haven't," Miss Fall replied. She began moving her fingers a bit more aggressively.

"What? What are you doing?" Carol asked.

"Close your eyes and relax. I'm going to make you feel good. I'm going to make you feel very good."

Carol did as Miss Fall instructed. She closed her eyes and lay back on the table as Miss Fall's skilled hands continued their work. Carol was not a stranger to the sensations; she had masturbated in the bathtub, and sometimes at night in bed. But this was the first time hands other than her own had evoked such feelings.

Suddenly, Carol felt a new, delightfully different sensation and she raised her head to see what was going on. Miss Fall had replaced her fingers with her mouth.

Carol felt the tongue darting in and around and each contact was like a tiny electric shock sending volts of pleasure through her body.

Carol lifted her long, slender legs and put one on each of Miss Fall's shoulders. She put her hands behind the older woman's head, then pulled Miss Fall's mouth and tongue into her, no longer giving herself, but taking what the woman had to offer.

There were two thoughts paramount in Carol's mind as Miss Fall performed cunnilingus on her. One was that someone might come in and catch them; the other was that what she was doing was very, very wrong. Despite those thoughts or, as she later learned, because of them, she threw herself willingly and eagerly into the pleasures of the moment.

Now, as Carol stood by the window looking out onto the motel pool, the sundance jewels that flashed from the water's surface brought her back to the present. She closed the blinds and walked over to the dresser to fix herself a bourbon and water, pouring it over the ice she had brought in from the machine a few moments earlier.

She wasn't dressed, but she had at least restored a bit of modesty by slipping on a black silk robe. Now, still wearing the robe, she waited patiently in the room for her appointment.

He was late. She didn't like it when he was late, but it didn't worry her. She had been seeing him for some time now and he was often late.

There was a light knock at the door. It wasn't the bellboy; it was a familiar knock. Carol smiled, put the drink on the dresser, then walked over to let him in.

"You're a little late," she said.

"I had some business to dispose of."

"Dispose of? That's a funny way to put it."

"That's the best way to describe this business. Anyway, what does it matter? You didn't start without me, did you?"

Carol glued herself to him, thrusting her tongue in his mouth, running her hand through his hair, mashing her breasts against his chest.

"Don't think I didn't have the opportunity. The bellboy was here. He caught me just as I stepped out of the bath."

"I know that was an accident," the man said. "I used to catch you a few times myself, if you recall. You used to drive me up the wall."

"Oh? You never tried anything."

"I couldn't. You were married then."

"You're married now."

"It's not the same with a man."

Carol laughed. "I didn't think there was anyone left who really believed that anymore."

"It's true," he said. "You can talk about the sexual revolution all you want, but the truth is, it's different when a man screws around."

"Let's not talk anymore," Carol said. "I haven't been waiting just to talk."

She kissed him again and felt him grow hard against her. His hands slipped under the silk of her robe and traced across her breasts, rolling the nipples between his fingers.

"Yes," she said. "That's what I've been waiting for."

He undid her robe and let it hang open, running his hands across her naked skin, feeling her smooth mound.

"Now," she said. "Let's do it now."

Carol slipped out of her robe and crossed to the bed.

She lay there looking at him through smoky eyes as he got out of his own clothes. A moment later he was in bed with her.

He took her aggressively and the pleasure moved through her in waves. She throbbed with more and more urgency, drawing up tighter and tighter like the mainspring of a clock until finally, in a burst of ecstasy, she reached the pinnacle of sensation. A cry of pleasure came from deep in her throat and she felt as if she lost consciousness for just an instant as her body jerked convulsively.

With a hoarse shout, he achieved his own orgasm then, and when Carol felt him shudder she was again struck by lightning when a new wave of pleasure burst inside her. This one was so intense that it swept away everything that had gone before it and brought her to a peak of fulfillment so exquisite that she could feel it in every part of her body. She hovered at the peak for several seconds, feeling the waves of pleasure pass through him, into her. Finally, he collapsed on her and, after a moment, rolled to one side, breathing hard.

"Sometimes you frighten me," she said.

"How?"

She laughed. "You get so carried away I'm afraid you're going to have a heart attack."

"Ah, but what a way to go," he said.

"Sure, for you — you'll be dead after a good fuck. What's it matter to you? But how do you think it's going to look for me?"

"You? I'm dead and you're worrying about you?"

"I can see the headline now," Carol said. "'Evan Hewlitt fucked to death by Carol McClarity.'"

Chapter Twenty

Houston — 1927

As the western sky turned from red to purple in the evening shadows, the cars began arriving. They moved slowly along a wide tree-lined drive, depositing their occupants under a portico where uniformed servants greeted them and escorted them into the house.

They were coming to a house-warming party to celebrate the opening of Cedars, the mansion Gamblin built after they moved. Here, in Houston, Rana, Gamblin, and Jason took their place among the wealthiest of the city, and Gamblin, in celebration of that fact, built a large house for Rana.

Rana didn't encourage the extravagance, but neither did she discourage it. She knew that it was something

Gamblin wanted, so she went along with it. She didn't even balk when he hired an authentic English butler named Smythe. Smythe had come to Texas to claim what he thought was a ranch. It turned out to be forty acres of property so worthless that he couldn't even sell it for enough money to make the trip pay for itself. He decided that, since he was in America, he would get a job, so he advertised for a position in the only field he knew. Gamblin heard about him and hired him. Both had been very pleased with the result.

The house-warming party was Rana's idea and, though she knew none of them, she had invited the entire listing of the Houston social register. The dust-encrusted young girl who had climbed out of the car in Texon just two years ago was now hostess of the biggest party of this, or any other, season.

The guests came for many reasons. Some came to genuinely welcome new blood to their society; some came just to see the people who had risen from nowhere to the sudden, dizzying heights of the ultra-rich; others came to ridicule, but no one came to be bored.

Cadillacs, Packards, Lincolns, and Dusenbergs moved over to join the fleet of luxury automobiles already in the guest parking area. The drivers then joined the other chauffeurs, who were having their own small party.

Inside Cedars there was a sunburst of gaiety. Women floated about in bright dresses, flashing earbobs, and sparkling necklaces. Men moved around them like bees darting from flower to flower.

In the main dining room a table that could seat forty in formal dining was now laden with hors d'oeuvres, glistening hams, and salads of every hue and design. French doors led from the dining room to a patio where three spitted steers turned slowly over a huge barbecue pit, filling the air with a delicious aroma.

Despite prohibition, there were several bars: one in the parlor, one in the game room, and another in the main ballroom, but the most popular one was set up in the enclosed courtyard where an open garden was created right in the center of the house. For those who didn't care to go to a bar, waiters glided from room to room carrying silver trays laden with various drinks.

The party attracted a wide spectrum of guests. There were the beautiful young people who showed up at all parties and, as far as anyone could determine, made that their sole occupation. The young girls flirted coquettishly with the older men, while the handsome young men titillated the sexual fantasies of middle-aged wives who were neglected by their wealthy, business-minded husbands. Later these same young men and young women would get together in the velvet-blue corners of the garden and laugh together over their episodes.

Wealthy cattlemen, businessmen, and other oil men were present at the party, as well as some of the most politically powerful men in Texas.

There were some who resented Gamblin and Rana's sudden entry into society. After all, Gamblin had been nothing but a seaman and a field worker before he struck it rich. Rana was the daughter of a boardinghouse owner in St. Louis and, it was said, had been pregnant when she and Gamblin were married. Some whispered that she had some connection with the legendary Josiah Hunter Ellison, but even he had died a pauper, so that was scarcely a recommendation.

The gossips weren't any kinder to Jason. He had been a four-flusher, a big frog in the little pond of Texon, and he had stretched his credit to the limit backing the oil company before the well came in. It was said that he was only twenty-four hours away from ruin when the well blew.

Nevertheless, Texon had paid off, and paid off handsomely. Now Gamblin and Rana could stand toe to toe with the wealthiest people in Houston and spit in their eye.

Gamblin began moving through the party, drifting from one small group to another. He had been so busy with his company that before tonight he had made no effort to meet any of the "right" people. Therefore, he knew very few of the guests at his party, and he was able to walk around unrecognized. He did make it a point to introduce himself, unless there was some reason that made it better for him to keep quiet.

"I tell you, no one really knows who the baby belongs to. It just missed being a bastard," Gamblin overheard someone say. He looked over to see an intense discussion being carried on by three or four men whom he didn't recognize.

"What do you mean no one knows whose kid it is?"

"From what I hear, it could be his, or Jason Hewlitt's, or their drill foreman's, or any of half a dozen others."

"Yeah, I heard she whored some up in St. Louis."

"Wouldn't surprise me none if she didn't whore to help raise the money they needed to get started."

"Shit! What the hell do you call what she did with Jason? You think he would've invested all that money if he hadn't been gettin' in her pants?"

"That's a lot of money for a piece of ass."

"Yeah, but she's a lot of woman. You tellin' me you don't get a hard-on just by bein' around her?"

"What about this Gamblin fella? Except for the fact

that he destroyed the town of Texon, nobody seems to know anything about him."

"They say he was the ruin of Clem Nester. He worked for Nester and he sabotaged a well. That's the way I heard it."

"Listen, Nester was a cheat. Hell, he damned near wound up in jail a couple years after that, and McClarity sure didn't have anything to do with it."

"Maybe not, but he was the cause of that mayor committin' suicide. That was just awful the way that happened."

"I heard a rumor that McClarity killed someone up in St. Louis. A preacher fella, they say."

"I don't believe that. Rana bein' a whore, I can buy that, but Gamblin killin' somebody, no, I don't believe that."

"You know, I've heard a rumor about this McClarity fella myself," Gamblin said, stepping closer.

"Yeah? What's that?"

"I heard that guests who come to his house who are uninvited, or who by their comments make themselves unwelcome, sometimes disappear and are never heard from again."

"I've never heard anything like that."

"Me neither."

"Believe it," Gamblin said. "I have this rumor from a very good source. I think you'd better pay attention to it."

The men looked at one another in confusion.

"Oh, Smythe," Gamblin called as the butler walked by.

"Yes, sir?" Smythe answered.

"Gentlemen, I'd like you to meet Smythe. He's an Englishman, as you can tell by his accent. He comes with more pedigrees than a prize bull. Tell them, Smythe."

"I am the fourth generation of Smythes to enter the service," Smythe said very formally.

"The service," Gamblin said. "That's what they call being a butler over there. Smythe is very proud of his profession and he's very good at it. Cost me a mint to get him to come to work for me, but I figure he's going to be worth it. Right now, though, he's going to show you gentlemen to the door and leave word with my groundskeeper that you are to be shot if you aren't off my property in five minutes."

The men looked at Gamblin in openmouthed shock. "*You* are Gamblin McClarity?"

Gamblin smiled but didn't answer. "Show these gentlemen out, Smythe," he said as he turned and walked away from them.

"It would be my pleasure, sir," Smythe said.

Jason was upstairs, dressing for the party. He had not wanted to come to this affair, feeling a little like a fifth wheel, but he knew of no good way to avoid it without hurting Rana's feelings. He felt no sense of exclusion as far as the business was concerned, Texon Petroleum was operated by the three of them in a way that made each of them equally important. But in their personal life there was really no place for Jason.

He did enjoy being around the baby and sometimes he even watched after C.G. for Rana. But Rana was Gamblin's wife and she was going to stay his wife. Jason was gradually getting used to that fact, though the best way to handle it was to pursue his own personal life as actively as he could.

Jason went out with many women, but he was in love with none. Gamblin sometimes teased him about it and asked if he intended to be a bachelor all his life. Beneath the teasing, Jason knew, was a little glimmer of insecurity. Gamblin was no fool; he knew that Jason was still in love with Rana, and though Rana had given him no cause for concern, he was sure she still had some feeling for Jason. It would be better for all concerned if Jason could find his own wife and start his own family.

Jason was staying in one of the many guest rooms, and though the party had already started, he was not yet dressed, hoping that if he took his time the party might come, and then go, without him.

Looking through his bag for his collar studs, he realized that he hadn't brought any. Thinking Gamblin would certainly have an extra set, he went off to Gamblin and Rana's bedroom. On his way down the hall, he heard a soft humming from the baby's room. When Jason looked through the doorway, he drew in his breath in a short gasp. The baby's nurse, a young Mexican girl, was holding the baby to her breast. She wasn't actually nursing the baby because she had no milk, but the baby was smacking and sucking quite contentedly.

The young woman was also getting some pleasure from the action, because her skirt was pulled above her knees and her hand was under her skirt. Her eyes were closed, her mouth slightly open. She heard, or sensed, Jason's presence and looked up with a start.

"*Señor*," she said. She pulled her skirt down and smoothed it. "I didn't hear you."

"I was looking for a collar stud," Jason said in a husky voice. "I didn't mean to frighten you." He couldn't take his eyes off her small, but perfectly formed, breasts. The skin under the nipple the baby was sucking was wet with the baby's saliva and it shone in the soft light of the room.

"Did you find one?"

"No," he said.

"Perhaps I can help, *señor*." The girl stood up and put the baby in his crib. The baby gurgled a couple of times, then satisfied itself with its own thumb.

The girl pulled her blouse together and buttoned one button, effectively covering her breasts. Jason smelled the faint scent of her as she walked by him to the dresser. He walked over to stand beside her, feeling a strong surge of heat in his loins. He felt himself growing large and he knew she knew.

"What's your name?" he asked.

"Rosita."

"You are a very beautiful girl, Rosita," he said.

"Thank you, *señor*," Rosita answered. She pulled out a collar stud. "Will this do?"

She raised it for his inspection and Jason took her hands in his. Her mouth opened slightly and she caught her breath, but she didn't speak.

"Rosita, I..." Jason began, but he couldn't finish.

"I know what you want, *señor*," Rosita said. She took a deep breath. "I do not want you to think I am this kind of girl. But I would like my mother to come to Texas to live with me. This costs money. Perhaps if you would..." This time she didn't finish.

"Yes," Jason said. "Yes, I'll bring your mother here."

Rosita smiled at him, and her deep, deep brown eyes glowed with some light way in the bottom. She sank to her knees in front of him, then, gently, opened his pants.

He sprang out at her like a jack-in-the-box. She looked at it for a moment, then smiled and took it in both hands, one behind the other. She touched the end of it with the tip of her tongue.

"Is this what you want?" she asked.

"Yes," Jason whispered huskily.

Rosita opened her mouth wide and took him inside. He felt the nibbling of her teeth, the tip of her tongue, the suction of her lips as she took him into her mouth. He put his hands on her hair and wrapped the black tresses tenderly around his fingers.

Rosita opened her blouse and moved against him, pressing her naked breasts against his trousers legs as she took him deeper, moaning and panting and clinging to him.

Jason felt a fire running through him then, and though he tried to stop, he couldn't hold back. He gasped in pleasure as she took him quickly, eagerly to orgasm.

Just outside the door, Rana leaned against the wall as her legs grew too weak to support her. She had come upstairs to find Jason, to see why he wasn't yet at the party, and when she heard Rosita moan she hurried down the hall to see what was going on.

Now she was trembling with repressed excitement. She turned and hurried quickly away. It wouldn't do to be discovered now. If Jason knew that she had been in the hall, had witnessed everything that had happened, he would be so embarrassed that he might never be comfortable around her again.

At least, that was what Rana told herself. In truth, she had been so aroused by what she just saw that she was afraid she would throw herself on the bed and beg him to make love to her.

And that was something she could never do again.

Chapter Twenty-one

Houston — 1929

By 1929, Texon Petroleum had made its three principals among the wealthiest people in Texas. It was the fourth-largest petroleum company in America, and its symbol, the blue, three-pointed star, was seen everywhere.

Although there was a board of directors and a corporate structure to Texon Petroleum in 1929, it was still an operation that was absolutely controlled by Rana, Gamblin, and Jason. Rana was the chief executive officer and Jason the chief of operations, but it was Gamblin who seemed to have the highest visibility.

Gamblin was perceived by outsiders as being the one in charge. He was the one profiled by the national news magazines, and on those occasions when disgruntled workers in the company would direct their ire at the "man on top," they always personalized it with Gamblin McClarity.

Jason never managed to lose the image of being the banker behind the scene. Publicly, he was quiet, though the ones who were really in the know never made the mistake of underestimating Jason's position of authority and power.

Jason and Gamblin were at opposite ends of a scale, balanced by Rana's stabilizing influence. Gamblin was the gambler, willing to take chances and seek growth along new avenues, while Jason advised a more cautious approach.

Rana guided the destiny of the company by taking the best from both men. Without Jason's commitment to caution, Texon Petroleum would probably come apart at the seams, the result of unwise and incautious business ventures. But without Gamblin's aggressiveness, it would become an impotent giant, doomed to die in its own sterility.

Thus far, Rana had been able to reason everything out between them, reach a compromise, and establish policy. She sided with Gamblin on some things, with Jason on others.

When Jason balked at buying Jefferson Motors, Rana and Gamblin bought the automobile-manufacturing company as a personal investment. When Gamblin wanted to buy a movie studio, Rana sided with Jason to talk him out of it.

Now Rana was being asked to mediate another dispute. They had realized an unexpected profit over the first half of 1929, when the price of oil jumped twenty cents a barrel at the well head, and brought two million dollars of windfall profits to the company.

Jason wanted to reinvest in real property, update equipment, and explore and drill new wells. Gamblin wanted to invest the money into the stock market to speculate with other companies.

Jason, Rana, and Gamblin met, alone, in the boardroom to discuss the problem. Gamblin, standing by a gold replica of Santa Rana Number One, jerked his head in Jason's direction.

Jason was over by the window peering through the blinds at the city. The boardroom was on the top floor of the Texon Oil Building, a fourteen-story structure. The edifice symbolized as much as anything else the growth and prosperity of Texon Petroleum over the last six years.

"I can't understand why you are so adamant," Gamblin said. "Two million dollars properly invested can bring back fifty cents on the dollar in a matter of weeks. And we don't have to do anything, Jason, except make good-faith indications. In actual fact, we'll still have the capital for other uses. It's just a paper investment."

"It's a paper profit, too," Jason answered. "I'll be honest with you, Gamblin: this stock market business is frightening. It's badly oversubscribed and undersupported. What's the basis for all these fortunes? The value of stock keeps going up because people are buying stock, not because the economy is experiencing actual growth. It's a pyramid principal where the capital is being artificially forced up."

"No matter what is forcing it up, it is going up," Gamblin insisted, "and we are fools not to get in on it. Now I think we should make major investments from our profits. After all, it's good for the nation's economy. And, besides, what could possibly happen? If the stock begins to slow up, we can withdraw our funds."

"I'll tell you what could happen," Jason replied. "A major loss of confidence could cause everyone to withdraw their funds. And that would be just like kicking the crutches out from under a cripple. There's nothing substantial supporting the economy except that artificial layer of invested funds. Remove them and the economy will come crashing down like a dynamited house."

"You don't want to do anything," Gamblin said. "I'm wondering now why you ever invested in Texon in the first place."

"I told you," Jason said. "I could smell money."

"And you don't smell it in the stock market?"

"Paper," Jason said. "It's all paper."

"Maybe so, but as long as that paper is money, it's fine with me. All right, if you don't want to invest Texon money, I'll invest money from Jefferson Motors. I'll speculate for a year or so and then Jefferson will be bigger than any other auto company. Bigger even than Ford."

"Ford is building assembly plants and modernizing its equipment. That's solid growth," Jason declared. "You can't match that by investing in the stock market."

True to his declaration, Gamblin began investing the Jefferson Motors profits into the stock market. Gary Somo, the C.E.O. of Jefferson Motors, telephoned Gamblin to ask him to reconsider his policy. Gamblin put him at ease and told him he was going to New York, but he would stop by Detroit and visit the plant along the way.

One reason Gamblin wanted to go to New York was to try out his new private railroad car. It took Gamblin and Rana three days and two nights to reach Detroit, and rarely was the country crossed in more luxury. They drank bootleg champagne, ate meals prepared by a chef who had learned his trade at the side of the great French chef Escoffier, and watched movies on the screen Gamblin had installed in the car.

Rana left C.G. with Sue Ellen. "Auntie Sue" and C.G. got along famously and, though separating from his mother for a week was a big thing for a six-year-old, C.G. handled it very well.

Gamblin suggested this could be a second honeymoon for them. Rana laughed and reminded him that it would be their first.

Though they had been married for six years, the excitement of the trip and the fact that they were alone made Rana feel like a newlywed. At night they made love while the wheels clacked softly against the moon-silvered tracks.

When they arrived at the station in Detroit, they stood on the platform in the October chill and looked around for the chauffeur who was supposed to meet them. Steam drifted around them, escaping from the valves and fittings, and people hurried alongside the standing trains, creating a carnival atmosphere.

"Mr. McClarity, sir?" a voice called. Gamblin turned to see a smallish man dressed in a chauffeur's uniform. "I'm your driver, sir."

"Where's the car?" Gamblin asked rather impatiently. "I'd almost forgotten how cold it gets up here."

"It's at the south end of the station, sir," the chauffeur said. "It's the black Crown."

"Lead the way," Gamblin said, putting his arm around Rana to help keep her warm.

The Crown was Jefferson Motors's proudest achievement. It boasted sixteen cylinders and a commodious interior with elegant upholstery. Considered one of the finest cars produced in America, it was fully competitive with Cadillac, Lincoln, Dusenberg, and Packard.

It began to rain just as they got into the car, and Gamblin sat back in the spacious rear seat, watching the drizzle fall from the slate-gray sky. The driver pulled away with the engine making a mere whisper.

Detroit was a city alive with evidence of America's vitality. The huge auto industry employed hundreds of thousands of people, turning out cars by the millions to feed the public's demand. Gamblin wished Jason could see this city. Never was there a more graphic demonstration of real prosperity than here.

Gary Somo was a man who kept himself in shape with daily workouts in the factory gym. He was five-ten, one hundred seventy-five pounds, with a muscular body that made him look like the Notre Dame football player he once was. He wore a neatly trimmed moustache and often touched it in a nervous gesture.

"I've prepared some charts to show you," he said to Gamblin and Rana. "I have a rather startling proposal to make, and I hope the charts back me up."

"All right," Gamblin said. He and Rana settled down on the brown leather sofa to listen as Gary gave his presentation.

"I want to completely retool," Gary began. "I want to drop production on the Sportster entirely and continue with the same model Crown only until the present inventory is sold out, then drop it as well."

"Discontinue the Sportster?" Gamblin replied. "And the Crown? Why?"

"For this," Gary said, pulling out an artist's rendering of a car. The car lacked the touch of elegance that had been the hallmark of all Jeffersons. In fact, the car was very plain-looking.

"That?" Gamblin asked, pointing to the picture with distaste. "Why, that's about the ugliest thing I've ever seen. It doesn't even have a radiator-cap ornament."

"It's functional, not ostentatious," Gary said. "But I think the average American will accept simplicity and clean design. Advertising sold them on elegance; it can sell them on simplicity as well. Especially for the price. We can sell this car for only seventy percent of the cost of our cheapest model now, and still make a profit."

"But why do you want to do this?" Gamblin asked.

"To keep Jefferson from going under," Gary said. "The Crown sold less than five thousand units this year; the Sportster, less than a thousand. Only our cheapest model kept us in the ball game, and Ford and Chevy beat us badly there. This car will make us competitive with them."

"What will you call it?" Gamblin asked.

"The Sixty-five," Gary said.

Gamblin rolled his lips back in disgust and tossed the picture on the table in front of the sofa. "The Sixty-five? Whatever happened to the good names we had?"

"They are all suggestive of money," Gary said. "The average-income person can't even consider a car with a name like Crown, Scepter, or Sportster. But the Sixty-five is something else again. It's utilitarian and it suggests economy."

"It's cheap," Gamblin said.

"No, it's economical. There's a difference."

"What do you think, Rana?" Gamblin asked.

"Gamblin, you know about oil," Rana said. "If this had anything to do with where to drill, I would listen to you. But Gary knows about cars. We agreed when we bought the company to let him run it. If he feels this is what needs to be done, then let's do it."

"All right," Gamblin said with a sigh. "But I don't know why, in the midst of the biggest economic boom in history, we have to sell cheap cars. Go ahead, do what you have to do."

"I can't," Gary said.

"You can't? Why not?"

"We don't have enough capital to retool. All our money is subscribed to stock investment."

"How soon would you have to have the money to meet the model for next year?"

"This is major retooling," Gary said, scratching his head thoughtfully. "I have all the preliminary work done. It's just a matter of getting set up. But I'll need the money before the end of the year."

"All right. We're going to New York from here. I'll pull out all of Jefferson Motors's funds. How's that?"

Gary smiled. "That's fine, Gamblin," he said. "I couldn't ask for anything more than that."

Gamblin shook his head. "The only thing, I hate to miss the rest of this year — 1929 is going to go down as the biggest year in stock market history."

Gamblin wanted to stay at the Waldorf, but Rana insisted upon the Algonquin because she wanted to be near the theater district. Besides, the Algonquin was the "in" place for all the actors, actresses, and writers, who gathered in the restaurant to eat the fantastic pastries and discuss the latest happenings.

Rana loved it. Tallulah Bankhead, Dorothy Parker, F. Scott Fitzgerald, and, of course, Zelda were likely to turn up at any moment.

Gamblin liked the chocolate cake.

On Monday, the twenty-eighth, Gamblin closed out the Jefferson Motors portfolio.

"Well, you certainly turned a handsome profit with that investment," John Tanner said after the transaction was completed. "Are you sure you don't want to let it ride for another thirty days? It could go up by another fifteen percent."

"No," Gamblin said. "I promised Somo I would return the money to the company, so I guess I'd better do that. It has been fun, though," he said with a big smile.

"Listen, have you ever been on the floor of the Exchange?" Tanner asked.

"No."

"Why don't you come down tomorrow? Tomorrow is Tuesday. All the weekend trading will be cleaned up and the end-of-the-month adjustments won't be on the boards yet. Tomorrow will be a good, average day. You can watch millions of dollars made in a matter of hours."

"That might be interesting," Gamblin agreed.

Rana went with Gamblin the next day, and when they arrived at the Stock Exchange, they were surprised by what appeared to be absolute chaos. People were milling around on the floor, bells were ringing, and people were shouting. It appeared to be a madhouse and Gamblin wondered how a nation's economy could be based on such a disorganized operation.

"So, here you are," Tanner said, greeting Gamblin and Rana when they arrived. "I'm glad you could come. Come along, let me introduce you around."

Tanner steered Gamblin and Rana through the floor, occasionally stopping people of note to introduce them.

"So, you are Gamblin and Rana McClarity of Texon Petroleum," one man said after he was introduced.

"Yes."

"Mr. McClarity, when are you going to put Texon on the big board? A strong company like that would be a gold mine."

"It is a gold mine," Gamblin said, chuckling. "And, like the prospectors of old, we've got ours and we aren't in any particular mood to share."

The man laughed. "You've got a good point there," he said. Then he looked at Tanner and grew a little more serious. "Have you been watching what's going on this morning?"

"Not particularly. Why? What are you talking about?" Tanner asked.

"I don't know, it's not something I can put my finger on, but I don't like the feel of things. Since Britain raised their interest rates, we've experienced a lot of wholesale dumping of stocks by foreign investors. Some of the domestic holders are beginning to move a little, too. Jefferson Motors sold out their entire portfolio."

Tanner chuckled. "Well, I can explain that. Mr. McClarity did that so he could invest the money in retooling. There's no mystery there."

"That doesn't explain the rest."

"Just a fluctuation," Tanner said. "It'll stabilize as soon as they adjust to the new rates and the foreign investors come back in."

"Nevertheless, since the weekend trading there has been some tension beginning to develop," the man said.

Gamblin and Rana wandered around the floor with Tanner, watching the activity. It was fascinating. Yelling, waving hands and papers, men pushed through the crowd to rush madly over to the big board, where they checked the latest figures.

Gamblin laughed and looked over at Tanner. "I'll bet a lot of people wouldn't feel so good about investing their money if they could see the way it was handled," he said. "This place is a madhouse."

Tanner was white-faced, his lips drawn into a tight line, and the pupils of his eyes pinpoints. Gamblin had seen the symptoms before. Tanner was frightened!

"Tanner, what is it?" Gamblin asked.

"This is insane," Tanner said quietly.

"What?"

Tanner held a shaking hand up toward the board. "They are selling like fools. The market is crashing. I've never seen anything like this!"

"What is it? What's happening?" Gamblin asked. He looked around and then for the first time noticed the same fear in the faces of the others that he had just seen in Tanner's. Gamblin had spent an active life, but he had never known the hair-tingling sensation of absolute panic that he suddenly experienced that morning, standing on the floor of the New York Stock Exchange. By the end of the day's trading, 16,410,030 shares were sold. Fortunes were lost, companies were wiped out, and the country plunged into a nightmare.

Gamblin and Rana returned to the Algonquin shocked by what they had seen. They walked through the lobby and looked at the people talking and laughing, unaware of what had just happened. It was as if they, alone, knew a terrible secret, watching as people rushed toward their doom.

"Jason was right," Gamblin said when they returned to their room. "I'll never doubt him again."

"Oh, Gamblin, what if we hadn't sold the Jefferson

portfolio yesterday? We would have lost four million dollars."

"I know," Gamblin said.

Rana leaned into Gamblin and he put his arms around her.

"Gamblin, what does all this mean? What's going to happen to the country?"

"I don't know," Gamblin admitted, holding her close to him. "I guess we'll just have to wait and see."

Chapter Twenty-two

The contrast between the Detroit Gamblin had visited in October of 1929 and the Detroit he was seeing now in 1931 was startling. Back then the streets had been filled with men hurrying to work. Now they were filled with lines of sullen men queuing up before unemployment offices and soup kitchens. Where factories had once hummed busily, silent smokestacks now stood like ghostly sentinels against the somber sky.

The Crown in which Gamblin was riding turned at the factory gate. Grim-faced men stood outside the gate watching the car as it came through. Gamblin stared straight ahead until the car stopped at the executive entrance to the Jefferson Building.

Gary Somo had begged Gamblin to come to Detroit to talk about his plan for saving the company. But

Gamblin had come to Detroit to close it.

"Who are those men out by the gate?" Gamblin asked as he settled into a chair in Gary's office.

"They are former employees," Gary answered.

"If they are former employees, why are they still here?"

"Where else would they go?" Gary asked, lighting a cigarette. "Sometimes we are able to hand out piece work, like today, when we are stamping out dies on a subcontract for Studebaker. We were able to put on an additional forty people."

"But there must be two or three hundred down there," Gamblin said.

"Hoping for something else," Gary answered. He looked at his watch. "Besides, we'll be serving coffee and doughnuts in a few minutes. Most of them will probably leave after that."

"It's a little frightening having masses of unemployed men hanging around like that," Gamblin said. "You never can tell what they might do."

"It's much more frightening for them," Gary replied. "Gamblin, I want to know what you've decided. If we can start production on the Sixty-five, we can tap some of the market still available. It'll put us on firmer footing and, equally important, we can start hiring again. I figure we can employ nearly ninety percent of our old force, and that's compared to less than forty percent now."

"That sounds very good," Gamblin said. "But Jefferson Motors is over two million dollars in the red right now. How would we finance such an operation?"

Gary shoved a stack of papers across the desk. "It's all here," he said. "We can get a government loan. All we need is collateral backing, and Texon can provide that."

"I have no right to commit any of Texon's funds to this," Gamblin said.

"I know," Gary replied. "But I've been in touch with Jason Hewlitt and he has promised to support you."

"Jason is getting married this week," Gamblin said. "Right now he would go along with anything."

Gamblin stood up and walked over to the window. A piece of paper blew across the large empty parking lot where hundreds of cars had stood on his last visit.

"It's hopeless," Gamblin said quietly. "There's no sense in throwing good money after bad."

"It's not hopeless," Gary said, slamming his hand down on the desk. "Damn it all, man! This country can get back on its feet again if the major industries will just make an effort."

"I was there, Gary," Gamblin said. "I saw the crash happen right before my eyes. I'm telling you if an animal had been in that room he could have smelled the panic."

"It was people like that who did this to the country," Gary said. "Everyone was content to sit back and play with the market until the trouble started. Then they took their marbles and ran."

"I would remind you that there weren't that many marbles taken," Gamblin said. "It was the heavy investors who suffered the most."

"Suffered?" Gary retorted. "Hell, they don't even know what suffering is!" He walked over to the window and jerked the blinds all the way up. Out in the street, men were beginning to crowd around the canteen truck, reaching for a paper cup of coffee and a single doughnut. "Goddamn it, that's suffering!"

Gamblin looked at the men in silence. He started for the door, stopped just before he exited, and turned to look at Gary. "I'm sorry," he said.

Gary slammed the notebook of his figures shut and turned his back to Gamblin.

Gamblin returned to the car and crawled sullenly into the back seat.

"Where to, sir?" the driver asked.

Gamblin didn't answer. He sat there thinking about his conversation with Gary.

"Sir?" the driver asked again.

"Oh," Gamblin said. "Uh, just drive around a bit."

"Yes, sir."

The car rolled through the streets of Detroit and everywhere he looked it was the same: small, pathetic groups of men milling around the street corner; apple stands with the vendors flapping their arms, or hopping from one foot to the other to try to keep warm. Occasionally, Gamblin would see someone dressed in an overcoat that was obviously designed for evening wear at a time when the owner had seen better days.

"Let me out here," Gamblin said.

"Where, sir?" the chauffeur asked, looking around in confusion.

"Right here, on the street. I want to walk some."

"Shall I follow you, sir?"

"No, go on back." When the chauffeur hesitated, Gamblin added, "It'll be all right."

The car stopped and Gamblin got out, then waved the driver on. He stood there for a moment, wondering why he had done it. It was cold and threatening rain, and this part of the city didn't look like it would be too safe a place to be after dark.

Gamblin started walking, and after a while, because it was getting colder, he turned into a small café for a cup of coffee.

There were four or five men in the café and they looked up when Gamblin entered. He had been a little concerned that they would see his clothes and be resentful of him, but he noticed they didn't pay too much attention to him.

Gamblin sat at a small table. The owner-waiter came over and made a few perfunctory passes over the table with a damp towel, then threw the towel over his shoulder.

"Coffee's a nickel," he said. "Bread's a penny a piece, but you can't use the catsup 'less you buy some kind of a sandwich."

"I just want coffee," Gamblin said. "I don't want catsup."

"I guess you're still too new to know that one," the waiter said. When he saw Gamblin's puzzled expression he added, "Guys come in here and buy a penny piece of bread, then slop it over with catsup. That way they get a cheap meal, but I'm out the catsup. I guess now that I've let you in on it, you'll be pullin' it on other cafés."

"Just bring the coffee," Gamblin said.

The waiter left and one of the other men came over to the table. He sat down without being invited and stuck his hand out. "My name is Jimmy," he said.

"I suppose you want some coffee?" Gamblin asked.

"Don't mind if I do," Jimmy answered cheerfully. "Figure I can pay for it with a little advice, seeing as how you'll be needing it."

"Why should I need advice?"

Jimmy pointed to Gamblin's clothes and laughed a short, mirthless laugh. "Well, it's pretty easy to see that it just happened to you," he said.

Gamblin looked puzzled.

Jimmy laughed again. "You want to know how I can tell, don't you?"

"Yes," Gamblin asked, curious as to what Jimmy had on his mind.

"Well, when you first get laid off, your clothes still look pretty good. Stylish, even. And cleaned and pressed and not torn or anything. And there's something else, too. Something that's even more noticeable."

"What?" Gamblin asked

The smile left Jimmy's face and he looked down at the table. "You've still got some pride left. You can see it in your eyes." He was silent for a few seconds. Then he said, "That leaves at about the same time you find that you have to wear your clothes dirty because you can't afford to get them cleaned. Or when you have to put old newspapers in the soles of your shoes. Or when you suddenly remember that it's been two days since the last time you had anything to eat."

The waiter brought Gamblin's coffee, then asked if Gamblin was going to buy coffee for Jimmy. Gamblin said that he would, then paid for both coffees and looked at Jimmy, who was sitting there with his head lowered and tears moving down his face and into the stubble of his unkempt beard.

"And then the pride is replaced by shame," Jimmy said quietly. His words were barely audible now and Gamblin had to strain to hear him. "And the shame of facing your family without being able to feed them is so great that you find you can no longer face them at all. So you leave."

Gamblin drank his coffee quietly. After a minute or two Jimmy picked up his coffee and began to drink it. He looked up and the expression on his face had changed back to an almost jovial one. "Forgive me for that little episode there," he said. "I was feeling a little sorry for myself, I guess. But I was feeling even sorrier for the country. And for you."

"You were feeling sorry for me?" Gamblin asked.

"Yes. You've still got it to go through. I've already come through it. Say, what are you doing for supper?"

"Would you like to eat?" Gamblin offered. "We can get something — "

"No, no, if you have any money, save it," Jimmy said, reaching across the table to prevent Gamblin from pulling out his billfold. "You'll be needing it later. Besides, they'll be having a real meat stew down at the kitchen tonight. It's good, really. Never ate better when I was flush."

"What do you...what did you do when you worked?" Gamblin asked.

"I was a test driver," Jimmy said. "Used to be a race-car driver. Finished third one year at Indy," he added proudly. "Then Jefferson Motors hired me. Anyway, when the squeeze started, my job was one of the first ones to go. They were pretty nice, gave me work in assembly for a while, but then those jobs started going, too, and I wasn't able to keep it."

"Did you enjoy your work?"

"I loved it," Jimmy said. "You know, I once got a Sportster up to a hundred forty-two miles per hour. God, that was power."

"They are fine little cars," Gamblin agreed.

"They're rich men's toys," Jimmy said with a surprising amount of bitterness in his voice. "That was the trouble with Jefferson. They built playthings and when the real world hit them, they were unable to take it. If they had built cars, real cars, instead of toys and luxury boats like that fat-cat Crown, I might still have a job. Along with a few thousand others."

"Perhaps," Gamblin said quietly.

"Hey!" Jimmy said suddenly. "You got a place to flop?"

"A what?"

"A place to sleep. A few friends and I have renovated an old building a few blocks down the street — that is to say, we've taken it over. It was condemned and marked for destruction, but the company ran out of money." He laughed. "Can you imagine not having enough money to tear something down, even? Anyway, it's still there and it gives us a place to stay. You're welcome to come in with us."

"I...uh...have a flop," Gamblin said.

"Well, if you have to leave for any reason, look us up. The accommodations aren't all that great, but you sure can't beat the rent."

"Thanks," Gamblin said.

"Come on, let's go be the first in line. If you're too far back, you don't get any of the meat, just the leavin's," Jimmy urged, swallowing the last of his coffee.

The kitchen had been a neighborhood activity center at one time. Since the Depression started, it had been taken over by the Salvation Army. When Gamblin and Jimmy arrived, Jimmy introduced his friends as Piney, Juke, George, and Billy Falk.

"Hey! You got a new recruit for us, huh, Jimmy?" one of them teased.

"Thought I'd bring him down to the best meat stew in town," Jimmy said.

"It's pretty good, all right, but the kitchen over on Southfield has better," Piney said.

"Yeah, but you've got to say about four prayers and

sing about twenty hymns before you get anything to eat over there," Juke complained. "All things considered, this is the best."

"Hey, you lookin' for a job?" Piney asked. "You wanna sell shoe soles for me?"

"Thank you, no," Gamblin replied.

"Piney's a real businessman, he is," Juke said. "He cuts shoe soles outta old inner tubes, sells them for two cents each. He's got about ten vendors workin' for him now. He gives 'em half of what they make."

"On a good day I'm makin' fifty, sixty cents," Piney said.

"Yeah, keep it up, you'll be eligible for the millionaire's loan Hoover is givin' out." Jimmy laughed.

"Millionaire's loan?" Gamblin asked.

"Large corporations can borrow money," Billy Falk said. "The idea is to stimulate the economy from the top down. In principle it's sound, but it goes down rather bitterly."

Gamblin suddenly recalled the loan Gary had mentioned.

"Billy Falk was a schoolteacher," Piney said. "Juke and George worked in an automobile plant like Jimmy. I worked in a bank."

"And you've all been reduced to begging," Gamblin said.

There was a sudden, stony silence. Then Piney stood up. "I am a businessman," he said sharply. He left the group and stalked off.

"I'm sorry," Gamblin said. "I didn't mean anything by that remark. I just assumed that...well...selling shoe soles cut from inner tubes is thinly disguised begging."

"So is drawing pictures on the sidewalk with chalk

and asking for a penny to see them," Billy Falk said. "But we don't look at it like that. We still figure that, in some way, we are earning our money. There is a precisely layered structure among us. Those who can get part-time work to survive are the highest. Those who come up on the street and ask for a dime are at the bottom. The rest of us are somewhere in between. We sell shoe soles, apples, stand on the corner and sing, do chalk rendering on the sidewalk. We have to feel that we are still a part of the human race. That's why I insist on being called by my whole name. It's the only thing that is truly mine."

"I'm sorry," Gamblin said. "I didn't mean to hurt anyone's feelings."

"That's all right, you're still new," Jimmy said, punching Gamblin on the shoulder. "None of the guys take it wrong. Piney, he'll be all right, too. He just has to pout a little."

"Naw, there's no hard feelings," Juke said. "By the way, what kind of work did you do?"

"I...uh...worked in an oil field," Gamblin said. "Before that I was a merchant seaman."

"Maybe we could start a new company here, called Experience Unlimited," Billy Falk teased. "We have such diverse backgrounds we could provide the experience for just about any job that would come up."

"Yeah," Juke said. "Yeah. Hey, Billy Falk, why don't you draw up the idea? Maybe we could do something like that, huh? I mean, who knows? Maybe it will go real good!" Juke grew very excited as he talked.

"Maybe," Billy Falk said easily, patronizingly.

Later, after they had eaten, Billy Falk was talking to Gamblin. "Don't pay any attention to Juke and his excitement over new projects," Billy Falk said. "He gets very enthused over every idea. We tease him about it sometimes, but I think we all secretly envy his ability to still have hope in something. In anything."

"You don't have hope in anything?" Gamblin asked.

"No," Billy Falk said. "I guess I just know people too well. I did my teaching at Michigan State University. I was a professor of philosophy."

"And you got laid off?"

"Philosophy is not a course that puts meat on the table. Everyone is going in for the practical courses now. I didn't have tenure."

"I'm sorry," Gamblin said. "But maybe you're too bitter. Maybe you'll be surprised."

"Not much surprises me anymore, Mr. McClarity."

"I don't know. You might — " Gamblin stopped in mid-sentence and looked at Billy Falk. "You know me?"

"I've seen your pictures. I know you aren't slumming. So what are you doing?"

Gamblin was silent for a few seconds. Then he looked up at Billy Falk and smiled a slow smile. "You're a teacher, Billy Falk. Let's just say I'm getting an education."

"I hope someone profits from it," Billy Falk replied.

Gary was awakened at about three-thirty the next morning, and when he went down into his study he saw Gamblin pacing back and forth.

"What is it, Gamblin?" Gary asked. "What's wrong?"

"How soon can you start retooling?" Gamblin asked.

Gary rubbed his eyes and brushed his hair back. "Well, right away," he said. "We've had the preliminaries worked out for almost three years. But I don't understand. Yesterday you said — "

"That was yesterday," Gamblin interrupted. "I've changed my mind. I'm not going to close Jefferson Motors. I want you to begin retooling immediately and get that new cheap car out. But I want it thoroughly tested. Hire back that test driver — you know, the one who used to drive race cars?"

"Jimmy Grant?"

"Yes."

"Where did you hear about him?"

"It doesn't matter. Is he any good?"

"Well, yes," Gary said. "But I don't even know where to find him."

Gamblin handed a sheet of paper to Gary. "He's at this address. I think you might be interested in a man named Billy Falk and a few of his friends, too."

"Yes, sir," Gary said with a big grin, taking the paper from him. "By the way, what changed your mind? I thought you said the situation was hopeless."

"I found out from a person named Juke that nothing is ever completely hopeless," Gamblin said.

But Gary wasn't listening. He had already picked up the telephone and was putting through a call to his plant foreman.

Rana went to the airport to meet Gamblin on his return from Detroit. She parked the convertible just outside the fence and sat there with Jane Ella and C.G., watching the airplanes take off and land. A Tri-motor Ford had just lifted its tail as it started down the runway, while behind it a biwinged Curtis Condor was drifting down on its final approach for landing.

"Is that Papa's airplane?" C.G. asked, pointing to the landing Condor.

"I don't think so, dear. That airplane says American Airways, and your father is coming in on Braniff."

"Can I go to the fence and watch the airplanes?"

"Yes, if you stay on this side," Rana said.

Without waiting for the door to be opened, C.G. climbed over the side of the car, then ran to the fence.

"I've never seen anyone as crazy about airplanes as he is," Rana said. "That's all he talks about."

"He's a wonderful boy," Jane Ella said. "Jason sure sets a big store by him."

"Who knows? Maybe you and Jason will soon have one of your own," Rana said.

"Maybe sooner than anyone thinks," Jane Ella added.

"Oh?"

"I'm pregnant, Rana," Jane Ella confided.

Rana smiled. "Why are you telling me in such a hushed voice?" she asked. "Do you think I'm going to find that so shocking that I won't want to be friends anymore?"

"No," Jane Ella said. "But when you hear the rest of it, you might want to reconsider."

"There's Papa's plane!" C.G. called excitedly, pointing to a Tri-motor Ford that was just touching down. "See? It says Braniff on the side."

"Maybe so, dear," Rana called back to him. She looked over at Jane Ella and saw the worry and fear etched on her friend's face.

"What is it, Jane Ella?"

"They're gettin' off the plane now!" C.G. interrupted. "There's Papa! See him, Mom? He's gettin' off right now! Can I go tell him where we are?"

"Yes, dear," Rana said. "But be careful, don't run in front of any of the airplane paddles."

"Propellers, Mom," C.G. said disgustedly. "They're called propellers."

"Now," Rana said. "What is it?"

"Rana, you know that I love Jason more than anything in the world. I love him so much that I'm willing to share that love with you."

"Jane Ella," Rana said, putting her hand on the other woman's arm, "I hope you don't think — "

Jane Ella held up her hand. "Don't misunderstand me, Rana. I know there's nothing going on between you two. I figure if Gamblin can live with it, I can, too. That's not what's bothering me."

"Then what is?"

"You must swear never to tell a living soul. Never."

"All right," Rana promised. "I swear."

"I hope you enjoyed your flight, Mr. McClarity," the stewardess said as Gamblin stepped down onto the concrete from the plane. The air had been rough and the flight had been bumpy. He was glad to be standing on solid earth again.

"These things might be faster than trains," he said, "but they sure as hell aren't as comfortable."

"Oh, airline travel is quite pleasant now," a fellow passenger said. "I remember the old days when the passenger had to wrap himself in leather and ride in an open cockpit."

"Papa!" C.G. shouted. He ran through the gate and Gamblin scooped him up. "Did the people look like ants?"

"In Detroit?" Gamblin asked.

"No, on the ground," C.G. said. "You promised me you would tell me what it's like, remember? You said you would tell me all about flying."

"Oh, so I did," Gamblin said. "Well, it was just like you said. The people, the cars, even the houses looked real small from up there."

"Say, young man, would you like to see the cockpit?" the pilot asked, appearing in the doorway then.

"Oh, yes," C.G. said, clapping happily. "Someday I'm going to fly an airplane just like this."

"Oh, not like this one," the pilot said. "By the time you grow up I imagine they'll be much bigger and much faster."

"The biggest and the fastest," C.G. said. "I'm going to fly it."

Chapter Twenty-three

Houston — 1935

The country was making good progress toward working its way out of the Depression, thanks to the efforts of men like Gamblin McClarity and Jason Hewlitt. It cost Gamblin several million dollars to retool his automobile operation and there was little promise of getting his money back for at least another ten years, but he did it anyway.

In the oil fields the situation was just as difficult. In order to employ as many men as possible, Texon Petroleum continued to pump at full capacity. That helped with the unemployment situation, but it also created the problem of oversupply. Texon was producing more oil than its distribution could handle.

To complicate things further, gasoline stations across the country were beginning to sell out to major refineries, so that Standard, Esso, Gulf, Texaco, Pure, and other chains began to replace the family-owned station. Advertising on a national level formed such public recognition of "name" brands that independently owned service stations were suffering.

Texon had never established a network of service stations, relying instead on the independent stations as a market for its oil. But with the independent stations hurting, there was a decreased demand for Texon oil at a time when Texon needed to move as much oil as it could.

Gamblin had studied the trend and suggested to Jason that Texon should take some steps to compensate. His idea was that they should introduce a chain of service stations that would feature only Texon products. Jason not only agreed, he even promised to introduce a new wrinkle that would help Texon catch up with the major stations on the business they were now doing.

"There is one problem, though," Jason suggested to the others as they sat in the library at Cedars. "It's going to take us from six months to a year to get enough stations built to make an impact on the market."

"Not necessarily," Gamblin answered.

"How will we beat it?" Jason asked.

Gamblin dropped a newspaper on the table and pointed to an advertisement. The ad read:

I.G.S. YOUR INDEPENDENT GAS STATIONS!

I.G.S. means the best deal in gasoline for the motorists on today's highways. We have united for efficiency, but are independently owned for thrift!

By buying our gasoline from nonaligned refineries,

we can save you money at the pump. So...when you drive, stop at a member station, and save!

"We're going to buy up these stations," Gamblin said. "We'll paint them blue and white, put the three-pointed star on them, and call them Texon Stations."

"Suppose they don't want to sell?" Jason asked. "After all, most of them are independent now because they wouldn't sell to a major company. They like keeping their own profit and being their own boss."

"But the majors are gradually running them out. If they don't join us, they won't survive," Gamblin said.

"We're going to have a hard time convincing them that they won't survive," Jason warned.

"Perhaps not as hard as you think," Gamblin said with a smile. "Bert Adams scheduled this meeting with us to talk about renewing the contract for the independents. I moved the meeting from the office to Cedars because I've come up with a little surprise for him. Take a look at this."

Gamblin opened a big box, then took out a building model and set it on the library table. He put a cigar in his mouth and lit it, then spoke around the edge of it. "I wanted you to see this. See what you think of the design."

"God, it's beautiful," Jason said.

The building was white, with one large and two narrow blue bands around the top. A tall, circular sign stood out front of the building, with the word *Texon* around the top of the circle, and *Petroleum* around the bottom, and the blue, three-pointed star in the middle. Even Jason felt a stirring of the blood when he saw it.

"Mama," C.G. said, coming into the room then.

"Yes, dear, what is it?" Rana asked.

"Can me 'n' Evan have some ice cream? I'll fix it for us and I'll be real careful, honest I will."

"You mean 'Evan and I,' don't you?" Rana asked.

"Yes, ma'am," C.G. said.

"Now, what do you boys want ice cream for?" Gamblin teased. "Evan told me he didn't like ice cream."

"No, I like it," Evan said. "I like it a lot, and I get the most."

"Why do you get the most, son?" Jason asked.

"'Cause I'm the guest," Evan said. "And Mama said you should always treat the guest best."

"But, Evan, you shouldn't take advantage of being a guest."

Gamblin chuckled. "Let 'im be, Jason. I like to see someone go after what they want."

"You can have some," Rana said. "But clean up after yourselves. I don't want to make more work for the people in the kitchen."

"Okay, Mama," C.G. called back as he and Evan ran happily to the kitchen.

Smythe came in right after the boys left.

"Yes, Smythe, what is it?" Gamblin asked.

"Mr. Adams has arrived, sir," Smythe said in his clipped British accent.

"Show him in, man, show him in," Gamblin said anxiously. Gamblin looked at Jason. "We're ready for him, right, partner?"

"I do believe we are," Jason replied, smiling broadly.

"Mr. McClarity, Mr. Hewlitt, how are you?" Bert asked, coming into the room behind an extended hand and an expanded grin. "Ah, and the lovely Mrs. McClarity will be joining us, I see."

Bert Adams was a large man with large hands and a bulbous nose that so dominated his face one almost had to look around it to see him. He had a rolling-thunder voice, so loud it made others tend to talk in quieter tones than usual, as if in that way compensating for the overall noise level. The result was that in any conversation Bert's voice was predominant. This gave the illusion of power and leadership, and when the League of I.G.S. was formed, the other owners elected Bert as their first president. He owned four of the stations.

"Bert, let me guess why you wanted to see us," Gamblin started easily. "It's about time to renew the contract."

"Yes, it is," Bert replied. He sat down and pulled out a cigarette. "Some of the men wanted me to talk to you about it. I'm glad you agreed to see me. We're going to have to make some changes, you know."

"Oh? What, exactly, did you have in mind?" Gamblin asked, holding a lighter to Bert's cigarette.

"Well, sir," Bert said, puffing on the cigarette and leaning back confidently. He was very sure of himself now. "The boys want more freedom on the gas they buy. The way it is now, you have a base number of gallons we must buy each month. Sometimes one of the majors is overstocked and they'll sell to the independents at a special price. Only our tanks are so full of your gas that we can't always take advantage of these kinds of deals."

"So what are you saying?" Gamblin asked. "What do you want?"

"We don't want a minimum," Bert said. "We'll still buy gas from you. A lot of gas, since you're our major supplier and we depend on you. But we don't want a minimum that we have to buy."

"You understand, don't you, that it isn't economically feasible for us to supply gasoline at a volume lower than the base we've established?" Jason asked.

"Well, sir, I'm sorry about that. I'm real sorry. But the station owners have made up their mind," Bert said, blowing out a long stream of smoke. "They figure you'll meet their demands since you don't have any other market available."

The smoke moved across the room and hovered over the table and the model of the station. Gamblin walked over to the model and picked up the roof to peer inside.

"I understand," he said finally. "We won't make any trouble," he added, almost as an offhanded remark. He repositioned the pumps, looked at his model, and changed angles, then looked at it again.

Bert leaned forward in his chair and squinted at Gamblin in surprise.

After a moment Gamblin looked over at Bert and, as if surprised that he was still there, asked, "Was that all?"

"You mean," Bert sputtered, unsure of his easy victory, "that you will renew the contracts without establishing a quota?"

"Well, no, not exactly," Gamblin said. He was still looking at the model and he carried on the discussion as if it were merely a diversion. "I mean we won't renew the contracts at all. What do you think of our new station design? I like it. I think it has an almost regal bearing."

"What?" Bert yelled, leaping up so quickly that his chair fell over with a bang. "You can't do this!"

"Tell him, Jason," Gamblin invited.

"Mr. Adams," Jason said calmly, seeing now where Gamblin was going, "I'm afraid we have no choice. As you can see, we're starting our own chain of stations.

I'm afraid our own outlets will be taking all the fuel we can produce."

"And," Rana added, "that leaves none for the independents."

"But... but we depend on you for over eighty percent of our gasoline!" Bert choked out. "If you don't sell us your gas, we can't stay in business."

"I suppose that's true, isn't it?" Gamblin remarked. "Of course, you could find another source of supply."

"There are no other sources of supply," Bert protested. "What are you trying to do to us?"

"I'm trying to explain the facts of life to you," Gamblin said easily.

Bert stood there for a moment. Then a smile broke across his face. "Oh, I get it," he said. "You're trying to force the owners to stick to the quota, aren't you? Well, you don't really have to resort to all this, you know. We aren't going to stick to that contract, but I'm certain we can work out something we can all live with." Bert sat back down, his confidence returning and his tone of voice easy again.

"I'm afraid not," Gamblin said. "It has nothing to do with the quota. I mean what I said about our own outlets. We won't be able to supply the independents any longer."

"What will we do?" Bert asked.

"You might consider selling out to us," Jason suggested.

Bert stood up and walked over to the model. He studied it for a moment. "You're serious, aren't you?"

"Very serious," Gamblin replied.

"I'll have to talk to the others," he said. "But as for myself — " he started to shout.

"As for yourself?" Gamblin asked, a confident smile on his face.

"As for myself, I see no alternative," Bert said in surrender. "I'll sell; I imagine most will. You were the last source of supply."

"Good, good," Gamblin said. He showed Bert to the door. "I expect you'd better get started on convincing the others, don't you?"

Bert looked back over at the model of the station. He took one final drag from his cigarette, then butted it in the ash stand by the door. "Yes," he said. "I guess so."

"There are over five hundred independent owners in that organization," Gamblin said after Bert left. "We can have them converted in less than a month. The only thing — I hate to be out the money right now. The new refinery equipment stretched our credit line pretty thin."

"No problem," Jason said. "I can work out a way for us to pay with oil."

"Good," Gamblin said.

"Now I have another idea," Jason said. "It's the wrinkle I told you about that would help us catch up to the others. I've been thinking about it for some time and I know it will work."

"What?"

"Account cards."

"Account cards? What are they?"

"It's a system of credit," Jason replied. "We issue identity cards to motorists and when they buy gas they can charge it."

"What's new about that?" Gamblin asked. "Gasoline stations have been giving credit to their customers all along."

"Yes, at individual stations where they know the customer," Jason said. "But my idea will allow a customer to get credit at any of our service stations anywhere in the country, just by showing his card."

"How will we convince the station managers to carry a stranger?" Gamblin asked.

"We don't."

"Then how is it going to work?" Gamblin asked.

Jason gave a little laugh. "You're going to like this, I'm sure," he said sarcastically. "We'll collect."

"We'll collect? How?"

"The stations will send the bill to us and we'll send the bill to the customer."

"And say please send us the money for the gas you bought in Dallas, or Austin, or who the hell knows where?"

"Exactly."

"Why the hell would we want to do something like that?" Gamblin asked.

"Because if we don't collect, the franchise holders won't extend credit. But if we guarantee collection, we'll increase our business by three or four hundred percent."

"And if we can't make it work, we've taken a hell of a risk."

Jason laughed. "I thought you were the one who was always willing to take a little risk."

"Little risk? If this doesn't work, we won't find a service station in the country that'll let us pump their goddamned gas. Hell, we could have ten or twenty million dollars out in credit before we figure out what's going on."

"Trust me," Jason said.

"All right, but it damned sure better work."

It did work. The idea of being able to drive hundreds of miles without having to pay for gasoline until the trip was over appealed to the motorists. By the time World War II started, Texon Oil was the second largest oil company in the nation, and the Texon Card was a part of life for millions of Americans.

Chapter Twenty-four

Houston — 1986

Rana opened the door and stepped into the Quiet Room, then closed the doors behind her. Heavy, dark-green drapes hung across the window and only a thin crack of light spilled in around the edges.

The Quiet Room.

It was always pronounced as if the letters were capitalized. It had been Gamblin and Rana's private retreat. They used to laugh that, in a mansion as large as Cedars, they would wind up spending all their time in a room that was as small as the tiny room Gamblin had lived in at the boardinghouse where he and Rana had first met.

But here they could be alone, totally isolated from

multimillion-dollar decisions, the bombarding by the press, and the pleas of presidents. And here they could find peace and quiet when they could find it nowhere else.

Rana pulled open the drapes. She knew just how far to open them to allow the sun to fall upon the painting of Gamblin. The painting was done in Gamblin's later years and it showed a handsome man with a granite-jawed face, steel-gray hair, and ice-blue eyes.

Rana liked paintings more than photographs. A photograph was only a microsecond of time, and one saw no more of a person than could be seen in the blink of an eye. A painting took time and the subject's personality came through the canvas. There was warmth and life to a painting, and Rana could feel Gamblin's presence, almost hear him breathing.

"Gamblin," she said quietly, "to quote you, I've got my ass in a crack. Deke, our Deke, is in love with Rebel. If they could get married it would be perfect, Gamblin. It would join you, Jason, and me together forever." Rana sighed. "But Evan's against the marriage and he thinks he knows how he can stop it. Well, he doesn't know as much as he thinks he knows, Gamblin, but if I set the record straight it's going to hurt some people. I don't want to do that...but I don't want to let him come between Deke and Rebel either. I wish you were here to talk this out with me."

Rana looked at the painting for a moment longer. Then she smiled. "I know what you are saying," she chuckled. "I sailed my own boat up this shit creek; it's up to me to paddle my way out. Thanks. Thanks a lot."

Across town in the offices of Texon, Deke was working at his desk when Paul Avoca, the office manager, stepped in.

"Deke, there's a federal marshal out here to see you," Paul said.

Deke looked up in surprise. "What about?"

"I don't know," Paul said. "He wouldn't say. He just said that he had to see you personally."

Deke leaned back in his chair and put his hands behind his head. "A marshal, huh? Is he wearing a star and a low-slung gun?" Deke laughed.

"No, sir, he's dressed in a very conservative business suit," Paul replied, not getting the joke.

"All right, show the marshal in."

Paul left and returned a moment later with a short, though rather powerfully built man who looked as if he really would be more at home in jeans and vest than in the suit he wore. He had brown eyes, creased by weather lines, and Deke guessed he hadn't spent his entire career in plush offices.

"Mr. McClarity?"

"Yes," Deke said.

"I'm U.S. Marshal Harold Tipton, Mr. McClarity. I'm here to serve you with an administrative order that prohibits you from doing any further business with Mexico."

"What?" Deke shot back. "Let me see that. I thought we had that all worked out."

Tipton handed the order to Deke. Deke read it, then let out a low whistle. "Damn! If I'm reading this correctly, we can't even buy a taco without being in violation of a federal order," Deke said. He looked up at Tipton. "All right, you've served me. Thank you, Mr. Tipton."

"You have fourteen days to either comply or appeal," Tipton informed him.

"Yes, I see," Deke said. "Thank you. Paul, if you'll show the gentleman out?"

"Yes, sir," Paul said. "Right this way."

Deke looked at the order for a few minutes. Then suddenly he laughed.

"All right, Evan," he said softly, "we'll do it your way."

"Everything?" Rana asked.

"Everything," Deke said. "Look at the wording. 'Texon and all divisions of the Texon Corporation, whether or not they are currently doing business in energy, are hereby enjoined to cease and desist in all operations that deal in whole or in part with any company that is based in Mexico, or with any company that does business in any way with any company that is based in Mexico.'"

"Well, that certainly should give us a basis for an appeal," Rana said. "Otherwise, we'll have to close down our entire operation. Even Jefferson Motors gets raw material from Mexico."

"Close them," Deke said. "Close them all."

"Deke, do you know what you're saying? Look at the number of people who will be out of work — not only our own people, but in the automobile industry. We aren't making cars anymore, but we are supplying components to all three of the majors. We could throw the entire industry out of — " Rana suddenly stopped and smiled at Deke. "Oh, you naughty boy, you," she said. "I think I see where you are headed."

"Right," Deke said. "Let's see how long this order

stands up when three and a half million people are laid off."

"You'd better call Paul and have him inform operations," Rana said. "We'll close everything down tomorrow — except for the personnel departments, of course. I think we should keep them going full-time to expedite the unemployment insurance for our people. We're asking them to bend a little, but I don't think they should take the whole brunt of the fight."

"I agree," Deke said.

"Oh, by the way, Evan is coming back today," Rana said. "I spoke to Jewel this morning. I've invited them for dinner. You'll be sure to bring Rebel, won't you?"

"Is it showdown time, Grandmother?" Deke asked.

"It may be closer than you think," Rana said. "I do want you there."

"I'll be there," Deke promised.

It was late afternoon when Rebel parked her little Mercedes in the V.I.P. parking lot of the executive aviation lounge at Hobby Airport. She was greeted the moment she stepped through the door.

"Miss Hewlitt, I just spoke to the tower. Your father's airplane is on the ground now. He should be here in about five minutes."

"Thank you," Rebel said. She walked through the lounge and out the front door, then stood just behind the fence to look out on the parking ramp at the private jets, turboprops, and twins that made up much of Houston's business fleet.

The top-of-the-line airplane for Texon was the stretch model DC-8. Evan was certainly authorized to use it anytime he wished, but he seemed to prefer the smaller, though no less luxurious, Gulfstream II.

Rebel could smell the hot jet fumes and hear the high-pitched whine of engines as she stood there looking out over the tarmac. She saw a lineman, dressed in yellow coveralls, step out into the middle of the area and hold up two batons. Then she saw the sleek white jet, with the blue three-pointed star, turning off the taxiway.

A moment later the air stairs were lowered and Evan climbed down, said something to the lineman, then, smiling, crossed the concrete pad toward Rebel.

"It was good of you to meet me," he said as she kissed him.

"You're so busy running around so much that about the only time I get to see you anymore is when I either take you to the airport or pick you up," Rebel said.

"Well, I'm glad, even if it does mean a ride in your Jeep."

"Jeep? What are you talking about? I'll have you know I brought my car," Rebel said.

"Did you now? Well, this is an occasion, then, isn't it?"

"Do you have any luggage?"

"Jerry will take care of it," Evan said.

A moment later they were in the car leaving the airport. Evan leaned his head back against the headrest for a moment, then looked over at his daughter.

"I wasn't sure you would even want to talk to me anymore," he said.

"Why? I'm the fallen woman," Rebel replied. "You caught me in a motel room with Deke. I've been waiting for you to be the outraged parent."

"No," Evan said with a surprising amount of gentleness in his voice. "No, honey, I'm not going to play the role of outraged parent. It's not like you're some little tramp with round heels. My God, sweetheart, I know you think you are in love with Deke."

"Not think — *am*," Rebel corrected.

"All right — *are* in love with him," Evan went on. He sighed. "But he isn't right for you."

"So you've said. Daddy, I want to know why we can't get married. What is it that Rana is supposed to tell us?"

"She hasn't told you yet?"

"No. She's telling us the whole story from the beginning, and you know how long her stories take. I'm dying to know the outcome, but you can't push Rana McClarity."

"I guess I can understand. It's going to be difficult for her. Believe me, it's difficult for me. But someone has to do something before it's too late."

"Daddy, what's it all about?" Rebel pleaded.

"I want Rana to tell you."

"And if she won't?"

"Then I will," Evan said. He was silent for a moment. "If that's what it takes."

"Because you're fighting Rana for control of the company? Daddy, do you really think I would vote with Rana on every issue? Nothing will change if I marry Deke."

"Honey, there are things you just don't understand," Evan said. He sighed. "I wish C.G. had lived. If C.G. was still around, there wouldn't be a problem."

"You're talking about Deke's daddy, aren't you?"

"Yes," Evan said.

"Did you and C.G. get along?"

Evan chuckled. "C.G. was my hero," he said. "I thought he was the greatest thing alive. I went to the airport with him to see him off when he left for the war. I wrote letters to him; I had a picture of his B-17 and the crew on my desk. On the wall I had a map of Europe, and I would plot each of his bombing missions with a long red line."

Evan was silent for a moment, and Rebel, because she was seeing a side of her father she didn't often see, allowed him his solitude.

"Then this woman came back from England," Evan went on.

"Thelma," Rebel said.

"Thelma."

"I remember her. I remember that I liked the way she talked. She sounded like people on TV or in movies, though she never seemed to talk too much. She was always... I don't know... just there. It was as if, after all those years, she still felt like she was imposing on people. I was sad when she died."

"Yes," Evan said. "She was a quiet woman, but in her quiet way she dropped quite a bombshell."

"What do you mean?"

"Well, can't you imagine what everyone thought when a strange English lady showed up after the war and had to be taken in as one of the family?"

"You mean no one believed her?"

"Oh, yes, everyone believed her. C.G. had written about her. And, of course, she had the marriage certificate, pictures — that sort of thing. But that wasn't the issue."

"What was?"

"She was pregnant," Evan said. "Six months to the day after she arrived in Texas, Deke was born."

"Daddy, why do you hate Deke so much?"

"I don't hate Deke."

"How can you say that?"

"I can say it because it's true. I don't hate him at all. I

think Deke is a fine young man — one of the finest I've ever known."

"But you are against my marrying him."

"Yes."

"Why?"

"I told you, it's best to let Rana explain that."

"Maybe she will tonight," Rebel said.

"Tonight? Why? What happens tonight?"

"She's having a small dinner party," Rebel said. "We're all invited — you and Mother, Deke and I."

"I see," Evan said.

"You will go, won't you, Daddy? It's very important that you go."

"Yes," Evan said finally. "I'll go. And I agree with you, it is important."

Chapter Twenty-five

England — 1944

It was raining when C.G. stepped off the plane at the London airport. It was a hard, drenching rain that blew across the runways, banged against the windows, and made rivers out of the small drainage canals on the field. The men, whose legs were cramped from eighteen hours on the plane, tried to run through the downpour to a large hangar where they would get transportation to their assigned airfields.

Second Lieutenant Charles Goodnight McClarity, United States Army Air Corps, was assigned to Dudleyshire Field and the 605th Bomb Group. C.G. flew B-17s, and the 605th was desperately in need of replacement B-17 pilots.

The hangar was a large building with a tin roof, and the rain sounded like a drum roll as it banged against it. The hangar was open at one end, where olive-drab buses queued up to take the men to their assigned bases. C.G. moved toward the open end, carrying his dripping duffel bag. He asked a transport sergeant which bus would take him to Dudleyshire.

"Dudleyshire?" the sergeant asked, chewing on a cigar which, because of the rain, wouldn't stay lit. He looked through the papers on his clipboard. "Oh, yes, Dudleyshire. That'll be bus number seven. Down at the other end of the hangar." The sergeant waved absently toward the far side of the hangar, then turned back to yell out the destination of the next bus.

"It would be the far end," C.G. muttered. He picked up his bag and trudged across the hangar, stepping over the men who were sleeping in various positions on the floor, until he reached the last loading dock. There was no bus there, not even a loading sergeant. C.G. put down his bag and looked around.

"You Lieutenant McClarity?"

The speaker was a captain who couldn't have been more than twenty-one, but when C.G. looked into the captain's eyes he lost all concept of how old the captain was.

"Yes, sir," C.G. answered, saluting.

"I'm Leo Greenly," the captain said, sticking his hand out and ignoring C.G.'s salute. "You'll be assigned to my crew."

"Very good, sir," C.G. said. "When do we go out?"

"Don't be in such a hurry, the war will last," Leo said. "The next bus is at ten tomorrow morning."

"Tomorrow morning?" C.G. complained. "What the hell am I supposed to do until then?"

"I intend to drink until then," Leo said. "Would you like to join me?"

"No, sir. Uh...thank you, sir," C.G. said. "I think I'll just get a hotel room and log some sack time. I'm beat."

Leo scratched his head and looked into C.G.'s face. "You're serious, aren't you? You intend to waste your time in London sleeping?"

"Yes."

Leo sighed. "Well, you'll never be able to find a hotel room. But" — Leo took out a piece of paper and wrote a girl's name and the address of a U.S.O. club — "here," he said, handing the paper to C.G. "Tell her I sent you."

"Who's this?"

"A friend."

"How do I get there?"

"Lieutenant, if you can't figure out how to get from here to the U.S.O. club, how the hell are you going to get a B-17 from here to Germany and back?"

"I'll figure out a way," C.G. said.

Leo smiled wryly. "I rather thought you would. Now, if you'll excuse me, I have some heavy drinking to do."

C.G. left his bag in a corner of the hangar, then went into the rain to try for a taxi.

He tried for an hour but none was available without a priority. "There's a war on, mate," the drivers said, as if informing him of something new.

C.G. finally managed to hitch a ride into town with a lorry driver. The rain had stopped, but the lorry had an open cab and C.G. had to sit in the wet seat as the truck inched its way through the heavy traffic. For the entire trip the driver cursed and ground the gears together until C.G. feared the transmission would fall out.

"Stop here," C.G. said when he saw the sign advertising the U.S.O. He offered the driver some money.

"Seein' as 'ow we're on the same side in this war, I don't know as I could take your money, guv," the driver said. "But if you've any cigarettes to offer, I'd be grateful."

C.G. pulled out a package of cigarettes, the last of three packs he had bought just before he left the States. He gave the driver the entire pack.

Inside the U.S.O. the air was heavy with the smell of wet wool uniforms, coffee, and tobacco smoke. Near one wall a girl was playing piano. She was surrounded by several men, and the strains of "Marisey Doates" floated through the noisy hall.

"Hello, Leftenant," a pretty blonde said as she greeted C.G. "Won't you have some coffee?"

"Yes, thank you," C.G. said. "Oh... uh..." He pulled out the paper. "... is there a girl here named Thelma Brosely?"

"Why, yes. I'm Thelma Brosely."

C.G. grinned. "I'm Lieutenant... I mean C.G. McClarity. Captain Greenly told me I should look you up and say he sent me."

Thelma looked puzzled. "Did he say why?"

"No," C.G. replied. "Not really. I just arrived today. I've been assigned to his crew."

A strange, faraway look came into Thelma's eyes. "Are you taking Doug's place?" she asked.

"Doug?"

"Never mind," Thelma said. As if making a physical effort, Thelma shrugged off the mood that had taken such a strange hold over her. She smiled again. "Come on, we'll drink our coffee and have a nice long chat. You must tell me all about yourself."

"Thank you," C.G. said. "Uh... listen, the truth is, I

was looking for a place to sleep. Even an empty couch. My bus doesn't leave until ten tomorrow morning, and I was on the plane for nearly eighteen hours."

"Oh, heavens, love, we close this place in a couple of hours," Thelma said. "I'm afraid you couldn't stay here."

"Oh," C.G. said. He sighed. "According to Leo, a hotel is out of the question."

"Quite out of the question, I'm afraid," Thelma said. "What will you be doing on Leo's crew?"

"I imagine I'll be his copilot," C.G. said.

"Like Doug Pyre."

"I'm sorry, I haven't met Doug Pyre yet."

"It's too late for that," Thelma said. "Here, take this key. It's to my flat in Wimbley House. That's just two blocks from here. The flat number is right on the key. Mind you, now, don't turn on any lights until the blackout curtains are pulled."

"I couldn't do that," C.G. said. "I don't want to put you out."

"It's all right, Leftenant," Thelma said, and the expression on her face was one of compassion. She touched C.G. on the arm. "Believe me, it's all right. Just go on to my place and have yourself a nice sleep."

"Gee," C.G. said, looking at the key, "I don't know what to say."

"Try 'thanks,'" Thelma suggested with a smile.

Wimbley House was a narrow-fronted building with a big black double door and a brass knocker right in the middle. A narrow stairway was tucked up against one wall and covered with a worn carpet that may have been a maroon color at one time. Now it was gray and brown where some of the inner weave was showing through.

Once inside the flat, C.G. checked the blackout curtains, then turned on the light. It was a single bare bulb that hung from a frayed cord. There were cracks in the ceiling and spots on the wall, but there was a big double bed and that was all C.G. really cared about.

There were a few other things in the flat, which was really just one room. A small refrigerator, a hot plate, a table with two chairs, and a sofa. There was a sink but C.G. didn't see a bathroom. A bowl of wax fruit and a basket of flowers provided the only splash of color.

C.G. stripped down to his shorts and climbed into bed. He was asleep in just a few moments.

"Good morning," Thelma said the next morning. C.G. opened his eyes and it took him a second or two to remember where he was.

Thelma was sitting on the edge of the bed wearing a sheer nightgown. Her long blond hair hung in luxurious folds across her bare shoulders and she was smiling at him.

"Good morning," he said. He rubbed his eyes. "Where did you sleep?"

"Right here, beside you."

"Beside me?"

Thelma chuckled. "I knew it would be safe. But you are a bit of a cover hog. Did you sleep well?"

"If you ask me, I slept too well," he said.

Thelma laughed again. "We must hurry if you're to catch the train to Dudleyshire. I'll walk you to the station."

C.G. looked around the room.

"Are you looking for the loo?"

"The what?"

"The convenience...the bathroom," Thelma said.

"Oh...uh...yes."

"It's right down the corridor, second door to your left. I'll just get dressed myself and fix us some tea and two. Then it's off to the station with you."

C.G. started toward the door. Then he stopped and looked back toward Thelma. "I don't know how to thank you," he said. "Maybe I can take you to dinner sometime."

"I'd rather not," Thelma said.

"No? Why not?"

"I'd rather not get involved."

C.G. laughed. "Who's involved?" he asked. "I'm just talking about dinner."

"It always starts very innocently. Then..." She was silent for a moment. "Please, hurry," she said, changing the subject completely. "There's only one train a day to Dudleyshire. If you miss it I don't know how you'll make it to your base."

"There's a bus from the airport at ten this morning."

"That's funny," Thelma said, laughing.

"What's so funny about it?"

"Dear, it's five after ten now."

The words "605th Bomb Group" were formed with white-painted rocks beneath the flagpole in front of the commandant's Quonset hut. It was easy to see how the rocks stayed white, thought C.G. as he watched a soldier with a can of whitewash and a brush. The "605" was gleaming white where the painter had just finished, but the other rocks were less dazzling. The soldier didn't even look up as C.G. passed.

C.G. reported to Major Briscoe, the group adjutant.

Briscoe was bald and wore glasses. He was an older man, probably overage in grade, with a friendly, though not cheerful, expression.

"Checked out in 17s?" Briscoe asked.

"Yes, sir."

"You'll go out tomorrow."

"I thought I was supposed to get an area check ride first," C.G. replied.

"We have neither time nor crews to spare for that sort of thing," Briscoe said.

A heavy rumbling, like distant thunder, rolled across the field. Briscoe stood up quickly. "They're coming back," he said. He walked over to the window and looked out at them. "Three short," he said quietly after a few minutes.

C.G. stood in the window with Briscoe and watched the bombers as they landed, their tires giving a loud chirp of protest as they touched down.

One bomber was trailing smoke. It didn't fly the landing pattern; instead, it made a long, low-level straight-in approach directly for the runway. As the plane came closer, C.G. could see flames streaming back from number-three engine cowling. The propeller was standing still, knife edge into the wind. Pieces of the airplane were breaking loose. Then, just when C.G. thought the pilot had it made, the airplane exploded into a rose-and-orange ball of flame.

"Sorry, son," Briscoe said in a quiet voice. "That's a hell of a way to get welcomed to the new unit." Briscoe ran his fingers through his hair. "Take the rest of the day off to get squared away. Briefing is at oh-three-hundred tomorrow morning."

C.G. found his room. Then he lay on the bunk for a

while and thought of Thelma. Without warning, she had kissed him good-bye at the train. It had been a lover's kiss, as if they had known each other for a long time. He put his finger to his lips and could still feel her there.

"Ah, there you are," Captain Greenly said. "I see you found your way."

"Yes," C.G. said. C.G. sat up on the bunk. "Captain, who is this girl, Thelma?"

"Didn't you find her?"

"Yes, I found her."

"Well, then, you know who she is. She's a friend."

"What kind of a friend?"

"Did she give you a place to sleep?" Leo asked.

"Yes."

"Did she charge you for it?"

"Well, no, but — "

"Then what the hell else do you need to know?" Leo asked. "I told you, she's a friend." Leo lay on his bunk and began looking at a magazine.

C.G. lay back down and folded his hands behind his head. After a few minutes he sat up and began digging through his gear for paper and a pen.

"Writing your girl back home?" Leo asked.

"I'm writing to Evan."

"Evan?"

"Evan Hewlitt," C.G. said. "He's a friend."

"Where's he stationed?"

"He isn't stationed anywhere. He's only thirteen," C.G. said.

"That's a good age to be right now," Leo said. "Unless you happen to live in Hamburg, Frankfurt, Würzburg, Nürnberg, or Düsseldorf."

"What do you mean?"

"Thirteen-year-olds die in those cities just like everyone else."

"Captain, are you saying we shouldn't be bombing Germany into submission?"

Leo laughed. "Into submission, huh?" he replied. "You're all right, kid."

It was funny. Leo called C.G. "kid," though there wasn't more than a year's difference in their ages. Somehow, even to C.G., it seemed to fit.

After briefing the next morning, C.G. rode in the back of a three-quarter-ton truck with several other men as they headed out to the flight line. The airplanes loomed like ghostly shadows in the predawn darkness. The name of the ship to which C.G. was assigned was *The Reluctant Virgin*.

Leo chuckled.

"What is it, Captain?" the navigator asked.

"We're going to bomb Germany into submission," Leo said.

"What?"

"That's right, isn't it, kid?" Leo asked C.G. "We're going to bomb them into submission?" he repeated.

"Yes, sir," C.G. answered quietly.

When C.G. climbed into the copilot's seat, he saw the name "Doug" in gold letters.

"That was the copilot," Leo said, pointing to the name. "He was good at lettering. He has labels all over the goddamned ship."

C.G. knew better than to ask about him, but Leo volunteered the information.

"He was killed over Würzburg."

"I'm sorry," C.G. said. "You must feel very bad about it."

"Better him than me," Leo said coolly as he moved the mixtures to start the engines.

C.G. leaned back in his seat so he could see the fireguard.

"Thelma mentioned his name. She didn't say much about him."

"They were in love," Leo said. He chuckled.

"Why's that funny?"

"Falling in love is for living people," Leo said. "We're dead, all of us. We're just looking for a place to lay down."

"If you feel that way, how can you fly?" C.G. asked.

"Hell, kid, it's the only way I can fly."

An hour later C.G. could taste the rubber as he breathed the oxygen through his mask. They were at twenty-five thousand feet and just crossing the coast of France. The sky was a bright crystal blue, lined with the vapor trails that extended from each bomber. The airplanes were enveloped in an avalanche of sound from the pounding engines and beating propellers. Far below green and brown fields stretched serenely from horizon to horizon.

They hadn't yet reached the point of radio silence and there was a great deal of chatter over the air.

"Seven, tuck it in a little. You're too wide."

"This is seven. Who's calling me? The flight commander?"

"No, this is three, on your wing. You're too wide. Tuck it in."

"This is ten. I'm going to check my guns now."

"Roger, this is flight commander. Okay to check guns."

The guns on *The Reluctant Virgin* exploded in staccato firing as they were cleared.

"Seven, you're still too wide."

"Where are the P-47s? I thought they were going to pick us up."

"Seven, tuck it in a little more."

"The fighter jocks are still in bed."

"Yeah, but with who?"

"I think that should be *whom*."

"Seven, tuck it in a little more."

"Three, I'm going to tuck it right into your asshole if you don't get the fuck off my back."

"Did you say *fuck* over the air?"

"Negative on the fuck."

"This is lead. Let's can the chatter now."

The plane-to-plane conversation fell off immediately. Leo turned the switch to Private so he and C.G. could talk.

"She's a good kid," he said.

"Thelma?"

"Yes. Adjust the prop trim. They seem a little out of sync."

C.G. changed the r.p.m., and a harmonic vibration, which was so slight that he could barely discern it, went away.

"Have you ever gone out with her?"

"Yeah."

"What happened?"

"What do you mean?"

"Why did you quit going with her?"

"She liked Doug better."

"But Doug's out of the picture now."

"Yeah."

"So why haven't you moved back in?"

"It doesn't work that way."

"Why did you send me to her?"

"You said you needed a place to sleep. I figured she could help."

"Captain, did you ever...uh, I mean you and Thelma...have you...?"

"What are you asking me, son? Have I been in her pants? Is that what you want to know?"

"No," C.G. said quickly. "It's really none of my business."

"You're goddamned right it's none of your business."

"Bogies, three o'clock high!" someone shouted.

"They're friendlies," someone else said immediately. "It's the P-47 escort."

The P-47s stayed with them for a while. Then, when their fuel ran out, they zipped through the formation wagging their wings. A little more than a blink of the eye and they were gone.

"Didn't do us much good, did they?" C.G. asked.

"We weren't jumped, were we?"

"No."

"Then they did us good. Be ready, the fun's about to begin."

Leo was right. Less than five minutes later the word rang out that bandits had been spotted at ten o'clock high. C.G. looked toward the area indicated and saw eight ME-109s flip over onto their backs and come roaring down a long, invisible track that led to the bomber formation.

"Here they come!" someone shouted.

"Hey! There's more climbing on us from six o'clock low!"

"They're all over the fuckin' place."

All the guns opened up and the sky was suddenly filled with brightly glowing balls of fire. The first attack wave slammed through the formation with no hits scored by either side.

"Christ! How do you keep from running over them?" C.G. asked.

"We don't," Leo said grimly. "We have to depend on Jerry. It's a cooperative effort. He's the only one maneuverable enough to avoid a crash. He doesn't want to run into us any more than we want to run into him, so we fly straight and level to allow him to make his move."

More fighters flashed through and the guns erupted with a roar. C.G. saw the wing break off the B-17 in the three slot. He was the pilot who had been so worried about a tight formation. Now his plane was making a five-mile plunge toward the ground, while the severed wing tumbled like a falling leaf, the propellers on the two engines still spinning.

From beneath C.G.'s plane a German fighter suddenly popped up, going away. The ball turret, the nose gun, and the top turret were all able to track on target, and C.G. watched as all three guns hosed into him. Smoke started streaming back from the engine cowl and suddenly the blur of what had been the propeller turned into black bars as it slowed to the point that C.G. could actually see it.

The plane was fatally hit and it rolled onto its back so the pilot could fall away. He rolled himself into a ball for the plunge through another bomber formation five thousand feet below. He was far from out of danger, as there were more than one hundred spinning propellers waiting for him, should he hit one of the planes in his fall.

In addition to the fighters, another danger presented itself. Anti-aircraft guns opened up and the sky ahead became a sickening mass of exploding flame, smoke, and jagged chunks of metal. The flak was everywhere. It tore off wings, smashed engines, and exploded inside the fuselage to rip the airplanes apart.

Fire, smoke, and exploding airplanes assailed C.G.'s eyes. There was a cacophony of sound as overrevved engines, exploding shells, screaming rockets, and shouts of terror filled the air. He could smell the smoke and burned oil, taste the bile of his own fear. He felt the shock waves of every explosion and his body itched with the pouring of sweat.

When *The Reluctant Virgin* settled onto the macadam runway at Dudleyshire, it was one of only fourteen to return from a group of twenty-two airplanes. Leo eased the plane into the revetment and killed the engines. C.G. leaned forward against the wheel. Twelve hours of pounding noise was over and only the gentle whir of the gyros could be heard as they spun down.

A truck backed up to the front of the plane in the next revetment and the bloody remains of what had been the bombardier was pulled from the smashed nose compartment. A three-quarter-ton truck pulled up alongside the wing of *The Reluctant Virgin* and the crew started loading tiredly onto it.

When they had loaded onto the plane this morning, C.G. felt like an outsider, detached from the rest of the crew. Now he was one of them. They had gone through the crucible together.

C.G. stopped the Jeep in front of the house. Southgate was a fifty-five-acre estate just south of Dudleyshire. It had rolling green hills, a verdant forest, and a small lake. The house was nearly two hundred years old, and when C.G. saw it he thought it was one of the most beautiful things he had ever seen. No matter how much money his dad or Jason Hewlitt had, they could never build anything to match the quietly stated elegance of Southgate. Cedars seemed garish and vulgar to him now.

It didn't seem possible that the girl who lived in the sparsely furnished room at Wimbley House also lived here. But Leo assured C.G. that she did, and when he was invited to spend the weekend with her, he decided to see for himself.

A butler answered the door and C.G. had to suppress a chuckle, because the butler looked like Smythe. C.G. was shown into a large room and asked to wait for a moment. Within seconds, a maid appeared with tea and he heard his name called.

Thelma was standing in the doorway, smiling. She was dressed in white shorts and a blouse and her hair was tied back with a red ribbon. She looked softer here in her own home than she had in the U.S.O. building, or even in her apartment.

"I'm glad you took me up on the invitation," Thelma said. "Oh, would you rather have coffee?"

"No, this is fine, thank you," C.G. said, holding up the cup. He looked around. "This is a beautiful place."

"Thank you," Thelma said. "It's been in the family for several generations. There are all sorts of neat family legends about ghosts if you're interested in such things."

"Not really," C.G. said. He chuckled. "Though I may change my mind if I see one."

Thelma looked around. "Didn't Leo come with you?"

"No," C.G. answered. "Was he supposed to?"

"I invited him for dinner. I thought he might come out with you."

"That's funny. He didn't say anything about it."

"Maybe he didn't feel it was necessary," Thelma said. "Come. I want you to meet my mother. I'm afraid you won't be able to meet my father, as he's fighting His Majesty's War in North Africa."

After C.G. met Thelma's mother, Thelma showed him the room he would occupy during his stay, then took him on a tour of the house and grounds. They walked around the lake and found a small lakeside cottage on the other side.

"This is my favorite place of the entire estate," Thelma said when they went inside. She walked over to the bed, then turned around with a smile on her lips and her arms outstretched. "Come here," she said. "I'll give you a demonstration of the bed."

C.G. stood there in momentary shock.

"Would you rather not make love to me?" Thelma asked.

"Uh... no... no," C.G. said. "I do want to make love to you. It's just that..."

"You aren't used to a girl getting so quickly to the point, is that it?"

"Something like that," C.G. agreed.

"C.G., things can't be the way they were before the war. There's no time now. Everyone is too old."

"Too old?"

"Like Doug. Doug was a very, very old man."

"I thought Doug was twenty."

"Doug is dead," Thelma said. "You don't get older than dead." Thelma put her hand to the buttons of her blouse. "Shall we?" she asked.

C.G. smiled and stepped up to her to help. "Turn around," he said when she took off her blouse. "Let me unsnap your bra."

Thelma turned around and C.G. marveled at the delightfully smooth skin of her back. He unsnapped the bra and she moved her shoulders forward to let it fall. C.G. reached around and cupped her breasts in his hands, feeling the congested nipples with his fingers.

Thelma turned her head back toward him and he kissed her open mouth, taking her tongue into his. C.G. pushed her down to the bed gently, then moved on it with her. Thelma's eager hands soon divested C.G. of his clothes. Then she pulled him over her and guided him into her.

They made love fully and completely, and finally a burst of wet warmth filled her and made them as one. They lay together quietly for several minutes and C.G. asked, "How well do you know Leo?"

"Oh, really, C.G., don't be an ass," Thelma said. She swung her legs over the edge of the bed and started getting dressed.

"I don't think it's such an unusual question to ask," C.G. said. "I mean, I could understand if — "

"You could understand if what?" Thelma asked, looking at him with a challenge in her eyes.

"Well, if he...I mean...if you were his girl."

"Why don't you just come out and ask me if Leo and I have made love?"

"It's none of my business," C.G. said.

"You're damned right it's none of your business," Thelma said. "It so happens that Leo is in love with me, but we've never made love."

C.G. was surprised to see tears in Thelma's eyes.

"Why not?" he asked.

"Your friend Captain Greenly is one of the war wounded who will never get a Purple Heart. It seems that he can't bomb people in the daytime and make love at night."

"You mean Leo is impotent?" C.G. asked, clearly shocked over the disclosure.

"Yes," Thelma said quietly.

"But he knew about Doug?"

"Yes. And he will know about you. I'll never say anything to him, of course, and I'm reasonably sure that you won't say anything. But he'll know."

"I guess there's a lot I don't understand about people," C.G. said.

Thelma smiled, then kissed C.G. gently on the lips. "You're a kind, loving person, Charles Goodnight. You'll learn. I'll teach you."

Chapter Twenty-six

Houston — 1945

The twin-engine Beechcraft banked sharply. Rana and Gamblin looked out the window as they passed over Houston. The sound of the engines lessened as the pilot throttled back for the landing.

"I'm sorry if the turn was too sharp, Mr. McClarity," the pilot called back through the open door. "The tower said if we expedite we can land now. Otherwise, we're going to have to wait another five minutes."

"Don't worry about us," Gamblin called back to him. "We're fine."

Gamblin leaned back in his seat as the flaps went down and the plane started its descent. This was the third airplane Texon had owned. They had learned ten years ago that it would be better to own their own airplane than to try to depend upon airline schedules. With the war, travel became even more difficult and the airplane became more necessary. There was a time, early in the war, when it didn't make any difference whether they had owned their own plane or not, because all private aircraft were grounded.

For Texon the grounding didn't last long, however. Oil was a war-critical item, and Texon's owners were given immediate priority to fly anywhere they wanted.

Gamblin and Rana were returning from Washington, having just attended a meeting with President Roosevelt. As a measure of the progress of the war, the topic of conversation never once touched upon war needs. Roosevelt was concerned about America's postwar growth. Specifically, he wanted to know how much longer America could count on energy independence.

"I'm interested in forty or fifty years from now," the president had said. "In 1985, will we be getting all the oil we need from our own supply? Or will we have to depend on imported oil?"

When Gamblin admitted that he didn't know, the president asked him to find out.

The airplane touched down, then taxied over to the private terminal. Rana looked through the window and saw Evan waving at them from behind the chain link fence.

"Well, Evan, how nice of you to come meet us," Rana said a moment later.

"I rode with Jennings," Evans said. He held up a letter and smiled broadly. "I got a letter from C.G."

"How's he doing?"

"He's going to get a medal," Evan said. "He's going to get the Distinguished Flying Cross."

"My, that sounds awfully impressive."

"I sure wish I could be over there with him," Evan said.

"Just be glad you aren't," Rana said. "One of my boys fighting this war is quite enough, thank you."

"Oh, you got a letter, too. I brought it for you."

"Thank you," Rana said. She took the incredibly thin Victory envelope that was being used for service mail. When they got into the car a moment later, she opened it and began to read.

"Oh, my," she said. "Oh, my."

"What is it?" Gamblin asked.

"I think you'd better prepare yourself for a little shock," Rana said. "C.G. is married."

"What?" Gamblin spouted. "Why, he can't do that, can he? I mean, without our permission?"

Rana laughed. "Darling, he hardly needs our permission."

"Well, who the hell did he find to marry? I mean some nurse or WAC, or what?"

"An English girl," Rana said. "Her name is Thelma Brosely. I take it she's from quite a good family."

"Why haven't we ever heard of her before?"

"I don't know. He says he met her the first day he arrived in England and has been seeing her ever since. They got married last week."

Gamblin groaned. "I can't believe it," he said. "With all the women in Texas, he goes halfway around the world and marries some foreigner."

"I wonder if her family feels the same way about C.G. At least there won't be a language problem," Rana said. "Now, Gamblin, you must promise me when he brings her home you won't act like this. You'll make her welcome."

The car turned up into the Cedars driveway then and they saw a taxi parked near the fountain.

"I'll be a good boy," Gamblin promised. "What's the taxi doing here?"

"I don't know. Perhaps one of the servants."

Smythe came out of the house to greet them when they arrived.

"What's Smythe doing out here?" Gamblin asked.

Suddenly, Rana's head began to spin and her stomach turned over. She gasped and put her hand on Gamblin's arm.

"Oh, Gamblin, no," she said quietly.

Gamblin looked at her in confusion. "What is it?" he asked.

"I'm frightened," Rana said. "I'm so frightened."

"Smythe, what is it?" Gamblin asked.

"There is a telegram for you, sir," Smythe said.

Gamblin ran up the steps while Rana, now feeling weak in the knees, moved more slowly. She welcomed Smythe's arm when he extended it to her. By the time she was inside, Gamblin was already reading the telegram.

"I'm sorry, Mr. McClarity, Mrs. McClarity," the taxi driver said. "I'm sorry I was the one who had to deliver it."

Gamblin read the telegram, then, with shaking fingers, handed it to Rana.

NA362 49 GOVT-WUX WASHINGTON DC
14 1031A
  MR GAMBLIN MCCLARITY
  REGRET TO INFORM YOU YOUR SON FIRST LIEUTENANT CHARLES GOODNIGHT MCCLARITY WAS SHOT DOWN OVER NURNBERG GERMANY ON
27 MARCH MISSING PRESUMED DEAD LETTER FOLLOWS WITH DETAILS
  KENNEMAN ACTING THE ADJUTANT GENERAL

Chapter Twenty-seven

Dallas — 1963

"To tell the truth, I don't even like Jackie. She's cold and standoffish," Rana said.

"She's the president's wife and she's keenly aware of her position. I think she's a very gracious lady."

"Bullshit," Rana said.

Gamblin laughed. "Bullshit? That's your opinion of the first lady? Bullshit?"

"I think that about sums it up," Rana said. "If it weren't for Lyndon, I wouldn't be here."

"Then just keep that in mind," Gamblin said. "Honey, you know there's talk Kennedy is planning to drop Lyndon next year. We owe it to Lyndon to be here to support him."

"He wouldn't really do it, would he, Gamblin? He needs Lyndon Johnson. How would he carry the South without him?"

"Truman won without the South in '48. Maybe Kennedy feels like he can win without them in '64."

"Well, if he feels that way, it's all the more reason I don't want to ride in his damned parade," Rana said.

"On the other hand," Gamblin explained, "perhaps we can give a demonstration of how much strength Lyndon really does have, and how much Texas loves him."

"All right," Rana said. She got up from the bed and started toward the closet. "But I hope Lyndon and Lady Bird appreciate how much I'm doing for them."

"I'm sure they understand," Gamblin said. "After all, no one plays the game better than they do. I've heard Lyndon say that being vice-president isn't worth a pitcher of warm piss, but he's doing it to keep a leg up for the race in '72."

"Do you think Lyndon has a chance of being president someday?" Rana asked.

"Yes, I do. You forget, before he got sidetracked in this dead-end job, he was majority leader of the Senate. That made him one of the most powerful men in America."

"He should've stayed there."

"When Kennedy offered him the vice-presidency, Lyndon asked Cactus Jack what to do, and Garner told him to take it."

Rana moved some of her clothes around.

"What should I wear?" she asked. "I wish I knew what Jackie is wearing. I wouldn't want to wear anything that would upset her."

There was a knock at the door and Gamblin went over

to open it. Jason and Jane Ella were on the other side.

"Jane Ella, let me see what you're wearing."

Jane Ella spun around to show off her white suit and pillbox hat.

"Oh," Rana said. "Yes, that's lovely. I wish I could make up my mind."

"Did you see the *Dallas Morning News*?" Jason asked.

"No."

"Listen to this. On page fourteen there's an entire page, bordered in black, blasting Kennedy. It accuses the president of the imprisonment, starvation, and persecution of thousands of Cubans. It accuses the president of selling food to the Communists who are killing Americans in Vietnam. It just out and out calls him a Communist and concludes by saying, 'Mr. Kennedy' — notice, not even Mr. President, but Mr. Kennedy — 'Mr. Kennedy, we demand answers to these questions, and we want them now.' "

"Goddamn it!" Gamblin said. "What the hell are those dumb sons-of-bitches trying to do to Johnson? It's going to look like he can't even prevent something like this in his home territory."

"I wonder if the president's seen it," Jason remarked.

"Hell, you know damned well he has. He makes it a point to look through the paper everywhere he goes."

"I guess so," Jason said. "By the way, I found out what car we're riding in."

"Which one?"

"We'll be two cars back from Kennedy and Governor Connally."

"Who's riding with Lyndon?"

"Yarborough," Jason said.

"How's this?" Rana asked, holding up a blue dress.

"Beautiful," Gamblin replied, looking out the window.

"Gamblin, you didn't even look," Jane Ella scolded.

"Never mind," Rana said. "When I show up butt-naked, no one can say we didn't give him the chance."

Gamblin looked around quickly. Then everyone laughed.

"Shit! It's raining," Jason said.

"Maybe it'll clear up," Gamblin suggested. "Come on, I think we're supposed to have breakfast with the president. I wouldn't want to be late."

Breakfast was in the Hotel Texas. When Gamblin, Rana, Jason, and Jane Ella arrived, they were seated promptly, but they had to sit for twenty minutes while the guests waited for the president and his wife to make their entrance. Finally, someone yelled out, "And now, an event I know you have all been waiting for! President and Mrs. Kennedy!"

The room erupted into cheers as the presidential party entered. All eyes were on Jackie Kennedy. She was absolutely radiant as she stood there, blinking a little under the glare of the bright lights. She was wearing short white gloves and a shocking-pink suit. Rana breathed a sigh of relief that she didn't choose her pink dress, because the similarity was striking.

After breakfast they were invited to the presidential suite. The president was on the phone when they arrived, but he waved at them, then hung up the phone and came over and greeted them warmly.

"Thank you so much for coming by," he said.

"It's an honor, Mr. President. I'm just sorry Texas couldn't offer you better weather."

"I think the rain has stopped," Kennedy said. "Last night, though, with the rain and the dark, it was a perfect night for intrigue, don't you think? Suppose someone was sneaking through the crowd, carrying a small pistol concealed in his coat pocket." President Kennedy assumed a half crouch and began walking on the balls of his feet, looking about furtively. "He could reach in his pocket, pull out the pistol like so, shove it into the president's side, and, *pop, pop,* then drop the gun, whirl away, and vanish into the night and the crowd."

"Oh, Mr. President!" Rana shuddered. "Don't say things like that. They make me nervous."

The president laughed and walked over to the window. "I'm glad it has stopped raining. It would have been a shame to have to put the bubble on the car. Where are you riding, by the way?"

"Just behind the vice-president's car," Gamblin said.

"Good. If he speeds, you'll be able to get his license number," Kennedy quipped.

"I'll try, Mr. President." Gamblin laughed.

"Mr. President, the plane is ready," someone said.

"Well, into the breach, as they say," Kennedy said, rubbing his hands together.

The presidential party flew from Fort Worth to Dallas, a flight of only thirteen minutes, then boarded the cars there for the motorcade through Dallas. Gamblin, Rana, Jason, and Jane Ella slid into their car and watched as the president and his immediate party got into the lead car. Someone had handed Jackie a bouquet of red roses and she was carrying them as she got in. She was on the left and the president was on the right. Governor Connally rode on the jumpseat just in front of the president. Jackie and the governor both wore hats, but the president was bare-headed.

At first the motorcade drove through streets that were nearly barren, and Rana and Gamblin sat back in the car holding their hands over their eyes to shield themselves against the sun, which had burned its way through the clouds.

"Jackie looks hot, doesn't she?" Jane Ella observed. "They should've put the bubble on. Then they could have used air conditioning."

"It would cheat the people," Jason answered. "The humidity would fog up the inside."

"What people?" Rana asked. "There's no one here." She pointed to the bare streets and stark billboards.

"There will be when we get downtown," Gamblin promised.

Gamblin was right. As the caravan moved downtown, the crowds began to get larger and larger until they were huge. They were waving and cheering and many of them held up signs. Most of the signs were friendly, though there were a few that weren't.

They rode for a few more minutes and then Jane Ella wiped her face. "Wonder what the temperature is," she remarked.

"I see a temperature sign," Rana said. "No, it's the time. It's twelve-thirty."

There was a sharp crack that snapped loudly, then rolled its echo down the street.

"What's that?" Jane Ella asked.

Jason and Gamblin knew at once what it was, and, as one, they pushed their wives down in the seats.

"It's a rifle!" Gamblin shouted.

"Mr. McClarity, the president! My God! Someone just shot the president!" the driver of the car shouted.

"Dear God, no, not in Texas," Rana said.

Gamblin looked up toward a building that had a sign reading TEXAS BOOK DEPOSITORY. Amazingly, he saw a man in a window very calmly taking aim with a rifle.

"There he is!" Gamblin yelled, pointing to the man, but his yell was futile. A puff of smoke and the rifle kicked back. Then the sound of the shot reached Gamblin's ears. The man disappeared into the shadows and John Fitzgerald Kennedy, thirty-fifth president of the United States, was dead.

Chapter Twenty-eight

Reagan County, Texas — 1967

The rims of the wagon wheels were covered with steel bands and they rolled through the hard desert sand with a quiet, crunching sound. The sun had not yet peeked over the hills, though the sky behind them was early-morning gold.

Gamblin McClarity rode on the highboard of the lead wagon through this hill country he loved so well. Of course, there was no question that Houston was home now. That was where he built his house and that was where C.G. was buried. Jason was buried there, too.

Gamblin missed Jason. True, there had been occasional differences between them all these years... and the question as to whom C.G.'s real father was had never been answered.

With Jason and C.G. both dead and buried, there was no reason now why Rana couldn't tell him, but he didn't want to know. He had grown used to sharing that mystery with Jason and he didn't want to change.

Gamblin looked out over the rolling terrain. In his mind's eye he was reliving the mornings he had spent out here in quest of the oil that had changed the lives of so many people.

What if he hadn't found oil? What if there had been no oil out here? Where would he be now? What would he be doing?

There were ten wagons in this wagon train, all loaded with football players—Deke's teammates—from the University of Texas. It had been Gamblin's idea that they have an old-fashioned "wagon train breakfast," in celebration of Deke's graduation from college.

At first the young men had laughed and joked among themselves, but soon they were too caught up by the beauty of the hill country and all were quiet, as if in a house of worship.

Rana put her hand on the seat beside Gamblin and left it there for a moment, neither intruding nor withdrawing. She hadn't spoken and Gamblin was glad, because he wanted the moment alone. He knew Rana realized that and he loved her the more because of it. Finally, he reached down and took her hand in his, squeezing it softly, inviting her into his cloistered world.

Gamblin held out his other hand toward the hills, taking them in with a wide sweep. He looked at Rana and tried to speak but the words wouldn't come.

"I know," Rana said softly. "You don't have to tell me. I know how you love it."

A rider came galloping along the length of the wag

ons, slapping the horse's neck gently with the ends of the reins. He yelled something to the first driver and the wagons began making a large circle. There were some tables and chairs already set up and several fires going.

The aroma of coffee and grilled steaks filled the air and Gamblin saw that there were already several people at work cooking breakfast.

The football players climbed down from the wagons and the solitude of the ride was broken as they began their banter once again. They were huge men, yet they moved with the easy grace of dancers.

"If you'll just sit there, sir, I'll bring breakfast over to you and Mrs. McClarity," their wagon driver offered. Gamblin thanked him and sat where he was instructed.

A little red-haired girl ran happily over to them. She held up her arms and Gamblin picked her up and sat her on his knee.

"Well, now," Gamblin said. "Who is this little waif?"

"I'm not a waif. I'm Rebel," the girl said, frowning seriously. "You know me, Gam'lin."

"Rebel? Why, so it is," Gamblin teased.

"Daddy said we're gonna eat breakfast out here," Rebel said. "Have you ever eaten breakfast outdoors before?"

"Why, sure. Haven't you?"

"I've eaten by the swimming pool," Rebel said. "But I've never eaten by the dirt."

Gamblin and Rana laughed.

"Rebel, get on back over here now and don't be bothering Gamblin and Rana," Evan ordered.

"She's no bother," Gamblin insisted.

"Wait until you try to eat," Evan said. "She'll drive you nuts."

Rebel hopped down.

"You'll come see us again after breakfast, won't you, Rebel?"

"Yes," Rebel said. She smiled, then ran back to join her mother.

"That one's going to be a heartbreaker," Gamblin said. "If Evan doesn't spoil her."

"Little girls are supposed to be spoiled," Rana said.

"That's not what I'm talking about. I don't want her to be mean-spirited like Evan."

"You aren't being fair. Evan isn't mean-spirited. How can you talk like that? Evan practically worships you. Ever since Jason died, you've been a father figure to him."

"Yes, but somehow he's managed to assume all of my aggressiveness, with none of his father's gentleness. It's left him hard, Rana, with no room for anything but blind ambition."

"Maybe you're wrong," Rana suggested. "He's still a young man. He'll mellow as he grows older."

"I hope so."

The sun climbed higher and the day grew warmer, though not unbearably hot. After breakfast the entertainment started and a band began setting up in the center of the circle.

"I can't stand to have all this spoiled by that," Gamblin said, pointing to the long-haired, bearded young men who comprised the musical group known as The Unwashed. "I'm going to take a walk."

"You want me to ask them not to play?"

"No. This whole breakfast was for the young people. I just don't want to listen to it, that's all."

"Want me to come with you?"

"No. I won't go far," Gamblin promised. He chuckled and held up his cane. "I'm not exactly in the same condition I was when I wandered all through here looking for oil."

Gamblin walked through the circle of wagons and down a small hill to a large rock. He sat on the rock and looked out across the rolling hills. There were dozens of pumps working, pulling oil from the ground, though he saw none of them. He was seeing the ground the way he saw it the first day he came out on it, nearly fifty years ago.

"Grandpa?"

Gamblin looked around at Deke's call. He smiled at him. "Thought you'd be back there with the rest of them getting your ears blasted out by that loud noise."

Deke smiled. "Am I to gather that you don't care much for that music?"

"Something like that."

Deke sat down on a rock across from his grandfather and picked up a stick. He began tracing on the ground. "I want to thank you for this breakfast," he said. "It's really nice of you to do it."

"Well, a fella doesn't graduate from college every day," Gamblin said. "I never did...your father never had the chance to. So far as I know, you're the first McClarity ever to make it."

"I'm glad I did," Deke said. "But not having a degree didn't slow you any."

"Nevertheless, education's a good thing. I've got an office ready for you, like we've been discussing all along. Got one of those fancy titles on the door, too."

"Thanks," Deke said. "But I'm afraid I won't be using it right away."

"Oh, hell, boy, you don't have to explain that to me. I understand. You just graduated, you need a little time to blow off some steam. I don't blame you. Why don't you take a trip? Maybe go to Europe or something."

"I'm going to take a trip," Deke said. He cleared his throat. "But I'm afraid I'll be going the other way."

"The other way? What are you talking about?"

"Vietnam."

"Vietnam? You're going to Vietnam?"

"Yes," Deke said. "I took the last two years of ROTC and got my commission. I'm going on active duty next month."

"How long have you known?"

"I've known I would have to serve some active duty time for two years. I didn't find out about Vietnam until about three months ago."

"Why have you been so quiet about it?"

"I didn't want to tell anyone. Mother's not in good health, and I didn't want you and grandmother to worry."

"This Vietnam war," Gamblin said, "it's not a good one."

"I don't suppose any war is good," Deke said.

"No, I don't agree. World War Two, now, that was a good war. It was a war that needed fightin', and when your dad was killed, Rana and I took some comfort in the fact that he was doin' the right thing. If anything happens to you over in that... Vietnam, I don't know as we could take any comfort at all."

Deke smiled.

"Then I shall make a concerted effort to see that nothing happens to me."

"See that you do," Gamblin said. "See that you do."

"Here's your coffee," Rana said, setting the cup on the table beside Gamblin's easy chair. They were in the

Quiet Room, having come here to read Deke's letters. As sometimes happened with overseas mail, they received four letters at once.

Gamblin chuckled. "Did you read this about the goat?"

"No, I haven't read that one yet."

"It seems the colonel got a goat and was going to barbecue it. But Deke's men made a pet out of it, named it Marsha, and gave it free rein of the place. Now they're standin' guard over it to keep the colonel from killin' it."

Rana wrinkled her nose. "Ugh! I can't think of anything worse-sounding than barbecued goat. Why would the colonel want to do that, anyway?"

"It's not bad," Gamblin said. "You ought to try it sometime. Maybe I'll give Lyndon a call and tell him to have one barbecued for you next week."

"Oh, I'd almost forgotten we were invited to the LBJ Ranch. I'd rather you call him and make some excuse for us not to go."

"I thought you liked going there."

"I used to," Rana said. "But it's different now. Lyndon is such a hounded man — the press, protesters in the street; it hurts me to be around him now. I feel so sorry for him, but there's nothing we can do."

"We can still be his friends," Gamblin said. "Don't you see? He needs this now, more than ever. The ranch is his only place of refuge."

"I guess you're right," Rana said. "Would you like a sweet roll? I'll call down to the kitchen." Rana picked up the phone.

"Do we have any cherry coffeecake? I'd like —"

Suddenly, Gamblin grabbed his chest and his face was contorted in pain.

"Gamblin!" Rana screamed, dropping the receiver. She ran over to him.

Gamblin coughed and reached for Rana.

"Richard!" she yelled.

Richard had been with them since Smythe died. His room was just down the hall from the Quiet Room. He hurried down the hall and opened the door.

"What is it, Mrs. McClarity?"

"Call the doctor, quickly!" Rana shouted. She rocked back and forth, sobbing, holding Gamblin's head against her breast. "Oh, Gamblin, hang on," she said. "Hang on."

"Rana," Gamblin said.

"Yes?"

"How is it you haven't changed in all these years? How have you stayed so beautiful?" He coughed, then drew one last, rasping breath.

"Gamblin?" Rana whispered quietly. "Gamblin?" she repeated a little louder Then, in an anguished shout: "Gamblin!"

"Please, send an ambulance to Mr. McClarity's residence at once," Richard said into the phone. "I'm afraid Mr. McClarity has suffered a heart attack."

"Oh, Richard, he's gone," Rana said. "What am I going to do? He's gone."

Chapter Twenty-nine

Houston — 1981

Deke stood in the library looking through the sliding-glass doors toward the swimming pool. Two dozen or more guests lounged around the pool; some were in it.

A white Porsche 911 was parked just beside the diving board, done up with a red ribbon and a big bow. A tag on the ribbon read: HAPPY BIRTHDAY, CAROL.

The car was a birthday present and the party a birthday party, but the guest of honor wasn't there.

Deke held a glass of bourbon-and-branch to his forehead and rolled it back and forth, feeling the coolness of it. He wished he could roll his headache away.

Things had not been going well in his marriage, and the car and the party were an attempt to change directions. And yet, even as he planned it, Deke realized there was little chance of salvaging anything.

"Hi, Deke. What are you doing in here?"

Deke turned to see Rebel standing just inside the door. Rebel was wearing an incredibly brief bikini. She was only seventeen, but there wasn't a woman at this party who wouldn't have given anything to have her shape.

"I must be getting old," Deke said. "The sun is too hot and the music too loud. I came in here to get away from it all for a few moments."

Rebel came into the room, then sat on the leather sofa. She smiled at Deke and brushed a fall of red hair away from her forehead. She laughed.

"I'm making you nervous," she said. "Good."

Deke took a swallow of his drink and looked at her over the rim of his glass.

"What makes you think you're making me nervous? And why is that good?"

"I can tell you're nervous because you're talking about how old you are. That's to contrast with the fact that I'm young, you see, though I'm not sure who you're trying to convince, you or me. And it's good because I want you to notice me as a woman."

"A woman?" Deke echoed with a scoffing laugh. "Listen, honey, don't be in such a hurry to grow up. You're a senior in high school. That's absolutely the best age to be. Enjoy it for a while."

"Now you're being patronizing," Rebel said.

"Privilege of age."

"There you go with the age bit again," Rebel teased. She got up from the sofa and walked over to stand beside him. There was about her a scent of warmed skin and a touch of coconut from the suntan oil she had used.

"I...uh...don't know what's keeping Carol," Deke said. "She should've been here by now."

"Carol's a fool," Rebel said. "If you belonged to me, I sure wouldn't embarrass you this way." Rebel put her fingers up to Deke's temple. "But I wouldn't want to share you with all these people, either. I'd keep you all to myself."

Deke cleared his throat. "Why don't we go back outside?"

Rebel smiled at him. "Why, Deke, I thought the sun and the music were just too much for your tired old body," she teased.

"Keep it up, kid, and you're going to find yourself thrown in the pool," Deke replied.

Before he could stop her, Rebel leaned into him and kissed him. She pulled away and laughed. "Poor, old Deke," she teased.

Carol stood just inside the door of the Blue Grotto and looked around. The place was crowded, but there was no one there from Deke's world.

That was good. She needed to get away from them every now and then. She needed desperately to be her own person, to make her own decisions, instead of subjugating everything to the "corporate structure" of Texon Petroleum.

She knew that Deke was giving a party for her right now and she knew that only the "right" people would be there. Well, fuck the party, fuck the right people, and fuck Deke.

"What'll it be?" the bartender asked.

"Bourbon and water," Carol said.

"Spoken like a true flower of Texas," a man said. "Make it two, will you, Mike? You don't mind if I join you, do you, miss?"

Carol looked at him. He had dark, wavy hair and deep brown eyes. He reminded her just a little of Burt Reynolds. She smiled at him.

"No," she said. "I don't mind at all."

The bartender put the drinks on the bar and took the money from a small pile in front of the man.

"I'm Russ Kolar," the man said.

"Carol Masters," Carol replied, using her maiden name. She wasn't particularly trying to hide. But she had learned that the name McClarity had a tendency to overshadow everything else. She never used it unless it was to her advantage to do so.

Russ held his drink toward her in a silent toast, then took a swallow. He studied her over the rim of the glass.

"I don't mean to sound corny, but have we met before?"

"No," Carol said.

"I've seen you somewhere."

As a McClarity, Carol's picture had often been in newspapers, magazines, and on television. Most people remembered seeing her, but few could make the exact connection. Carol had a way of getting around that.

"I did some nude layouts for a few magazines," Carol lied. "Maybe it would help if I got naked."

The man smiled and snapped his fingers. "Now that's an idea," he said. "You think we could arrange it?"

"Let's don't rush things," Carol replied.

"Maybe you're right," Russ said. "That's the trouble with the world today. Everyone's in too big of a hurry. Me, I like to stop and smell the roses."

"My God, how poetic," Carol teased. "You ought to write that."

Russ laughed and looked at his watch. "Hey!" he said. "I know where there's a very good party going on. You interested?"

"Not particularly," Carol replied. "I came here to avoid a party."

"I'll bet it wasn't like this one," Russ said. "This is an occult wedding."

"An occult wedding?" Carol repeated. "What on earth is that?"

"Why don't you come along and see for yourself?" Russ invited.

When they arrived at the party, the house was lit only by green indirect lighting that gave a ghostly glow to the proceedings. Music, if the strange sounds coming from the many speakers could be called that, filled the house with a deep, sensual throb. They were greeted by a girl, a striking redhead, who was wearing a dress made of net. There was nothing beneath it and she may as well have been nude since all the points of interest were clearly visible. The girl looked pointedly at Carol and licked her lips. She ran her hands down the sides of her thighs as if in invitation, and Carol felt a stirring of excitement.

"Come on," Russ invited. "I'll introduce you to the bride and groom."

Carol followed Russ through the house into a den where the bride and groom stood greeting their guests. Both the bride and the groom were totally naked.

Carol gasped.

"Didn't I tell you this was a far-out party?" Russ asked.

"I must confess it's different from the one I'm avoiding."

Carol felt wet lips on the back of her neck, and when she turned around the lips moved to her mouth. She was being kissed by the red-haired girl who had greeted them, and she could feel the hard little nipples of the girl pressing into her.

"Hey!" Carol said, pushing away.

"Don't mind Candy," Russ said, laughing. "She's into feeling."

"Fine, as long as she's not into feeling me," Carol said.

They wandered around a bit more. Then a young man handed Carol a glass.

"Thanks," Carol said, accepting the drink. She tossed it down, then put the empty glass down on a table.

"Hey, babes, you better find a place to sit down," the young man said.

"Why?"

"You just dropped a passion bomb."

"A what?"

"Jerry," Russ said angrily, "you gave her that without telling her?"

"Hey! I just told her, man."

Carol felt a slight light-headedness, and a tingling sensation in her knees.

"What... what did I take?" she asked.

"Passion bomb," Russ said. "It's a combination of L.S.D. and methamphetamine."

"No," Carol said. "I don't do drugs."

"You just did," Jerry said. "Get ready, mama. You're goin' on a trip you won't believe."

"What did she take?" Candy asked, coming back over at that moment.

"A passion bomb."

"Oh, honey, are we going to have fun!" Candy said. "Come with me."

By now Carol felt as if she were floating. She was feeling other things, too, tinglings and a strange heat. She didn't resist Candy when she led her over to a large blue sofa.

"Sit here with me," Candy invited. "Don't be afraid. I won't leave you."

"Candy," Carol said. "The sofa. Can you hear it?"

Candy laughed. "Hear it?"

"Yes. It's humming. The color blue...I never knew that blue was such a pretty sound."

Carol leaned her head back on the sofa and looked around the room. Over in the corner she saw someone playing a flute. She was sure that the flute player would be interested in hearing blue, so she tried to call him over. When she looked at him, though, she could hardly believe her eyes. There were bright red colors splashing from the end of the flute. The colors sparkled and danced and shimmered as they hung in the air.

Candy! Candy was having intercourse with the music! One of the bright drops of color was making love to her. She had taken off her net dress and was leaning over backward so that her hands were holding on to her ankles. Her hips were thrust forward and the color was moving in and out of her vagina. It was a solid, three-dimensional color and the thrusts were deep as Candy opened up for the fornication.

Carol was amazed. How are they doing this? She thought it was beautiful and she envied Candy.

While she was envying Candy, some of the color moved over to her. Carol knew why it came and she took off her clothes, then spread her thighs appreciatively. The color entered into her and she gave herself over to it. It was an all-encompassing thing and she felt all her erogenous zones being sensitized.

Carol was swept with washes of color and the blue of the chair continued its music as she climaxed. There were several climaxes coming wave after wave, so close together that she couldn't distinguish between them.

Her entire body dissolved into one massive climax and she felt herself breaking into pieces...pieces of climax that had taken her personality and now drifted across the room, borne on the fragrant wafts of incense.

How was she doing this? She was cognizant of several different entities. She was here and she was there, all at the same time, yet every entity was still sensitized by the explosion of the last climax. It was as if she had captured the most divine feeling at its peak and stayed with it, not letting it go. Only it was greatly multiplied because the climax had shattered her personality into several parts, each with the same sensation.

From her new perspective, Carol watched the others in the room. She now knew who she was. She had moved into the aura of latent sex that hung over the room and had breathed life into that aura: the life spawned by her orgasm.

Ah, here was an interesting point of view. She was part of a man's penis. Odd, she didn't feel as if she were in the penis, she felt as if she were a part of it. She could feel the throbbing of the veins, the rush of blood, and the tightening of the skin as it grew larger. She felt her temperature rise and issue forth a drop of precoital fluid.

While she felt all this, she could also feel herself a part of the stiff protrusion encased in the velvetlike folds of Candy's vagina. It was warm and damp, a pleasant dampness, like the warm water of a scented bath. There was a twitching of nerves as the entire sexual area had sharpened the senses of the nerve endings. Carol felt the head of the penis, both as it contacted the first part of Candy's mound, then as it entered, proud and smashing around, splashing within the juices and forcing its way deep into the tubes.

In her new perspective, Carol was able to feel the intercourse conducted by these two lovers through her entire body, not just in the sex-organ areas. When the penis finally erupted in a hot spurt, Carol felt herself being shot into the tunnel, carried along like a board on the surf, cascading off the vagina walls.

The two lovers were spent, so Carol found herself leaving them. She resumed her position in the sexual aura until she could find another beckoning well. She found an interesting trio in one corner and became one with a girl who was having sex with two men at the same time.

Carol rode out the climax, climbing to the peak again with each one as they reached orgasm, one after the other. She left them then, the girl sore and heavy, the men spent and limp.

Carol contacted other fragments of climaxes released by the copulating masses, but she found that none of the others had personality. Somehow, only she had managed to enter this state of perpetual orgasm.

She drifted about the room collecting the other pieces of herself, then returned to her body. When all had returned, she felt herself falling through and into the cushion. She tried to stop herself but she couldn't. Soon all the colors, the music, the fragrances were gone. She was in a forest of great blue trees. She looked up to see the sky, but there was none. There was ony the jungle of blue fibers making up the cushion of the chair. She fell to the bottom and her eyes closed. She was swallowed by an amoeba and deposited on a dust mote. She drifted without mind, without body, slowly and unseeing for a time that had no beginning and no end.

"He's over there."

Deke was standing by the poolside bar when he saw two policemen talking to one of his guests. The guest was pointing Deke out to the officers.

"Something I can do for you gentlemen?" Deke asked.

"You Deke McClarity?"

"Yes."

"We have a woman downtown who says she's your wife. Carol McClarity?"

"Yes, yes, she's my wife," Deke said. "We've been waiting for her. What happened? Has there been an accident? Is she hurt?"

"No, sir, no accident," one of the officers said.

"Mr. McClarity, would you like to come downtown with us?"

"You want to tell me what this is all about?"

One of the officers looked around and saw that they were separated far enough from the others that he could talk in a low voice and maintain some degree of confidentiality.

"Your wife is in jail, Mr. McClarity."

"Jail? What for?"

The officer cleared his throat. "For starters, under the

influence. Also indecent exposure and public performance of a sexual act."

"What?"

"She was picked up at a drug party, Mr. McClarity. About an hour ago. As soon as we found out who she was, the judge set bail."

"How much is her bail?"

"Five thousand dollars."

"All right," Deke said. "I'll be right down. Let me put on a shirt and some trousers."

"We'll be waiting in the car out front. You can follow us down if you want."

"Thanks," Deke said.

Deke watched the policemen leave. Then he started toward the house.

"Deke? Deke, is anything wrong?" Rebel asked.

Deke looked at Rebel and shook his head. Behind her he saw the Porsche 911, still gleaming in its ribbon and bow. He walked over toward the car and jerked the ribbon off.

"What is it, Deke?" someone asked.

Deke said not a word. With his mouth clamped tightly shut and his jaw jutting out angrily, he opened the door and slid in behind the wheel.

The car was brand-new and he could smell the leather and glues and paints. He looked through the windshield out over the sleek hood. Then he turned the key and started the engine. The exhausts purred the deep-throated purr of an expensive sports car.

Rebel had no idea what the police had said, but she knew that Deke had been upset by their visit. She was concerned for Deke and she came over to the car and leaned down to the window. "Deke? Deke, where are you going?" she asked.

"Watch your feet, little one," Deke said as he slipped the car into gear.

"Deke!" Rebel called in alarm as the spinning rear wheels left rubber on the concrete patio that surrounded the pool.

"Deke, where you goin', buddy?" someone called. "Hey, watch out, you're..."

The warning came too late, though Deke wouldn't have heeded it anyway. He intended to do just what he did. Like a stunt car in a television action movie, the Porsche leaped over the coping and flew several feet out toward the middle of the pool. It hit flat on the surface in ten feet of water, throwing out a huge spray that doused everyone and everything.

Men shouted in alarm and women screamed. A couple of people laughed, though the shock effect was such that the laughter died in their throats.

Deke swam away from the car as it went down in a boiling caldron of water. Huge bubbles broke on the surface as the car settled to the bottom of the pool.

Without so much as a word or a glance to anyone, Deke climbed out of the pool and went into the house as his guests stood around in shocked silence.

Rebel, her heart pounding, ran inside the house and down the hall after Deke. Opeing the door to his bedroom, she found him just inside the door as he stepped out of his wet bathing suit. She saw the ugly puff of scar tissue where the VC bullet had hit...and she saw a great deal more. Deke was totally nude.

She gasped. She hadn't meant to intrude on him this way. She wanted only to help.

"I'm going down to the police station to bail my wife out of jail," Deke said as he dried himself. He made no effort to cover his nudity. In fact, he treated it as if it were perfectly normal for Rebel to be standing in the room with him while he was naked.

"What did she do?" Rebel asked in a small voice.

"Murder."

"Murder?" Rebel gasped.

"Yeah. She murdered what was left of our marriage," Deke explained as he stepped into his trousers.

"Deke...I'm so sorry," Rebel said. "I...I wish I could do something."

Deke smiled at her. "You might see if you can figure out some way to get that car out of the pool," he said. "That son-of-a-bitch set me back twenty-six thousand dollars."

Rebel walked back through the house with Deke, then watched as he drove away to follow the policemen downtown. She started to return to the pool when she saw a piece of paper lying on the floor, dropped from Deke's pocket. She picked it up and saw what he had written upon it:

> Words are spoken, but there is no conversation. Semen is spilled, but there is no satisfaction. Because of this, there is something hidden inside me, deep and untouched, crying for recognition. And in a quiet moment there is the silent sound of the dying of my soul.

Tears slid down Rebel's face as she read the words. She wished with all her heart there was something she could do to ease Deke's pain. But he didn't even know that she loved him.

Chapter Thirty

By the time Evan reached his Houston office, there were already half a dozen telephone messages for him from Stewart Jackson.

"Mr. Wainwright wants to see you the moment you arrive," an attractive, middle-aged woman said.

"Okay, Nancy. Tell him I'm back. And you may as well get Jackson for me."

Evan was still hanging up his jacket when Wainwright, his personal accountant, came in.

"Have you heard?" Wainwright asked in a nervous, excited voice. "They've shut down everything."

"They've shut down everything? Who are 'they,' and what have they shut down?"

"My God, you haven't heard, have you? All the closings are on the news already."

"I haven't seen any news. I got a late start this morning. Then I flew back from Washington. Rebel picked me up at the airport and we talked."

"It's awful, Mr. Hewlitt. I don't know what we're going to do."

"Dwayne, would you quit moaning and wringing your hands and tell me what the hell this is all about?" Evan asked in an irritated voice.

"Rana has closed down all our operations. I mean everything: oil production, refining, shipping, chemical processing, manufacturing — everything Texon has anything to do with has stopped."

"Why the hell would she do something like that?"

"It's that restraining order," Wainwright said. "The way it's worded, they are just doing what they were ordered to do."

"The restraining order? You mean the one Jackson put out? I thought that was just to keep them from dealing with Mexico."

"Yes, sir, it was supposed to be. But here's a copy. I've underlined the part that's causing the problems."

Evan sat down and looked at the order. The phone buzzed and he picked it up.

"Mr. Jackson, sir," Nancy said.

Evan punched the glowing button.

"Goddamn it! Can't you do anything right?" Evan demanded. "You've made a mess with this restraining order."

"I'm...sorry...Mr. Hewlitt," Jackson stammered from the other end of the line. "I was trying to keep them from finding loopholes that would let them deal with Mexico through one of the subsidiary companies. I had no idea that they would take such a literal interpretation of the wording."

"I see. You thought they would just roll over and play dead, did you?"

"Well...I thought we had them against the wall. I thought —"

"You didn't think at all, Jackson. That's the whole problem," Evan said abruptly. "I told you not to underestimate Rana McClarity. All right, what happens if we let them play it out? What if we call their bluff?"

"You mean...let them close down everything?"

"Yes."

"Mr. Hewlitt, we can't do that. You must realize that when Texon shuts down everything, it affects dozens of other corporations as well. If this goes on, the United States could have as much as thirty percent of its work force off the job within a week. I've already got half a dozen senators calling for an investigation now."

"Can you amend the order, change the part that lets them shut everything down?"

"I'm afraid not," Jackson said. "All I can do is rescind it. And once I rescind it, we'll be right back where we were."

Evan ran his fingers through his hair and sighed. "Jackson," he said finally, "you're worthless as tits on a boar hog. Rescind the goddamned order."

"What...what do we do next?" Jackson asked.

"Next? We do nothing, you dumb shit. We've lost the fight. You stay the fuck out of it from now on. I'm going to be busy mending a few fences and I don't want you in the way."

"Whatever you say," Jackson replied meekly.

Evan hung up the phone, then looked up at Wainwright. He chuckled and shook his head. "I'll tell you one thing," he said. "When Rana dies, she's going to heaven."

"Why do you say that?"

"'Cause the devil won't want anything to do with her. She'd jerk a knot in his ass before he could get the fires stoked." He sighed. "Draft a letter, Jake. Offer Rana my complete support in getting Texon back to full production. Tell her I'll vote with her on any measure that might come up. Then prepare a news release saying something like: 'Though Rana and I often differ on internal policies, we always have and always will present a united front when the company is threatened.'"

"You won't fight the Mexican deal anymore?"

"No," Evan said. "I'm willing to cut my losses there." He sighed. "But there's one place where the battle line stays drawn."

"Where's that?"

"I don't intend to let my daughter marry Deke McClarity, and I'll stop that marriage, no matter whose toes I have to step on."

Deke was sitting in a chair in the corner of the living room at Cedars when Rebel and her parents arrived for dinner that night. He stood as they came in and returned Rebel's kiss, despite Evan's scowl.

"Good evening, Evan, Jewel," Deke said.

Jewel, Rebel's mother, was a quiet, reserved woman. Though Rebel had an entirely different personality, she did inherit her mother's looks. Jewel was only seven years older than Deke. Frequent visits to health salons and expensive beauty shops helped maintain the image. Tonight, auburn wings of hair swept up and back over her ears to gather into elaborate coils and curls. The color was partially her own and partially the creation of a skilled colorist who had blended a shade that was used exclusively for Jewel.

"Hello, Jewel, Rebel," Rana greeted them, stepping into the living room. "I'm so glad you could come."

"It was gracious of you to invite us," Jewel replied.

"Well, shall we have a drink?"

"I'll pour," Deke said.

"There's no need. Richard will pour," Rana offered.

"Let me," Deke said. "I know what everyone likes. Besides, I think we have some talking to do, and it might be better if we talk alone."

"All right," Rana said. "Before we start, though, I want to thank you, Evan, for offering your proxies to me this afternoon."

Evan took his glass from Deke, then saluted Rana with it.

"That's the way of it, isn't it? To the victor go the spoils," he said.

"Nevertheless, it is reassuring to know that the battle is over. We shouldn't fight, Evan. Gamblin and Jason left us with a trust, and we owe it to them to be true to it."

"I agree," Evan said. He raised his glass. "In fact, I would like to propose that we drink a toast to the two loves of your life...Gamblin McClarity and Jason Hewlitt."

"I would be proud to drink to them," Rana said.

The five drank silently. Then Evan put his glass down on the bar. "The question is," he went on, "which of them was your real love?"

"What do you mean?" Deke asked.

"You know what I mean, don't you, Rana? You know why these two can't get married."

"Rana?" Rebel asked with a catch in her voice. "Rana, what's Daddy talking about? Is there a reason we can't get married?"

"Your father seems to think so," Rana said.

"Are you going to deny it?" Evan burst in. "Are you going to deny that Deke's father was my half brother?"

"What?" Deke asked sharply.

Rebel gasped. "Daddy? What are you saying?"

"Tell them, Rana," Evan said. "For God's sake, tell them the truth. You've won the battle, I'll vote for anything you say, support you in any board action. But please do the right thing. Tell my daughter and your grandson that they can't get married, because they are first cousins."

"Why are you doing this, Evan?" Rana asked. "Why are you pushing this so?"

"Why shouldn't I push it? I've known from the time I was a small boy that you and my father were lovers. I used to hear the snickering remarks... I saw my mother hurt, my father's reputation ruined by it. And now you would carry the sin further by allowing Rebel and Deke to marry. How can you do this?"

"Grandmother, is it true?" Deke asked.

"No," Rana said.

Evan slammed his glass down angrily.

"Rana, you and I have been on opposite sides before. But you have always fought an honest fight. I can't believe I'm hearing you lie now. I can't believe you would deny that you and my fathers were lovers. What is your gain?"

"All right," Rana said with a sigh of surrender. "Jason and I were lovers. I loved him, perhaps even as much as I loved Gamblin. But Jason and I never made love again after Gamblin and I were married."

"What difference does that make?" Evan asked. "It's well known that C.G. was born the night Santa Rana One came in. Look in any history book in the world and you find out that was only five months after you and Gamblin were married. Am I right?"

"Yes."

"I've heard the story many times of how my father actually delivered C.G."

"C.G. might have died if Jason hadn't been there," Rana admitted.

"And, isn't it a fact that my father knew he was C.G.'s father?"

"He believed he might have been, yes," Rana said.

"Then...it is true," Rebel said in a small voice. She looked at Deke and her eyes were flooded with tears. "We can't get married."

"Yes, you can," Rana said.

"But you just admitted that Jason was my grandfather," Deke said.

"No, I didn't admit that," Rana said. "What I said was that he *believed* he was C.B.'s father. But Gamblin believed he was the father."

"How could they both believe it?" Deke asked.

"Because it could have been either one of them, and I never told them which one it was."

"I don't understand," Deke said. "Why would you not tell them which one was the father?"

"If I had told, it would have split us up," Rana said. "It was better to let them both believe than to have one of them hurt. They went to the grave, each of them convinced that he was C.G.'s father."

"Obviously, only one was," Evan said. "But the impediment remains. If you don't know which one was the father, Deke and Rebel can't marry."

"I know which one was the father," Rana said. She put her hand on Evan's hand and squeezed. "Believe me when I say it is all right for them to marry."

"Daddy, did you hear that!" Rebel exclaimed, smiling through her tears. "There's no reason we can't get married."

Evan looked at Rana for a long, silent moment.

"Rana, for God's sake, I plead with you to tell the truth."

"Evan," Rana said, "as you say, there's no business reason for me to want them to marry, just as there is none for you to prevent it. If they love each other and want to marry, then who are we to stand in the way of their happiness? I swear to you on the graves of Gamblin and Jason, there is no reason why Deke and Rebel can't marry."

Rebel walked over to Deke and let him put his arm around her. "You heard her, Deke. What about it? Will you marry me?"

Deke brushed her hair back from her forehead and kissed her there, lightly, then looked at Evan and Jewel.

"I want the blessing of your parents," he said.

Rebel looked at her mother.

"If Rana said there's no reason why they can't get married, I believe her," Jewel said.

Finally, Evan put his arms around Rana and pulled her to him in an embrace.

"All right, Rana," he said. "If you say there's nothing to keep them from getting married, that's good enough for me. They have my blessing."

"Oh, Daddy!" Rebel said, leaving Deke's arms and rushing to her father. "Thank you! Thank you!"

"But you'd better treat her right," Evan said to Deke. "I'm not the kind of man you ever want to cross."

Deke smiled. "I know," he said. "Believe me, I know."

"Now," Evan said, rubbing his hands together, "I

thought you invited us over for dinner. I take it that means we are going to eat sometime soon? I'm starved."

Late that night, after Deke and the others had left, after the servants had cleaned up and the house was silent, Rana went into the Quiet Room. She sat in the easy chair that had been hers and looked at the empty chair Gamblin had always used. In her mind's eye she could see him sitting there. She sighed.

"I need to talk to you, Gamblin. Tonight I'm afraid I chose the coward's way out. I refused to answer any of Evan's questions. I simply said there was no reason why Deke and Rebel couldn't get married."

Tears welled in Rana's eyes, then began to slide down her face.

"No one could ever have asked for a better husband, or a better father, than you. You made my life worthwhile, and if I had it to live over again, I would live it exactly as we did. But...forgive me, my love. You weren't C.G.'s father. Jason was."

Rana leaned her head back on the chair as the tears continued to slip down her face.

"I know," she said. "You are wondering how I could let Deke and Rebel marry if Jason was C.G.'s father. Well, that's the real irony of it.

"Do you remember the day Jane Ella, C.G., and I met you at the airport, just before Jane Ella and Jason were married? She had something to tell me that day, something that she made me swear I would keep secret for the rest of my life. Since I had a secret of my own to keep, I found no difficulty in the task...until Deke and Rebel fell in love.

"When they fell in love I knew I was going to have to

do something. I was either going to have to betray Jane Ella, or betray you and Jason. In a way, I guess I betrayed you and Jason, since I let them believe that you were C.G.'s father."

Rana sighed.

"What is the old saying? 'What a tangled web we weave when first we practice to deceive'? The truth is, Gamblin, it doesn't make any difference who C.G.'s father was, because Jane Ella was already pregnant by someone else when she and Jason got married. That was the secret she told me long ago."

Across town in the Adams' Mark Hotel, Deke and Rebel were celebrating in their own way. From the moment they reached the room they began teasing and tormenting each other with tongues, lips, and teeth.

Though still clothed, they sat on the edge of the bed. Then Deke pushed Rebel back against the pillow and moved over her.

Rebel felt his weight upon her, his hands moving eagerly over her shoulders and arms, drifting down to cup her breasts, caressing her nipples with his fingers.

She wanted more, ached for him, and she moved against him in a way that clearly expressed her desires. Deke responded by trailing his tongue across her earlobe, then closing his teeth gently on that delicate piece of flesh.

"Deke," she said. "I love you, Deke. I have always loved you."

Even though she was gently restrained by his weight upon her, she could still move. She reached up under his shirt and stroked his back, rubbing her fingers over the skin and muscle she knew so well and which, despite the familiarity, were always exciting to her.

"I love you," Deke said. Suddenly, he moved away from her. "But we're overdressed."

Rebel got up to stand beside him and began removing her clothes as he shed his own. Within a moment they were standing face to face, bare breast to bare breast, loin to loin.

"I love to look at you," Deke said.

"Will you still love to look at me when we are married?"

"I'll love to look at you when we have been married twenty years," Deke answered.

"Only twenty? What happens then?"

Deke smiled. "I don't know. I'll be sixty then. I'd like to reserve my options," he teased.

"Maybe you have a point," Rebel replied. "I might want to change you in for two thirties then."

"Nevah hoppen," Deke said, reaching out to pull her naked body to his.

Rebel felt a powerful tremor run through him as their bodies melded together.

"God, you feel good," Deke said huskily. "Your skin is so smooth and so incredibly hot."

"When we're like this, it's like we're one," Rebel observed.

Once again Deke's lips and tongue probed Rebel's mouth. It wasn't just a kiss of passion, but of exploration and wonder. Gently, he laid her back on the bed.

As Deke's hands enveloped her, her skin tingled with a thousand teasing little fires. New strokes of pleasure swept her up, second by second, as Deke's body took charge of hers, his fingers deftly working their way downward, molding her smooth skin between them until finally they slipped into the welcome dampness between the soft folds of flesh.

Deke moved into position over her again, only this time there was no barrier of clothes between them. She felt the connection being made and pleasure shot through her body like a bolt of flame, generating enough surging heat to ignite a rocket and catapult her into space.

Deke kept at her, pushing, pushing her body on, upward from ecstasy to ecstasy, until she felt her body leap in its final, shattering, white-hot explosion; and she knew she was falling, falling away through the endless corridors of time and space.

She could literally bear no more; and at last the empty shell of her body did truly fall away from Deke, leaving her shaking and senseless, utterly satiated at last.

Back in the Quiet Room, Rana sat in her chair with only the small lamp that illuminated Gamblin's painting for light. The room was mellow and golden, and she felt Gamblin's presence. It was loving and understanding and Rana realized that, at long last, the circle had been completed.

DON'T MISS READING
PaperJacks BESTSELLERS!

___ **ARIANA** — Edward Stewart (Fict.)   7701-0427-4/$4.50

___ **DIVIDED SOUL: THE LIFE OF MARVIN GAYE** —
David Ritz (Bio.)   7701-0423-1/$4.95

___ **FOR LOVE OR HONOR** — William Saxon (Fict.)
7701-0431-2/$4.50

___ **HARD DRIVING: MY YEARS WITH JOHN DELOREAN**
— William Haddad (Bio.)   7701-0477-0/$3.95

___ **KHADAFY** — Harry Gregory (Bio.)   7701-0532-7/$3.50

___ **"LAST" NAZI: THE LIFE AND TIMES OF DR. JOSEPH MENGELE** — Gerald Astor (Bio.)   7701-0447-9/$3.95

___ **NOT IN VAIN** — Gerald Green (Fict.)
7701-0373-1/$3.95

___ **REPUBLIC: A NOVEL OF TEXAS** — E. V. Thompson (Hist. Fict.)   7701-0479-7/$3.95

___ **WIND AND THE SEA** — Marsha Canham (Hist Rom.)   7701-0415-0/$3.95

Available at your local bookstore or return this coupon to:

BOOKS BY MAIL
320 Steelcase Rd. E. 210 5th Ave., 7th Floor
Markham, Ont., L3R 2M1 New York, N.Y. 10010

Please send me the books I have checked above. I am enclosing a total of $ _____ (Please add 1.00 for one book and 50 cents for each additional book.) My cheque or money order is enclosed. (No cash or C.O.D.'s please.)

Name _____
Address _____ Apt. _____
City _____
Prov./State _____ P.C./Zip _____

Prices subject to change without notice.   (BS1/LR)

DON'T MISS READING
PaperJacks BESTSELLERS!

___ **BELOVED OUTCAST** — Lorena Dureau (His. Rom)
 7701-0508-4/$3.95

___ **CONGLOMERATE** — Rita Jenrette (Fict.)
 7701-0581-5/$3.95

___ **HAUTE** — Jason Thomas (Fict.) 7701-0379-0/$3.95

___ **HOLLYWOOD CHRONICLES: THE SILENT IDOLS**
 — Sam Dodson (Fict.) 7701-0574-2/$4.95

___ **HOLLYWOOD CHRONICLES: THE GOLDEN IDOLS
 BOOK 2** — Sam Dodson (Fict.) 7701-0588-2/$3.95

___ **MASS** — Jack Fuller (Fict.) 7701-0573-4/$4.95

___ **SLEEP** — Lynn Biederstadt (Horr.) 7701-0572-6/$4.50

___ **TRAUMA** — J. Fried & J. G. West, M.D. (Fict.)
 7701-0453-3/$3.95

___ **THREE AMIGOS** — Leonore Fleischer
 (Movie Tie-In) 7701-0566-1/$3.50

___ **WHITE JAGUAR** — William Appel (Fict.)
___ Cdn. 7701-0571-8/$4.95
___ U.S. 7701-0493-2/$3.95

Available at your local bookstore or return this coupon to:

BOOKS BY MAIL
320 Steelcase Rd. E. 210 5th Ave., 7th Floor
Markham, Ont., L3R 2M1 New York, N.Y. 10010

Please send me the books I have checked above. I am enclosing a total of $ _____ (Please add 1.00 for one book and 50 cents for each additional book.) My cheque or money order is enclosed. (No cash or C.O.D.'s please.)
Name _____
Address _____ Apt. _____
City _____
Prov./State _____ P.C./Zip _____

Prices subject to change without notice (BS2/LR)

William Appel

BRINGS TO YOU HIS NEWEST AND
MOST EXCITING NOVELS YET!

THE WHITE JAGUAR

WHITE POWDER. GREEN DEATH.
BLACK EVIL.

____ CDN 7701-0571-8 $4.95
____ US   7701-0493-2 $3.95

WaterWorld

Out of dark dreams and cold hallucinations a questionable death surfaces.

____ CDN/US 7701-0530-0 $3.50

The Watcher Within

A prisoner of fear against an Angel of Madness.

____ CDN/US 7701-0552-1 $3.50

Prices subject to change without notice

BOOKS BY MAIL

320 Steelcase Rd. E.   210 5th Ave., 7th Floor
Markham, Ont., L3R 2M1   New York, N.Y. 10010

Please send me the books I have checked above. I am enclosing a total of $_____ (Please add 1.00 for one book and 50 cents for each additional book.) My cheque or money order is enclosed. (No cash or C.O.D.'s please.)

Name _____
Address _____ Apt. _____
City _____
Prov./State _____ P.C./Zip _____

(WA86)

YOU WON'T WANT TO MISS THESE BIOGRAPHIES ON

HOLLYWOOD'S FAVORITE STARS

___ **AUDREY: THE LIFE OF AUDREY HEPBURN**
— Charles Higham   7701-0354-5/$3.9

___ **BURTON** — Hollis Alpert — The boozer, the brawler, th husband, the lover, the genius, the star, THE LEGEND...TH TRUTH.   7701-0545-9/$4.9

___ **LAUGHING ON THE OUTSIDE, CRYING ON TH INSIDE** — Judy Carne — Autobiography
          7701-0494-0/$3.9

___ **RED: THE TEMPESTUOUS LIFE OF SUSAN HAYWARD** — Robert Laguardia & Gene Arceri
          7701-0429-0/$3.5

___ **A VALUABLE PROPERTY: THE LIFE STORY O MICHAEL TODD** — Foreword by ELIZABETH TAYLO — Michael Todd, Jr., & Susan McCarthy Todd
          7701-0299-9/$3.9

Prices subject to change without notice

BOOKS BY MAIL
320 Steelcase Rd. E.   210 5th Ave., 7th Floor
Markham, Ont., L3R 2M1   New York, N.Y. 1001C

Please send me the books I have checked above. I am enclosing a total of $_____ (Please add 1.00 for one book an 50 cents for each additional book.) My cheque or money orde is enclosed. (No cash or C.O.D.'s please.)

Name _____
Address _____ Apt. _____
City _____
Prov./State _____ P.C./Zip _____

(BIO/LR

PaperJacks *Presents*

BILL PRONZINI

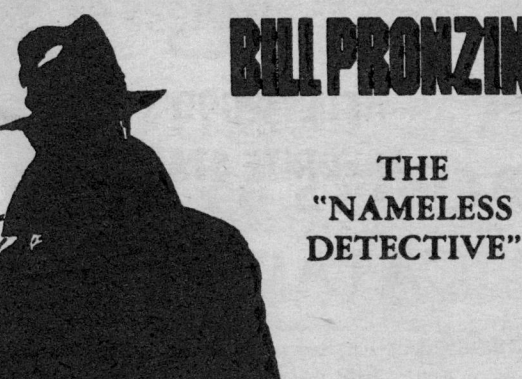

THE "NAMELESS DETECTIVE"

__ **BONES** — An old grave opens a new case of murder. 7701-0451-7/$3.50

__ **LABYRINTH** — One smoking pistol points to a clear case of conspiracy. 7701-0432-0/$3.50

__ **HOODWINK** — A Pulpwriter's Convention becomes the setting for Real-life blackmail and murder 7701-0549-1/$3.50

Prices subject to change without notice

BOOKS BY MAIL

320 Steelcase Rd. E. 210 5th Ave., 7th Floor
Markham, Ont., L3R 2M1 New York, N.Y. 10010

Please send me the books I have checked above. I am enclosing a total of $_____ (Please add 1.00 for one book and 50 cents for each additional book.) My cheque or money order is enclosed. (No cash or C.O.D.'s please.)

Name _____
Address _____ Apt. _____
City _____
Prov./State _____ P.C./Zip _____

(PROZ/LR)

FREE!!
BOOKS BY MAIL CATALOGUE

BOOKS BY MAIL will share with you our current bestselling books as well as hard to find specialty titles in areas that will match your interests. You will be updated on what's new in books at no cost to you. Just fill in the coupon below and discover the convenience of having books delivered to your home.

PLEASE ADD $1.00 TO COVER THE COST OF POSTAGE & HANDLING.

BOOKS BY MAIL

320 Steelcase Road E.,   210 5th Ave., 7th Floor
Markham, Ontario L3R 2M1   New York, N.Y., 10010

Please send Books By Mail catalogue to:

Name _____
(please print)
Address _____
City _____
Prov./State _____ P.C./Zip _____

(BBM1)